The flames danced across the lunar landscape of the desert night.

Movement caught his eye; spinning quickly toward the movement, Bexar raised his rifle. Three people outside the fence were running toward the gate. The tip of the red triangle in the optic tracked just ahead of the leader. Two smooth pulls on the trigger, and the first person fell; the second person tripped over the body. Bexar drove the rifle to the person at the rear, who stopped and turned to run away. Another two shots and the rounds pierced his back, blood erupting out of his chest where the rounds exited, the man crumpling to the ground in mid-stride. The remaining person of the assaulting force stood, arms raised. An odd-looking tube was slung across his body; it looked vaguely familiar to Bexar, but he wasn't sure why. Anger pierced the air between them. A fraction of a second passed, but for Bexar it felt like ten minutes. Through the reticle all he saw were the eyes and the hatred they held.

WINCHESTER UNDEAD BOOK 5
WINCHESTER:STORM

« DAVE LUND »

A WINLOCK PRESS BOOK

ISBN: 978-1-68261-207-1
ISBN (eBook): 978-1-68261-208-8

WINCHESTER: STORM
Winchester Undead Book 5
© 2016 by Dave Lund
All Rights Reserved

Edited by Monique Happy Editorial Services
Cover art by Dave Lund of www.f8industries.net

WINLOCK PRESS

Join Winlock's spam-free mailing list to find out about the latest releases and giveaways.

www.winlockpress.com

Please visit Winchester Undead on Facebook

CHAPTER 1

April 1, Year 1

Andrew banked the bright yellow Aviat Husky left and deftly held the aircraft in a lazy orbit above the scraggly lake in the Ozarks. Bentonville, Arkansas, as far as he could tell, belonged to the dead. *Which is too bad,* Andrew thought as he glanced at the twin-needled fuel gauge. Avgas was hard to come by, but regular unleaded gas with an octane booster seemed to be working fine. He reached into the back seat and felt in his bag for the big spiral bound Hema road atlas. It wasn't good airmanship using a road atlas to fly his way cross country; certain hazards definitely applied, such as tall towers now unlit. It was true IFR flying for a country pilot like himself . . . *I Follow Roads.* When disorientated Andrew would push his bush plane down, skimming the rooftops of the cars on the largest highways he could find, looking for highway signs and road signs to help him figure out his location.

With the wings level, Andrew held the aircraft impossibly slow in the crisp air above the lake. If his altimeter was still correct, he was roughly seven thousand feet above sea level, and with his uncalibrated eyeball he would call it closer to five thousand feet above the lake. Oreo nudged his hand as he dug for the atlas; a quick scratch between his best friend's ears and the atlas came out of the bag. Squinting, he read the small print naming the lake *Beaver Lake*.

The atlas didn't name the little community below him, nor did it show a little airplane to indicate an airport, but the black tarmac stood out from the brown trees and roof tops. Smoke billowed softly from a few of the chimneys, blowing lazily south. Replacing the atlas in the bag by Oreo, he dug around and found his binoculars. The runway numbers were easily seen without them, *thirty-one and thirteen; chimney smoke trailing south.* The choice was easy to land toward the north. What grabbed Andrew's attention wasn't the smoke or the runway; it was a small boat a few hundred yards off the shore to the east of the runway. Banking the aircraft over and again starting a lazy orbit, Andrew peered through the binoculars at the man in the boat, who was pulling in a floating jug line and looked up at the circling aircraft and waved.

"That's a good sign, Oreo. He's waving at us."

Oreo nudged Andrew on the shoulder with his snout, which was responded to with another scratch between the ears. The engine sputtered, Andrew reached for the fuel selector and cycled the tanks, smoothly adjusting the throttle and pushing the light aircraft's nose forward. A few more coughs and the spinning propeller outside of his windscreen slowed and jerked to a stop, a white tip of one of the propeller blades staring at him in defiance.

"Well, shit. Like it or not buddy, this is where we land."

Andrew's bush-plane-turned-glider edged through the air, nearly silent, the passing wind the only noise in the cockpit. With no radio to listen to, no other pilots to broadcast, no mayday call to claim his ownership of the small landing strip, and no other airplanes to jockey for position, all he had to do was land safely.

"Crunch this one in, and this community better be friendlier than that one in Tennessee."

Oreo whimpered and looked out of the window. Sitting straight in the seat behind Andrew, his eyes were open and bright, ears perked up. With more flight hours as the dog-second-in-command than most people pilots log in a lifetime, Oreo showed blazing awareness to their tense situation.

Andrew cut across the middle of the field from the east, banked, and made a sweeping left turn to put the big tundra tires on the tarmac and let the aircraft roll to a stop to save wear on the brakes. The engine off from fuel starvation long before putting the tires on the ground, Andrew turned off the ignition to save the battery and flipped open the clam-shell window and door, and stuck wheel chocks under one tire while turning a three-sixty, scanning for any threats . . . living or dead.

CHAPTER 2

Chivo lay near the cliff's edge, a wool blanket pulled over him to break his form up if he were seen from a distance. This was nothing like the ghillie suit he would have preferred to have, but it was better than nothing. Since the night more than a week ago when Doc was killed, the group hadn't had another run in with the other survivors' splinter group, which was the good news. The bad news was that his hand still ached, and Bexar was still in a cast. With a pencil and a notebook, Chivo took his time to plot all the dirt roads between the compound and where their truck lay in burned ruin. He was just too far to see the truck with any sort of detail; the truck was roughly a mile and a half away. He could see its rough shape, and he could tell that it had burned, but he couldn't tell if the debris around it included his rifle case. South of the compound lay the Interstate. After his previous experience with that section of road, Chivo wanted nothing to do with it until he absolutely had to go back there. The enormous horde of dead had thinned out over the past few days, still not as bad as the night of the attack or the day they'd wrecked the truck, but still enough of the reanimated corpses that it would be suicide to go down there.

The past two days Chivo had lain near the cliff's edge at different times during the day, using the different angles of the day's light to better observe and take notes. His first duty, though, was a range card for his M4 on the approach to the compound from the west, up the driveway or over the rocky ground. His distances and elevations were set. With the shorter distances of fire to protect the compound, he was confident in his ability to quickly respond to another attack. His self-imposed duty now was to map a way to the truck that, with Angel's help, he could reach the truck via horseback or on foot if need be. The big Barrett 50-caliber rifle would be a huge asset for counter-insurgency operations against the splinter survivor group, assuming the rifle survived.

Chivo, relating the current situation more along his original missions in Northern Afghanistan, thought of the survivor groups as tribes. The list of people in the friendly tribe read only twelve names when they were pulled off the Interstate and out of the clutches of death. The list, now one person short after Doc was killed, still had promise and had some along for the ride. Chivo's focus wandered through his internal lists, moving each piece into a plan to stabilize the tribes and get out of dodge sooner than later.

Angel, some tactical skills, skilled with horses and designer of the compound and Guillermo, friendly registered nurse and now the defacto group medic since Doc died are the tribal leaders, the first family. John is the beer guy and the quartermaster of dry foods. Brian is the group armorer with general tactical knowledge. Heath takes care of the systems in the compound. Marylyn and Frances, another couple, are both in charge of long-term food storage, meal planning, and inventory. Coach, no real name known, heads security. Stan is the group's mechanic and general handyman. Gary has no real skills that I've seen, but his ability to tell a story is incredible. His daily journal might be of interest to a future historian, if there are any left to care. Jennifer is a bit of a mad-scientist seamstress. She's the one who modified Bexar's pants for the cast and Doc. Doc is dead. If this tribe is going to barter with the other tribe, they need to barter skills, not goods, if at all possible. Jennifer and Stan are the most valuable for that task. Surely every other tribe in the region needs something repaired, something sewn, and something patched.

He and Bexar had wasted enough time sitting in Utah, so close to Groom Lake and reuniting Bexar with his wife, Jessie, but even as anxious as Bexar was to get moving, he needed to be out of the cast on his leg first. Luckily, he was starting to put a little weight on his leg and cast, if only for short periods, but it was a start.

Rifle, insurgents, vehicle, and leave.

Simple plan, only three parts and a drive, but Chivo knew that even the simplest of plans often didn't survive first contact with the enemy.

Yuma, AZ

Aymond sat in the back of the hardened ordinance storage structure. Near the covered aircraft storage and flight line, just a year ago the air would have been full of Marine Aviators ripping across the desert sky, but now all they had was silence and the soft hum of the Chinese radar truck. The remaining men of his Marines Special Operations Team, or MSOT, had settled into the new routine of their new temporary home. Enterprising as they were, they'd found a cache of HESCO barriers and a front-end loader that Jones was able to get running. A little over a week ago, they'd left San Diego in a rush and in ruins, hopefully slowing the Chinese invasion, but Aymond doubted it. He needed more than the eight of them who remained alive to fight off an invasion; he needed more Marines or anyone who could carry a rifle really.

I need patriots, minutemen ready to fill the gap between the Chinese and the dead.

Walking into the hard mid-day sun, Aymond squinted from the contrast. Even in April, the air was already warm, and, as much fun as he'd had while temporarily stationed at the Marine Corps Air Station Yuma when he was a young Marine, he really didn't want to stick around for the triple-digit temperatures of summer. HESCO formed a protective U-shaped wall around the north, west, and south sides of the group of hardened bunkers. A chain-link fence with barbed wire surrounded them, but chain-link wouldn't stop the Zeds, and chain-link would give them no protection if the PLA somehow showed up.

Hammer and Gonzo were on a recon patrol in one of the M-ATVs with Kirk. Jones manned the radar truck, marker-smudged tape placed over the Chinese labels with what the switches did, as best as the men could figure out. Aymond monitored the radio, ready to shake loose Davis, Snow, and Chuck from their sleep cycle if Hammer and his merry band of raiders ran into trouble. The second M-ATV sat at the ready, loaded for the war they would bring as the Quick Reaction Force. Happy stood on the top of the HESCO near the radar truck and east-facing entrance, binoculars to his eyes as he scanned the housing complexes in the distance.

The early patrols found signs of survivors having been on base at some point, improvised positions, obvious signs of battle, but so far no other living person had been found.

"Anything yet?"

"Nothing but Zeds, Chief, although I'm fairly sure this is where they come to check the accuracy of carpenter levels."

Beaver Lake, AR

"I know he waved, but keep cool. Like sirens luring sailors, we can't trust until we verify."

Oreo nudged Andrew's hand.

"Yeah, I agree."

Andrew pulled one of the bags out of the small cargo hold, a backpack that looked like something a high school kid would have stuffed in a locker, shouldered the bag, and jogged to the broken split-rail fence line and to the metal building off the end of the runway. Panting from jogging uphill, he noticed his breath hung in the cool air. Each of the four roll-up garage doors was locked in place. The regular door on the side of the building was locked too. Oreo whimpered softly. Andrew looked at his dog and then in the direction he was looking.

"Come on," Andrew tersely whispered as he ran to the back of the building and into the tree line. He took the backpack off and lay still in the shadows among the trees. Oreo lay on the ground next to him, sniffing the air, ears forward toward the road going down the hill, and he tilted his head as dogs do when trying to decipher something unexpected. A house on their left appeared vacant and closed; another house directly across the road, partially hidden by the trees did not. Taking in his surroundings, Andrew saw faint smoke rising from the chimney. His heart was beating behind his ears, straining to listen to any sound outside his own body, but the more he attempted to listen the less he could hear.

Oreo's tail swept back and forth before he sat up and suddenly ran out of the trees toward the house. Tail wagging, he stopped across the road where the driveway met and sat eagerly. A little girl, who appeared to be no older than ten, walked from behind the trees and overgrown brush. A pistol that seemed impossibly large for her small body tugged at her belt, and in her hands she held a rifle that appeared to be a Ruger 10/22 with a camouflaged stock colored in bright pink.

At sight of her, Oreo stretched and waited like an eager puppy. The girl looked at Oreo and smiled and said something Andrew couldn't hear, but Oreo trotted to her and sat in front of her to enjoy a happy scratch behind his ears. The girl knelt and looked at the tag on his collar, "Oreo is your name? Did you fly that plane here, or who are you here with?"

The girl scanned the wood line, squinting with the look of a seasoned hunter. Andrew took a deep breath, stood, and walked around the side of the building into view. The girl reacted immediately and raised her rifle. Oreo trotted off toward Andrew who stood a few hundred feet away with his hands out and away from his body.

"Mister, don't you move uh inch."

"My name is Andrew, and I won't, and this is Oreo, who you just met."

"What'cha doin' here?"

"Ran out of gas, and it's sort of hard to pull to the side of the road when you're five thousand feet up."

The girl didn't say anything; she glanced over her shoulder at a much older man who walked up the driveway.

"Gran'pa, this man says he ran out of gas."

The man nodded and squinted, examining Andrew. "Where you from there, mister?"

"You don't have to call me mister, mister. The whole world calls me Andrew."

"What?"

"The old country song, you know? Well, sorry, no, my name is Andrew. This is Oreo. We're from Florida."

"Wha'cha flying around for?"

"Just searching, looking for others."

"We've had some problems with *others*, Andrew."

"Yeah, well, so have I."

"Come on up here so we don't have to holler at one'nuther. We don't wanna be attract'n those damn things."

Andrew walked slowly toward the man and the girl with his hands open and away from his side, her rifle still trained on him. The last thing he wanted to do was spook someone and get shot at . . . again. Andrew stopped in the middle of the road, about twenty feet from the girl and the man. Oreo never stopped wagging his tail as he walked to the girl and nudged her in the leg to get another ear scratch.

"Where ya head'n?"

"Truth be told, I'm not really sure. I'm just wandering here and there hoping to find something, someone who can fix this mess. I guess I'm looking for help, the military, the government, someone or anyone who can tell me that *they* are on top of it, and we'll all be OK."

"Son, I'm afraid that just ain't gonna be the case . . . why don't you lower your rifle, princess. My name's Warren, and this little one is my granddaughter, Mary."

Andrew smiled and nodded at each in greeting. Mary, now with a hand free, finally acknowledged Oreo's insistence and petted him. Warren glanced at Oreo and then stared at the plane. "We ain't got no hundred low lead for your plane."

"It'll run on car gas. I have some bottles of octane booster in the cabin I mix with the gasoline."

Warren nodded slowly and looked at the sky for a moment. "Well, come on inside, and we can talk trading. First, I'll trade you lunch for news or stories, and then we can talk about get'n some gas for your plane."

"Sounds like a plan, Warren. Thank you."

They walked in silence, Mary and Oreo ahead of them with his tail wagging while her ponytail bounced with each step. Warren frowned and glanced over his shoulder toward the parked Husky bush plane.

Groom Lake, NV

The peaceful desert morning and cool air grew worse with every passing minute. Bill struggled to finish the riggings for the homebuilt antenna he hoped would give him the chance to communicate over the horizon with other survivors, if only he could complete his task. A radio is nothing without the right antenna.

"I like the fresh air and all, but seriously, fuck this weather."

"Erin, darling, relax. We're outside, and Brit isn't with us . . . so what if it's windy."

"Jessie, it isn't the wind. It's the damn sand that's blowing!"

Jessie shrugged and walked against the howling wind sandblasting the small group on the desert floor. Wind ripped across the mountains and into the dry lakebed, picking up sand and some surprisingly large rocks. Bill's antenna was finally erected, but it took so long that the nice weather had changed dramatically since he first started.

It isn't that it took so long; it's that the weather changed that suddenly. First zombies, now extreme weather . . . Erin's right.

Jessie coughed. Goggles that the world had previously seen on the dusty helmets of military men and women in the first Iraqi war were pulled tight against her face, and a dark shemagh was wrapped over her head and around her mouth in a vain attempt to keep the dust out of her lungs. The last thing Jessie needed was to get a lungful of dust and spend the rest of her pregnancy below ground with miner's lung.

Erin usually liked to lay on the roofrack of the FJ with the big Barrett rifle, but today she opted to stand on the ground, or attempt to in the gusting winds, with her short-barreled M4. It didn't seem to matter what firearm Erin had in her young hands, she was not only fast but wickedly accurate.

I'd hate to piss her off.

Since the first time Sarah had ridden up on her motorcycle and warned that her daughter was holding over-watch with a rifle, Jessie'd had a bit of a soft spot for Erin. Although a young girl who should be worried about school dances and homework, the bouncing ponytailed country girl in jeans was a stone-cold machine, constructed in the ruins of society out of necessity.

Jessie frowned, not that anyone could see it, and looked at Sarah, who was standing next to Bill. *She has the intelligence, poise, and confidence that I know my little Keeley had; she just never had a chance to grow into it.*

Bill moved in more of a fast waddle than a walk back toward the FJ. Sarah circled her hand above her head, meaning *Time to leave.*

At least none of the damned had shown their undead faces this time, Jessie thought.

The last time anyone had seen Brit was shortly after the first attempt to erect Bill's homebrewed radio antenna. Jake said he'd spoken with her, and she'd said she had the flu. Sarah and Jessie thought she was too embarrassed to be seen in the public spaces after nearly getting bit. Erin took it upon herself to passingly "mention" the episode to all who ventured near her. When Sarah asked her to stop, that it would cause nothing but discord, Erin gave her mother the middle finger and walked off.

The interior of the FJ was warm, which was nice, but not as nice as being free from the sand and dirt that flowed across the dry lake like a monsoon. With every bounce, every jostle, dirt floated off their clothing and covered the inside of the well-used overlanding-rig-turned-bug-out-vehicle.

"So after testing the antenna and the radios, the airmen will broadcast a loop on shortwave that they recorded detailing how to construct a spark-gap radio. The secondary shortwave channel will have a looped ten-minute tutorial on CW," Bill explained.

"What's CW?"

"Continuous wave, what they used to call Morse code."

"Huh." Sarah's look was one of curiosity. Although she would have enjoyed a longer explanation, she really didn't want one as long as Bill was ready to give. She didn't want a lesson; she wanted the cliff notes, which Bill seemed physically incapable of providing for any subject. The rest of the slow ride was passed in silence. Driving the Toyota, Jessie wanted to drive much faster, but visibility was not much beyond the end of the hood due to the dust storm. Eventually they drove into the gaping cavern of the hanger that housed the main entrance to the underground facility. Jason was standing by the blast door, happily returned to his previous job as greeter. *He needs a blue vest . . . and maybe some shopping carts to go with his shotgun.* Jessie smirked at the thought.

SSC, Ennis, TX

Sweat stung her eyes. Panting and trying to catch her breath, Amanda moved with all the energy she could muster. This time she would make it. This time she would succeed. She had to succeed—she could not fail. Failure could be death. Amanda dove under the big armored truck. Rolling to the other side, she stood quickly and jumped as high as she could with her hands stretched far above her head.

Her feet fell to the pavement, her knees bending to absorb the impact. Amanda touched the cold tarmac and jumped as hard as she could, hands reaching toward the roof of the MRAP and back down to the asphalt.

One . . . two . . . three . . . four . . . .

Amanda counted out twenty burpees before dropping to her hands to bang out twenty-five push-ups. On her feet, she began the circuit again. Every single day she worked one of a half-dozen of her own workouts of the day. The extensive facility had a well-equipped gym, a weight room that would make a Division I football program proud, but what she shunned in pushing iron, Amanda made up for in conditioning and body strength. She had a plan. It was a simple plan, but it would require the best of her. Outside the protection of the concrete-lined walls deep underground was the real world, the world that belonged to the dead, and the world she'd unwittingly inherited by being the last one alive in the Presidential line of succession. No, the citizens, her fellow citizens and the U.S. Constitution she'd sworn to protect needed a leader, a strong leader to bring them through this dark time. History would remember her name as someone who gave beyond their best, or history would remember nothing at all but the empty ruins of an extinct civilization.

CHAPTER 3

Saint George, UT
April 1, Year 1

"Brian, do it again, please."

Brian moved with the practiced poise of someone who had once been an athlete. Obviously his mind retained the vigor of his youth, but the body of a middle-aged man simply didn't respond as quickly, as gracefully as a younger man, nor did it recover as quickly from such a physical experience as the end of the world as we know it.

A butter knife in Chivo's hand was the closest thing that the group could come up with for an analogue to a rubberized training knife, but with Chivo, they would be as safe as they could be for the new training.

Chivo glanced suddenly to his left over Brian's shoulder, who in response turned his head to follow Chivo's gaze and look of surprise. In less than a blink of an eye, Chivo's ruse worked, and he was in Brian's guard, knife to his throat. "Had you scanned the surroundings before we started?" Chivo asked.

"Yeah."

"Then why did you look when you knew nothing was there?"

"I don't know."

Chivo nodded. "Know what you know and act accordingly."

These sorts of Yogi-isms seemed to gush forth unwittingly from Chivo when he was playing the role of instructor. Ever the quiet professional, he had no problem teaching his peers and fellow Special Forces soldiers, but teaching civilians was a different ballgame altogether. It required an air of overt confidence that Chivo typically tried to play off, but at least with Guillermo and Angel's group of survivors, preppers who did it right, he found eager and willing students.

"OK, Brian, set it up again."

These people have no idea. Their war is coming. It will be brutal, and they will have to be ready to fight. Fight or surrender; if not against this enemy, the opposing group of survivors, it will be the next one or the ones after that. The dead don't envy the living; they have no mind but to feed. No, the fall of man will be from man's own mind and flesh . . . Lord help us all.

Chivo lunged at Brian with the butter knife. Brian stepped off line with a sharp block to the radial, rotating through with an elbow to Chivo's face. The knife fell from Chivo's hand, and his hand bent into a hard wrist lock, which Brian used to simulate breaking his elbow.

"Good job," Chivo said, while shaking his hand and retrieving the dropped butter knife.

Step by step. Knife defense, disarming, escape, survival, fighting . . . this is an unconventional force of conventional people.

Chivo's face betrayed nothing, but he doubted whether their new friends and one-time saviors would be able to become saviors unto themselves.

Lost Bridge Village, Beaver Lake, AR

Burning wood popped and hissed in the fireplace. With the fire pushed to one side, the other side glowing with the white hot coals gave heat to a medium-sized dutch oven. The living room's dark shadows belied the afternoon sunlight outside. Wool blankets were tacked to the walls, stretched over the windows, and old newspaper in thick crumpled clumps filled the space between the blankets and the windows; the homemade insulation helped to keep the fire's meager heat from escaping the home too quickly.

"Come summer, we're gonna have to pull down the blankets and hope to get some air through, but these modern homes just weren't meant for it."

Andrew nodded, wrapping his hands around the mug of hot tea, a wonderful treat after the weeks of hopping from camp to camp via his airplane.

"You're not the first to say that to me, Warren. A number of others I've found have all said the same. They wished for the old homes, but with that said, the old homes aren't as well insulated, and many of them are near the center of towns, historic homes and neighborhoods. It goes without saying that being close to downtown anywhere is a bad idea."

"Most folks been accommodating?"

"Eh, well, I'd say most have been cautious. Some groups were quite reluctant to allow an outsider in their midst; one couple seemed to want to cook Oreo here for dinner. I couldn't even imagine. Needless to say we took flight very quickly after that suggestion. It isn't all death and despair though. I found a group of farmers in Georgia who'd banded together and have established an intermittent mail route between about a half-dozen smaller camps. They even have a trade day every other Sunday!"

"Amazing, how can they do that safely? We tried to venture out toward Rogers, near Bentonville, using the lake, but all we found were the dead. Not one sign of another living soul that way. The other way up the lake are a few other groups. All in all they been the friendly sort, but then some of 'em we knew before too. The damnedest thing was ole' Highway 12. One day, I saw what had to be a thousand of the dead marching 'cross the bridge. They even pushed some cars over the edge and into the water, the dead going with them. They sank like the cars, but I don't think we'll be swimming in the water come summer. Not with the dead mucking about in the water."

"You should see the giant migrations of dead; massive, miles long. Some of the other groups have seen them, a couple even talked about other groups they had contact with wiped off the earth by the mass of migrating dead."

"You bump across any government or military or anything like'n that yet?"

Andrew tilted his head. "Sort of. Nothing what I would have hoped for, but I've seen some groups of military vehicles, tents, and such. I've steered clear; they make me a little uneasy, Warren, and truth be told that is what I'm searching for. There are survivors, more survivors than I could have imagined when I flew out the first time, but nothing is organized. I don't know if it could be organized. There just aren't the resources or the people . . . I take that back, there might be enough people if we had someplace safe to center the efforts. A leader, a mission, equipment, and purpose, but no, so far everyone is just trying to keep their friends, their families, and their own little communities alive as long as they can."

"What about them fellers over in Nevada? You listen to them yet?"

"Listen how? I don't understand, the others said there was an EMP, and my radios didn't work anymore."

"I suppose that's true, Andrew, but . . . Princess, go grab my shortwave out of the pantry. Some things survived. I don't know why, but this guy was in an old metal ammo can in my garage, stuffed in with my hunting gear. Bought it years ago for the weather radio, but it picks up the shortwave stuff too."

Mary left her warm and cozy place sitting on the hearth to quickly return, handing Warren a crank-powered radio before returning to her warm spot and checking on the meal cooking in the dutch oven. Oreo yawned and lay back against her legs.

Warren cranked the radio while explaining the looped broadcasts, starting with the BBC news broadcast from just after the attack, which had since gone off the air. "Then some station came on blabbering nonsense, just a bunch of numbers or letters, and then it disappeared, no idea what was the reason, but strange all around."

Stopping, Warren extended the antenna and turned on the radio. "The reception is better at night, but maybe we can find you som'thing right now, and then we can try again after supper."

The radio hissed, static rolling between each change in frequency before Warren stopped on a tinny voice that sounded miles away with the weak reception ". . . the letter D is dash, dot, dot; the letter E is dot; the letter F is dot, dot, dash, dot . . . ."

"Hey, that's Morse code!"

Warren nodded. "Sure'nuff is. First time I've heard that on the radio. Usually they talk about how they're a safe haven, all are welcome. They also say we got ourselves a new President . . . a woman."

Andrew quickly dug around in his pockets before pulling out a bright orange Field Notes notebook and a pen. "Would you mind letting it play. I want to write this all down. Maybe they'll start over, and we can get what we missed."

Warren nodded and set the radio on the end table next to his recliner. The transmission continued through the alphabet, following some basic protocols for when transmitting so messages could be understood. An example broadcast of Morse code was transmitted very slowly along with what it all meant.

DAVE LUND

"This has been an official United States of America radio broadcast, authorized by the President of the United States Amanda Lampton and broadcast from the safe facility in Groom Lake, Nevada. For information on how to construct a radio and antenna out of parts scavenged from everyday items you can find in your home or neighborhood, please tune to the shortwave frequency . . . ."

"President Amanda Lampton is her name, so they say. Ever heard of her, Andrew?"

"Warren, I have no idea, but if you wouldn't mind, I would like to try to make contact. Would you change the frequency so we can get the assembly instructions?"

Warren looked at Mary. His soft eyes betrayed a kindhearted man contained behind the hard weathered face. Her possible future broke his heart every time he considered it. Silently nodding in response, Warren tuned the radio to the second frequency, turned the generating crank a few more times, and set it back on the end table. Andrew smiled, excitement from a glimmer of hope twinkling in his eyes as he took careful notes in his small durable notebook.

CHAPTER 4

Yuma, AZ
April 2, Year 1

The beep crackle of a radio transmission snapped Aymond awake. The hardened structure that was his berth inside their HESCO built firebase was the safest he had felt since leaving the Mountain Warfare Training Center. Faintly glowing, the hands of his analog wrist watch, a classic military field watch, showed 0400.

Rifle fire filled the radio transmission. Aymond was not awake enough to understand the words, but the gunfire in the background coming through the handset vividly brought back memories of deployments in northern Afghanistan.

What the hell?

"No copy, say again your last, over!"

Now standing, Aymond squinted in the darkness at the other Marines that weren't on patrol or holding fire watch.

"Chief, contact, PLA, request QRF, repeat Quebec Romeo Foxtrot, how copy?"

"Good copy!"

Aymond turned his head and yelled "QRF, SHAKE IT LOOSE!"

A small chorus of mumbled "fucks" was heard as the Marines leapt off their cots, shrugging on their battle rattle and slinging rifles.

"Clear copy, QRF, location, status, over?"

"The eight north of the river, at business eight, mounted patrol, one dozen APCs, one radar truck, about a platoon in strength, how copy?"

"Clear copy, strobe friendly, ETA ten mikes."

"Roger, ten mikes, out."

The hard thump of a 50-caliber rifle was heard in rapid succession over the last radio transmission. Hammer, Happy, and Snow were the patrol team in contact. Jones and Chuck held fire watch, leaving Gonzo, Kirk, Davis, and Aymond in a rest cycle with one M-ATV and their lone radar truck. Jones and Chuck came running toward the M-ATV, Gonzo already behind the wheel, the diesel engine rumbling and ready to go. Two minutes later, the armored truck tore out of the compound, leaving it open, unguarded, and in a condition Aymond would have preferred not to leave it, but there were only nine Marines left, counting himself. Master Gunnery Sergeant Aymond had no other choice.

Kirk spun the remote turret that commanded the mounted M2, a 50-caliber machine gun, forward. Next to the heavy automatic weapon were the sensors and camera. The Marines in contact were instructed and knew to deploy IR strobes that the rest of the MSOT could see with their NODs, or night optic devices, assuming that these Chinese and Korean forces were like the ones they'd fought in California, without any night-vision capability. The problem was that unlike the previously contacted units, this PLA unit was operating at night.

SSC, Ennis, TX

Amanda jogged past her chosen MRAP in the cold tunnel, the overhead lighting casting hard shadows. If not for her familiarity with the tunnel and daily workout routine, she would have been concerned with all the dark spaces, but in the weeks that they had been in the secret underground facility not a single walking corpse had threatened them.

No, my threat is from a single walking man . . . I can't believe how stupid I was.

Frowning, Amanda quickened her pace, sweat falling from her face, steaming in the cool air. Upon reaching the paved-off wall at the end of the tunnel, beyond which lay the publicly known section of tunnels that had been filled with gravel and water; she turned and began her jog back to the main facility. What started off as a one-mile jog with more walking than jogging weeks ago was now a steady five-mile run. Amanda, who was now in the best shape of her life, felt fear and uncertainty fall away from her thoughts. With each footfall, her plan became clearer, and her resolve strengthened.

Tomorrow morning, tomorrow is the day.

A faint smile slipped through her mask to her face. Passing her chosen MRAP, she ran her fingers along the hull as she passed.

Foreign and domestic . . . .

The oath of office . . . Clint had sworn her in as President, with video-conferenced witnesses from Groom Lake . . . but the oath, a blur at the time, still resonated in her mind.

Foreign AND domestic . . . domestic, created by the Presidents before me . . . the Constitution . . . back to the basics . . . the basics.

The plan she'd made secretly from Clint's eyes, due to her burgeoning distrust of him, had to happen. She would make it happen, and it would begin in twenty-four hours. The list of items she had prepped scrolled through her thoughts, and she checked items off the list as she visualized the memory of placing each into the MRAP for her journey.

Groom Lake is well stocked. I just have to get there. All I have to worry about is ammo, fuel, and some food and water; the rest they will have in their stores.

Reaching the makeshift pull-up bars, Amanda stopped and caught her breath before jumping up and hanging from the athletic-tape-wrapped steel bar.

Groom Lake, NV

Jake sat in the mess hall slowly sipping at his black coffee while he read the *Alien Dispatch*, which was the Groom Lake newspaper of sorts. Every other day, the front and back printed sheet of copy paper was produced for all the residents. Containing what little news they had, the rest of the copy was full of stories, jokes, and a surprisingly engaging serialization about "what really happened in Roswell." A few people griped that the paper and copier toner used to produce the paper was a waste, but besides beans and bullets, the facility had a surprisingly large cache of office supplies. Which made a little sense in contrast to the square footage given to office space, cube farms still smeared with the dried gore of the original undead outbreak in the facility that Cliff had singlehandedly cleared.

It really seemed like Cliff should have returned by now.

The thought hung in Jake's mind as he watched a trio of women walk into the mess hall. Earlier than the usual crowd; only a few dozen people sat in small groups across the expansive room. *Her husband too . . . Cliff, her husband, and the other guy; the ragtag rescue party's radio traffic was weeks ago.* Jessie was barely beginning to show her pregnancy, which Jake found to be a strange juxtaposition of visuals: a pregnant woman with tactical kit and a rifle. It was one he wasn't accustomed to seeing but realized that it was the current and their future in their post-apocalyptic life.

Even in contrast to the other survivors, those women have an intense vibe radiating in every direction.

Jake tried not to stare as they walked between the tables. The women were armed, but everyone was armed at all times as a standing rule. The rifles, magazines, and tactical gear weren't what set them apart from the rest. It was their bearing, their focus, and even the way they walked that screamed of an intensity that the others didn't have, except for Cliff and the lost Para-Rescue Jumpers. They were similar, except they weren't pregnant. Fading inward to his thoughts, Jake didn't realize at first that the women were walking toward his table.

"Morning, Jake, we have a question."

Blinking and returning to the present, Jake set his coffee on the table. "I'm sorry, could you repeat that?"

"We said good morning and that we have a question."

"Well, good morning to you, Jessie, Sarah, and Ms. Erin. What is your question?"

"Bill told us that no one has fully explored the facility. The weather topside turned miserable yesterday, bad sandstorm across the lake bed, so we think the underground facility should be explored to create a map of sorts."

Jake nodded. Jessie was correct in that none of them knew the full layout of the facility, where every door went, what every room was, only that Cliff said he had cleared the entire facility and that it was safe. So far he was right, except Cliff wasn't here, and so now they had no idea.

"You'll need a full access key card."

"That's why we're talking to you."

Jake pulled the lanyard over his head, which held his ID card with his photo printed on it like some high school student, and handed it to Jessie. "If you find a door that won't open for my ID, then I don't know what to tell you."

Jessie put the lanyard around her neck. "Any hints before we get started?"

Jake described the layout of the facility as far as he understood it. "The labs are all the way down on level seven, but who knows. Cliff told me there was only enough food for two hundred people to survive on for a year, but he was wrong, well, not wrong but not right. There's enough MREs in the supply level to feed that many for perhaps longer than a year, but the dry storage we found is what we are eating now."

"Which will last how long with this many people?"

"The estimate is nearly five years, and we have fourteen hundred thirty-nine and a half residents," Jake said with a smile, glancing at Jessie's stomach.

Erin stood turned away from the table, listening to the conversation while watching for any threats that could approach the group. "How's that work out with all the bunk rooms?" she asked.

"Those weren't bunk rooms. Those rooms were all office spaces, cube farms, and, before you ask, I have no idea why, but strangely the supply cache had all the collapsible bunks and bedding. It was almost like the planners guessed that something like this would happen."

"I'll bet it wasn't a guess."

Jake sighed. "Probably not. Supposedly the labs on seven were working on the problem we currently have. I can't remember what Cliff called the project name, but there was only one of the scientists still alive when he arrived. His name was Lance, but he was killed in a lab accident."

"Like he blew up?"

"No, Erin, he was bit."

Saint George, UT

"Sure, but that's a big what if."

"I know it is, mano, but we've got to try. I mean we owe our lives to these guys. We repay that debt and the pop smoke, though first, I need to get my rifle."

"If it survived the wreck."

"Sure, Schrodinger's cat, right? It neither survived or was destroyed until we open the box."

"You have issues, dude."

"My biggest issue is your lack of balls and being a pussy about your leg."

"Hey!"

Chivo smiled, their whispered discussion before the rest of the house woke up being exactly what they needed. A plan, a means, and a bad attitude; everything required for success was put into motion.

"So get Angel, his guys, the horses, and we boogie down to the crash site and then come back. Then I can recon the other group. Kill those fuckers, find new wheels, and we get you to Area 51."

"What if we don't find new wheels?"

"Then we steal the horses."

"That's how you get hung, guy."

"I'm already hung, so what?"

Bexar smirked and shook his head. "OK, fine, Señor Machismo, so what's your timeline?"

"Five days? Seven tops. If my rifle survived, then I can simply put the other group under from across town. If it didn't, I'll have to improvise."

"More napalm?"

"Hell no, well, maybe, mano, you never know. We have to stay loose, improvise."

"Why do I feel like every time you improvise, something blows the fuck up?"

"Remember, smile, be kind . . . ."

". . . and be ready to blow everyone the fuck up?"

"Exactly."

Lost Bridge Village, AR

Oreo nudged Andrew, waking the pilot from a comfortable sleep on the sofa near the fireplace. Once Andrew sat up, Oreo walked to the back door and sat, tail happily swishing back and forth across the tile.

"OK, buddy, sniff it out first though."

Andrew pulled his boots on before unlocking and opening the back door, stepping onto the back porch with Oreo. Muzzle in the air, Oreo sniffed the air before deciding it was safe to go out into the grass for his morning constitution. The eastern sky glowed with the coming sunrise. When they stepped back into the house, Warren was in the living room, stirring the white coals in the fireplace before setting a blue enamel kettle on the glowing embers.

"Good morning, Pilot Andrew and Oreo."

"You're up early, Warren."

"If you have the chance to grow into an old man like myself, you'll find that early is normal. Besides, we need to get started early so we can meet up with the others by the lake."

"And do what?"

"Welp, 'ole Tom used to be one of the radio hams, I'd bet he'd want to look at the plans you wrote down yesterday. Then we find someone you can barter with for some gas-o-leen. Once Mary wakes and after breakfast, we'll head on down there, but for now I want you to tell me whereabouts them other survivors with the trade days were located."

Yuma, AZ

The hard fast thumping of the big M2 tore the air apart around the M-ATV. Nothing else sounded like one, and there was a reason why Ma Deuce has seen every war the U.S. has officially and unofficially fought in since John Browning designed it in the early twentieth century. Roughly five hundred rounds per minute ripped through all that stood in front of it in the practiced short controlled bursts fired by Kirk.

Twilight was beginning to break into dawn, removing the MSOT advantage of night optic devices. One of the APCs lay in ruin on the bridge; another had fallen off into the river after trying to evade the third, which lay burning to the north, blocking any escape the PLA forces had wanted to take. At least two dozen of the dismounts lay in ruin on the bridge in view. It was unknown how many were killed in the downed armored vehicles, but Aymond knew one thing for sure: there were nine more APCs, a radar truck, and some of the PLA bodies were starting to get up again. Quite undermanned and underarmed to be a true quick reaction force, the arrival of the second M-ATV helped Hammer and Snow break contact and gain some ground while the PLA's attention was diverted. It was all taking too long. They were stuck in a drawn-out battle, something they could not keep up for much longer.

"Hammer, kill the radar truck if you can, over!"

"Roger!"

Another 50-caliber round tore through the air, this time from the east, center punching the big rectangular antenna of the radar truck and rendering it useless.

"Good kill!"

Small arms fire thumped against the armored hull of the M-ATV.

"Chief, we've got to get moving or we're not going to have much of our ride left!"

Aymond nodded, his face set in stone, no emotion showing, just the hard eyes of an experienced operator thinking through a problem.

"Hammer, Snow, Happy, haul ass east on the eight, rendezvous at the Avenue 3E bridge, how copy?"

"Uh, Chief, Happy has the truck and is on the west side of the bridge."

Aymond grunted, the first outward sign of any emotion given during the battle. "Clear copy, Hammer. Happy, pop green smoke to pull attention away from Hammer and Snow, and then get north to Hammer and Snow. I don't care how you do it, just do it, how copy?"

"I'm clear, Chief, green smoke going out the door now, moving!"

"Kirk, one more burst, and then stop until I tell you different. Jones, get us moving back south. Go slow at first. We're going to rabbit them through town to our rendezvous point. Everyone clear?"

Various grunts and noises of positive affirmation could be heard among the Marines overcrowding the already cramped interior. The big M2 fell silent, and Jones sat stationary, the truck facing the north. Without the added benefit of the electronically zoomed display that Kirk had at the remote turret station, the APCs on the bridge appeared tiny. Slowly, green smoke began rising into the desert air to the west.

"Chief, it looks like they're splitting the mounted patrol into two groups."

Aymond nodded. "Kirk, give them a few more bursts to keep their attention."

The only answer given was the sound of Ma Deuce sending 50-caliber freedom prizes to the newly welcomed guests of America.

"Jones, pull forward about half a click. Then, Kirk, open up again. If they don't take the bait, then we'll have to drive back, motivate them a little, and then disengage and haul ass."

The heavy truck lurched forward more nimbly than would be expected before the tires chirped to a stop on the baked asphalt. The heavy machine gun opened fire again, and the staccato notes of return fire hitting the armor welcomed their presence.

"OK, turn us around and haul ass. Kirk, give our friends one more burst after we get moving, and then keep an eye on our six. I'm not really sure of the top speed of those APCs, but I want them kept close enough to feel like they're winning, but far enough away that they don't hard-kill the truck."

"Aye, Chief."

DAVE LUND

Jones shot forward, turning the wheel and bounding over the center median before slowing and speeding up again like someone trying to entice the fish to bite the bait on their line.

"We have six of the nine in pursuit, Chief."

Aymond nodded and keyed the radio. "Three unaccounted for, Hammer."

"Roger!"

Jones drove south on Business I-8 and into the heart of Yuma. "Chief, this is going to go right by our FOB."

"Yeah, I know, Jones. Assuming this works, we'll go back for the radar truck and our gear. If it doesn't, then we'll have to improvise a bit."

Internally, Aymond cringed. Improvising wasn't something he preferred to do. He planned and tasked, with plans to back up other plans and plans to back the back-up-plans.

"Save your ammo, Kirk, as long as they keep up the chase."

"Got it, Chief."

Jones swung the big truck from curb to curb, dodging Zeds and abandoned vehicles in the road. Aymond watched the road signs go by, trying to imagine the layout of the town he used to be familiar with.

"Jones, left now!"

Jones ripped the steering wheel hard left, the big M-ATV leaning on the long travel suspension, tires squealing on the pavement.

"Sorry, I remembered what street we needed when I saw the shopping center."

Jones shrugged, the classic shrug of an indifferent grunt just doing what he's told.

"Chief, they made the turn."

"Good, Kirk, maybe they think we're trying to shake them."

"Uhhh . . . maybe, they've sped up and are gaining on us now."

Aymond keyed the radio. "Snow, SITREP."

"Situation is we're rolling; the report is that we didn't toss smoke because Hammer left the APCs with glory holes for the Zeds to fuck them through."

Aymond nodded. The smoke was a diversion; he was hoping to make the Chinese and Koreans believe there were more of them, or that air support was coming in to chew them up. Anything, as long as it distracted them long enough for the Marines' play to unfold and disappear.

"ETA?"

Happy keyed the radio. "Call it five mikes, five clicks."

WINCHESTER: STORM

Aymond didn't have to say be careful; running one hundred kilometers an hour or roughly sixty miles per hour on the Interstate would have been slow last year. This year it was ludicrously fast while trying to dodge Zeds and vehicles.

"Jones, speed up and then take Pacific southbound. Try to keep it at about fifty clicks."

"Roger that, Chief."

The M-ATV sped up slightly before braking hard to make the right turn onto Pacific Avenue.

"Take it to Business 8 and turn left, and then we're going to go left on 3E, clear, Jones?"

"Clear, Chief."

Aymond looked at his watch and then at the map in his head, calculating the time for their path and Happy's path. *This might just work.*

"Happy, when you get to the bridge, park it, set a hasty ambush, and check in."

"Clear, good copy."

Aymond's overloaded truck swung left back onto Business I-8, running alongside the north fence line of the air station. As they passed the end of the main runway, the intersection of Avenue 3E was in view. Discipline kept Aymond from keying the radio to request another situation report. He knew the SITREP would come when it came; he had to trust his teammates.

Jones turned the truck north on 3E, speeding back up once he was pointed in the right direction.

"Jones, once Kirk gives the word that the PLA made the turn, I want you to floor it."

"The lead vehicle just made the turn, Chief."

Jones didn't wait for any other instruction; his right foot slapped the accelerator pedal to the floor, and the big turbo diesel roared. They were quickly nearing the railroad tracks and then the bridge for the hasty ambush. With nothing but radio silence, Aymond was internally wishing for the radio call to come across the speaker.

"We're set, Chief!"

Cold, with no emotion in his voice, Aymond replied, "Roger. Keep your speed, Jones. Once we clear the overpass, try to make a turn off and get us up on the highway."

Jones nodded.

. 30 .

The bridges flew overhead, a gray concrete blur as Jones stood on the brakes, frowning at the abuse his truck was taking. They would need to get comfortable and give him at least three days to work over the M-ATV in a location that had the tools and parts he needed or the truck would end up as a combat loss. They already had too many asses in the truck for seats; the remaining three Marines would make one truck nearly impossible to travel with as a team.

Skipping the desert to avoid having to drive through some fences, Jones made the turn off onto the north frontage by bounding through the ditch and back onto the pavement. Reaching the Interstate, Jones bounced the truck through the center median as he raced to the other truck, Kirk already bringing the mounted M2 into the fray.

Five APCs lay in ruin, charred corpses falling out of the trucks that were burning. The second truck's 50-caliber M2 caught the pursuing PLA by surprise and at close range. The heavy rounds punched through the armored personnel carrier's light armor like cardboard.

Aymond keyed the mic. "OK, back to the FOB. We get the other truck, get our gear, and we get our asses out of Yuma. If the PLA have radio contact, then it might be raining APCs in a short time."

SSC, Ennis, TX

Steam filled the cavernous shower room. Like a high school locker room, stainless-steel shower heads protruded from the tiled walls and columns.

More like a damn prison.

Hot water poured off Amanda's nude form. Her hands against the tile wall, her head and neck under the shower spray, Amanda felt her tight muscles begin to release from the morning's PT session. She examined what she could see. With her legs lean and muscular and her stomach flat, this was the best shape she had ever been in and the hardest exercise program that she had ever attempted. Apparently, after the world ends and you're trapped in an underground prison sheltering you from the storm that rages on the surface, there's time to exercise.

Clint often joined her in the shower. Today he didn't, and she was thankful he didn't. Amanda knew she was leaving tomorrow, and she wasn't sure if she was capable of keeping up the ruse much longer. Especially if her boyfriend . . . ex-boyfriend . . . was trying to get laid.

Using the checklist in her mind, she clicked off all the items that she had loaded into her MRAP. There wasn't much, just the essentials of some food, water, fuel, and as much ammo as she could scavenge without being noticed.

The little notebook in the pocket of her battle rattle held the long key code to open the main door on the surface, the secret rising platform built into a forgotten shed in a small park on a small lake in the middle of Texas. If she found any other survivors, she could write down the number and give it to them with directions to the facility. Clint be damned, she was going to save her country at all costs.

With a flick of her wrist, the shower went from steaming hot to ice cold, sending a momentary shiver through her body at the sudden change, Amanda took a deep breath and felt awake, more alive than she had in weeks. Everything felt more real now that she had an actual plan and she was going to be able to actually help people. Turning the water off, Amanda pulled the crappy military-issue towel from the hook on the wall, brushed away most of the water, and wrapped her hair into the towel before picking up her rifle, which hung by the sling from another hook on the wall. As she walked past the sinks and mirrors, she stopped to admire her fit athletic body. The scars of child bearing shone red against her pale skin. Her heart sank momentarily while thinking about her children. Frowning, Amanda walked into the bunk area adjoining the showers and to her footlocker. Digging through the contents, she came up with a pair of scissors that she had pulled from the supply cache after first arriving.

Standing in front of the mirrors over the sinks once again, Amanda removed her towel and began cutting at her long hair.

Lost Bridge Village, AR

Warren walked near Andrew. Oreo kept watch up ahead with Mary as they walked down the hill alongside the tiny airstrip. Mary was nearly twenty yards in front of them. Oreo's ears were perked up and on watch duty, his tail wagging slightly; he would nudge Mary every so often to have his head scratched. In her hands, she held the pink rifle from the day before. Warren had his rifle slung over his shoulder nonchalantly as if this was all perfectly normal for life in the United States.

Well, it is normal now.

"Our little community here kept together before the end, but looking back I should have pushed to organize everyone better. We lost a lot of people to the dead at first. Welp, we're nearly there, just a bit further now."

They passed by a fenced-off pool and building.

"What's that, Warren?"

"That was the civic center. Now we use it mostly for our weekly meetings. Outside of that, the pool is practically worthless, so much chlorine in it that it would pro'bly damn near kill a man if he tried to live by drinking much of it."

"Couldn't you distill it?"

"Sure'n we could, but don't need to really. A few of us have wells dug, and the rest can take water from the lake. We made filter buckets out of rocks and sand to pour water through, and then we boil the water to kill off anything we can't see. Works all right."

"Seems like you and the others were well prepped when the end came."

"Welp, we was thinking we was, but sure enough, we have so much that would make life better if we had it."

Mary stopped at a driveway, the home's backyard ending at the shoreline. A lone metal tower behind the house stood out of the tops of the trees against the blue sky. She waited with Oreo for Warren and Andrew to walk up as well.

"OK, little one, go'n ahead and knock."

Mary walked up the drive and knocked smartly on the front door. A few moments later, a balding middle-aged man who looked like he'd lost a significant amount of weight recently opened the door. He smiled at Mary, looked puzzled by Oreo, and was shocked when he saw Andrew standing with Warren.

"Morn'n, Warren, Mary. Who's the stranger?"

"He flew in yesterday. His name is Andrew."

"Flew? How'd you fly in here, flap your arms real hard?"

"He's got an areoplane up on the strip, out of gas and needs unleaded, but he's met other survivors . . . he also has something for you to look at."

"Like what?"

"Plans for a homemade radio, picked it up on the shortwave, them peoples over in Nevada broadcast it along with instructions on Morse code."

"CW, yes, sir, I know it already. Y'all come inside and let me see the plans you wrote down. We'll see what it is, and then we'll try to find some gasoline for your plane. It's just that what we've got left, we're trying to keep for the boats so we can fish and eat."

Andrew nodded. "I can respect that. Just remember that fuel goes bad, and fuel with ethanol in it goes bad even faster."

"Yup, we know," Will said with a hard glance at Warren, who acted like he didn't hear the discussion.

As they walked into the house, candlelight flickered in the living room. Dark curtains hung over the windows in Will's house just like they did at Warren's house.

"What kind of radio you have in your plane? Does it still work?"

"I have nothing. It didn't work, so I took it out to save weight."

"Huh. Well most of my shit got fried by the EMP . . . sorry, Mary. My radios were fried by the EMP. All I have left are a couple of cheap Chinese dual-band handhelds, for all the good they'll do you with only four watts of power and no way to charge them. Besides, who you going to talk to on two meter? All the repeaters are down, too, at least all the ones I could reach with those little things."

Andrew joined Will as he brought the candle from the living room and sat down at the dining room table. After handing Will the notebook and his notes, they all watched in silence as Will copied the notes onto a legal pad, nodding his head with a crooked smile.

"Yes, sir, top band with a spark-gap radio . . . this will work, this will work just fine. We're gonna have to get creative to build this antenna. First, we need to build a power source."

"They have directions for that too. I wrote them on the next page."

Will nodded and turned to the next page, reading intently.

"No, that design won't work. Well it will work, but it will just be hard to use. I have a better idea."

Saint George, UT

"Let's get a move on, vaquero."

Chivo grunted at Angel's remark. Angel led the afternoon's happy trail ride of two. Chivo followed Angel as they rode down the jagged desert hillside about a quarter mile north of the compound. This was the flattest descent and the only one the horses could take to head east without going back to the Interstate. Moments later, the horses' hooves clopped along the sunbaked asphalt of the now-defunct neighborhood.

"We cleared about half of these homes before giving up on finding anything useful. We evaluated the risk for the reward and decided to leave whatever forgotten supplies sat in these homes until we needed them, assuming that there is even anything worth needing left in the first place. I think our perspective of what we need might change in a couple years."

Chivo nodded, the reins of his horse held softly, which both surprised and didn't surprise Angel. Angel had heard rumors that Special Forces in Afghanistan had been using horses. It seemed like a random skill for a top-level operator to have, but Angel knew he was biased since he loved his horses. Snaking their way through yards with desert landscapes and crossing unfinished cul-de-sacs with half-built homes made it feel like they could be riding horses on Mars, except for the random homes in which the dead thumped against the windows trying to get out at a fresh kill as it passed. Trapped in their homes for all eternity. Chivo didn't know which was worse, living in the new world or the possibility of never quite being able to die.

Reaching the eastern edge of the subdivision, the pair were again crossing red dirt and desert. This time, they were close to I-15, much closer than Chivo would have liked, but the geography made them take this route. If they'd taken a different route further north, it would have added hours to their journey, increasing their time of exposure to danger and leaving the compound less protected longer than if they were there.

Chivo looked at the shimmering Interstate. The dead still owned this stretch of road, but their numbers were thinning with each passing day. He knew that every day that lapsed was another day that the other group could launch another surprise attack. Next time, they might not be so lucky as to only lose one member of the group. Operations such as this were a delicate balancing act, running down the high wire at full speed with no net to catch you. One little mistake could be the end. Chivo felt his horse tense up, quarters quivering, close enough to the dead to smell the rotting stench. The air around them buzzed with black flies. Petting the side of his horse's neck, Chivo tried to keep his mount as calm as he could. If his horse bucked him off, he would fall off the high wire. If the horse bolted, he would fall off the high wire. If a number of things out of his immediate control happened, he would fall off the high wire.

Rounding the edge of the hillside, their path turned more northerly and away from the teeming mass of death to the south. Truck yards full of CONEX containers sat in their path; the chain-link fences, CMU-made walls, and barbed wire fought to keep intruders out of the trucking firm's property, which made sense before the end.

"Angel, you guys could scavenge all these fences and build an outer perimeter or a series of concentric rings. The cliff on one side trumps it all, but adding layers of security will slow down future attacks."

Angel looked at the fences, nodding. "That's a good idea, but it would be hard to accomplish on horseback. We need a truck or a trailer that we could team the horses to, but we don't have any harnesses for such a thing."

"Then get a truck."

"Sure, but you had a truck, and look where you are now."

Chivo shrugged and kept riding as they passed outside a trailer park wall; they turned to ride around the side of a duplex and into another subdivision. This was their last hurrah before reaching the wrecked truck. More homes held the dead, or so it seemed, for the sounds of the dead throwing their bodies and their heads against the windows to get out increased in frequency. Some of the homes were burned-out shells. The lack of emergency services after the fall of society left homes to burn to the slabs and fire to spread as the wind blew it. Modern cars sat dormant in the twin driveways of the duplexes, except for one lone old Beetle that had been converted into a Baja-style Bug. Chivo didn't say anything, but he made a mental note to check the car on the way back.

Eventually, the pair reached the back of the squat convenience store and gas station on the corner, the last bit of cover before possibly having to enter the open area and be dangerously close to the Interstate and the chumming swarm of death it held. Dismounting, Chivo handed his reins to Angel. Still around the back of the convenience store, Chivo snuck around the edge to check for any threats before really reconning the area. The traffic lights were knocked over, the truck was a burned-out shell, and the bodies of the undead had melted and charred into the blackened pavement near the truck where they had caught fire. The scene was as gruesome as Chivo had ever seen in a long professional career of unique combat experiences. Binoculars now held up to his eyes, he scanned the scene in more detail. The fuel cans were nowhere to be found, presumably burned into the pavement, but Chivo expected nothing less with such a fire. Following the line from the damaged bridge railing where the truck had taken flight to where the truck crashed, he continued scanning along that path to find where the contents of the truck bed might have landed.

In the rock-lawn landscaping of the convenience store lay his prize, a long Pelican case, still latched. Behind one of the large rocks in the landscaping was a bit of green poking out. Chivo hoped it was some of their gear. Angel and his husband had a lot of gear cached, but anything extra would be an added benefit. Besides, Chivo didn't want to use up too much of the group's resources. They might need them after he and Bexar left.

Chivo returned to Angel and the horses. "Tie'em off. I found it. I'm going to dart out there to get it; I need you to hold cover for me just in case I missed something."

"Got it." Angel tied the reins to the electrical box on the back of the building and took a kneeling position on the edge of the corner. Chivo gave him a thumbs up and darted in a low crouch to a space between two palm trees in the store's landscaping. Waiting and scanning for a moment before darting again, Chivo reached the Pelican rifle case and found one of the gear bags they had brought from Cortez. Shouldering the bag, holding the rifle case, Chivo made one hard sprint for the building. Dead were falling off the bridge to a hard crunch on the burned pavement below. Trying to reach their new prize, the dead streamed out into the open from around the gas station across the street, their awkward, shambling gait slow but never ending. Chivo could hear them, but he didn't look back to see them as he sprinted, not slowing down until he passed Angel and the relative safety of the back of the building.

"No times to check your gear now, a bunch of dead are giving chase to the little Mexican that could."

Chivo smirked, tied the rifle case to the side of the saddle, and wedged the gear bag under his elbows and sort of in his lap. They left in a slow trot to gain some distance from the advancing dead, which made it around to the back of the convenience store just as they left.

Groom Lake, NV

The concrete at the bottom of the stairwell was darkly stained, blood smeared the walls, and it all smelled wretched. Jessie coughed and threw up at the smell. Leaning over the handrail of the stairs, she finished with a couple of dry heaves before spitting and trying to wipe the spittle and snot from her red face.

"Sorry. Pregnant nose."

"What?" Erin looked perplexed.

Sarah smirked: "Pregnancy is weird. You have to pee all the time, you can't remember what you were doing or why you came into a room in the first place, and your nose is really sensitive. Morning sickness is a cruel joke. It is really all-day sickness and with your newly found superpower of supersmell, it doesn't take much to set off losing what food you were able to keep down in the first place."

"That sounds horrible."

"It is," Jessie gasped, still trying to regain her bearings. "OK, well I think I'm done with that for now. The bottom floor is supposed to be the lab. Let's see what's behind door number one."

Jessie held the keycard against the RF reader, and the little LED light on the reader turned from red to green, the door lock releasing with an audible click. Jessie opened the door and held it open. Darkness greeted them. Erin loudly slapped her hand against the door frame a couple of times, but nothing stirred in the darkness.

"We should have brought something to hold the door open with."

"Mom has a point."

"She does, so if we see a door stop or something that we can use for one, grab it, and we'll take it with us."

Sarah and Erin nodded in agreement with Jessie as they switched on the lights mounted on their rifles. The bright lights piercing the dark room brought no surprises. No alien corpses, no dead, nothing but a dank-smelling foyer that could have been in any government building in America. Erin stepped into the dark room, flicking the light switch on the wall up and on, only to be greeted by another locked door with an RF reader for access.

Two for two, Jake's ID opened the doors they'd found, and the trio of women found themselves in the most secret lab of the U.S. government. It was empty, and Erin was again disappointed that there were no aliens.

"You would think with all the technology and the secrecy that there would have to be an alien in the mix somewhere."

Jessie looked at Erin as they pulled open the cabinets looking for anything interesting.

"Come on, what about the pyramids? Didn't you ever see that guy on TV talking about that?"

"The guy with the crazy hair?"

"Yeah."

Sarah raised her hands in front of her face like she was on TV. "But what if . . . aliens."

Jessie and Sarah both started laughing, until Jessie snorted, and then all three of them began laughing so hard that Jessie had to sit down.

Catching their breath, they turned out the lights and shut the doors behind them as they left. Standing in the stairwell once again, looking at the dark stains and now puke on the floor, Erin asked the question that all three of them were thinking: "Has anyone seen a zombie go upstairs before?"

Jessie shook her head. "No, but it doesn't matter. Always take the high ground. Make them fight up to you if they're dead or alive. Now I need to get out of this horrible stairwell before the dry heaves start up again."

Starting up the stairs, Jessie wondered how this pregnancy would go. Keeley's was easy, or at least her memory of the pregnancy was that it was easy. She knew about the blessing of giving birth; once you hold your newborn in your hands for the first time, all the memories of the terrible trials of pregnancy and childbirth begin fading away.

SSC, Ennis, TX

Amanda sat on her bunk eating her dinner. After her shower and haircut, she'd cleaned her rifle and pistol, disassembling each magazine one at a time to clean them and check the springs. Her gear reassembled and ready for the morning, she ate quietly and wondered where Clint had been; she hadn't seen him all day. The facility was quite large for being underground, but being the only two people in it meant that you tended to bump into each other a lot unless you disappeared on purpose. Even when she tried to do that, Clint would magically find her, *accidently* of course, and inquire as to what she was doing. Today he had been a ghost, until he walked into the bunkroom.

"I see you got your hair done. Get your nails did too?"

Amanda held up a hand, calloused from the pull-up bar and weight room, in front of her face and feigned blowing on her fingernails, which were cut short and unpainted.

"Yup! Now I'm just waiting for my facial and cucumber wrap while I eat my organic locally sourced MRE while wearing a pistol on my hip."

"There you go; the President deserves to be pampered a bit now and again."

"Where were you all day? Run to the store or something while I was getting my hair done?"

"Nope, I took the day off and spent it on the lake fishing."

"Seriously?"

"No, but I did spend some time up top pulling down some of the HESCO, so it looked more weathered and wouldn't give us up with SATINT."

"With what?"

"Satellite intelligence,. Remember, I have to assume that the Chinese and Koreans are jamming our ability to update imagery, but they probably still have full access to theirs. We need to keep ourselves under a dark rock for a good while until everything blows over, and having the entry gate completely blocked would stick out like a poodle at the dog track."

"Did you contact Groom Lake and warn them?"

"No, you know we can't do that. We have to run completely dark. Cliff knew what was up; he should have warned them before he left."

"He didn't know he wasn't coming back."

"Well, he should have finished up his task by now; hopefully he'll be back in the next few days. Depending on his outcome, we might be able to come out of the shadows."

"Why is that?"

Clint's expression didn't change, but he didn't answer.

"No, seriously, what was his mission, or what is his mission? After all we've been through together you still keep secrets."

"Don't we all?"

Amanda tried to keep her facial expression neutral, but she doubted she did it as well as Clint, who seemed to flip his emotions off and on like a light switch. "Honey, I'm an open book, and you're always a dark hallway."

"I'm sure."

Clint striped out of his utilities and walked into the shower room naked, dark scars on his back betraying his fit body.

Shit. He knows something is up. Will he try to stop me? Should I leave early? What if he blocked the exit while he was topside?

Her mind spun faster and faster before she finally took a few deep breaths and realized there was nothing she could do about it at the moment. If she tried to leave now, it would tip her hand. If she waited until just before sunrise as planned, nothing changed, except if her path was blocked. If Clint had taken steps to stop her, she might have a chance to figure it all out before he realized she was trying to leave.

So many problems, and all of it caused by one asshole at the end of the world.

Yuma, AZ

"Marines, we have a choice. We can't go west because that's where we came from. I don't want to go south because we'll quickly be in Mexico, and we need to find friendly forces to help bring the fight back to the tangos. Do we go north or east?"

Aymond stood next to the loaded trucks, which idled loudly, his team standing in a half circle around him.

"We don't have much time to chat about this, gentlemen. We have to assume the PLA is about to make it rain and we're out of umbrellas."

"Did you actually just say that out loud, Chief," Gonzo replied.

A mixed response of "north" and laughter was all that came after from the rest of the men.

"OK, north it is, but why north?"

"Fucking Vegas, Chief. We're going to get us some shore leave and party."

"Sure, Happy, of all the places in the world that survived, Vegas would be it."

"We could also see the Hoover Dam, Chief."

"I've always wanted to hit up Area 51; I want to see some spaceships."

"And aliens."

"Hammer, Snow, fine. You two can hold hands and go be fucking tourists in the ruins of our country. Maybe as high rollers, you'll get comped a room. The rest of us are going north with purpose. Load it up!"

Nothing else was said. The Marines took their spots in the two M-ATVs, while Jones took the driver's seat of the radar truck. They drove out of their HESCO-lined position to the wilds unknown. Aymond wondered if the Hoover Dam might be a good place to take a low-key defensive position under all that concrete, before realizing it would be catastrophic if the dam were bombed or if it failed for some reason.

Pulling out onto Highway 95 and pointed northbound, Kirk finally asked, "So where are we headed, Chief?"

"You chuckleheads want to go to Vegas, we'll go to Vegas, but I want to see if any PJs are hanging around Nellis. We could use some of them in our merry band of raiders."

"That we could, Chief, that we could."

Lost Bridge Village, AR

Andrew enjoyed the best dinner that he and Oreo had eaten in some time and all out of a household fireplace, cooked in a single Dutch oven. It was amazing. Either it was amazing or his standards had slipped significantly since the fall of man; regardless, he felt welcomed and happy amongst his newly acquainted fellow survivors, which was better than some of the receptions he'd had in the past few weeks.

"Andrew, where was you saying that you saw the military units?"

"I'm not sure they were actually military units. They were driving military vehicles in a short convoy and appeared to be wearing camouflage uniforms, but I gave them a wide margin for fear they weren't military and weren't friendly. Overall, I've had much better luck landing next to small communities that have built up and walled off."

"Walled, how walled?"

"Well, I've seen a little of everything, Will. The best I saw was a ring of those metal shipping containers that they put on train cars. The guards could walk on top of them and shoot from an elevated position if necessary."

"I can see it. Those containers are hard to come by 'round these parts. Besides we got no way to move something heavy like that."

"Do you need it, with the lake at your back?"

"We need sumth'n. We get about a dozen a week falling down the hillside into our neighborhood here."

"A dozen? You should be so lucky. Tomorrow I can show you my atlas. I've been tracking massive swarming herds of the dead, like bison of the old frontier, roaming the countryside but destroying all they find. I've see cars pushed off bridges, lights knocked down. I even saw a couple houses knocked over from the sheer relentlessness of them all together. Scariest thing I've seen so far. I can't imagine how someone would survive if caught in the middle of a swarm."

Will and Warren both looked at Andrew with surprised expressions.

"The worst part," Andrew continued, "is the smell and the flies. Sweet Jesus, the flies are bad, like a thick dark cloud. I made the mistake of trying to figure out what the pulsing cloud was when I first saw it and flew down next to it all. Took me a solid hour to wipe all the dead flies from my windshield and the leading edges of my wings."

They all sat in silence for a moment, Warren and Will imaging what Andrew was describing and Andrew reliving the scene in vivid detail.

DAVE LUND

"So, uh, Will, what is your plan for a better power supply for the radio? What's wrong with the one they described?"

"Their plan means that you have to keep cranking with one hand while you tap out your message with'n the other. Nope, I'm going to use a bicycle on a stand to turn an electric motor from my workshop to charge a car battery. All I'm have'n to do is modify the motor and the bicycle and make a stand. The rest is the easy bits."

"So what first?"

"First is you go on back up the hill with Warren before it gets dark. First light, I'll be up to start build'n, and you come on down here and help. Sound good to you, Warren?"

"Yes, sir, it does."

"Great, be see'n you in the morning. God's speed to you all."

Will stood up and scraped the remaining food on his plate back into the Dutch oven, set the plate on the hearth, and walked to the back of the house.

"Mary, it's time to go, Princess."

Mary stood, checked her rifle, and walked to the front door, Oreo plodding along beside her with his tail wagging. Outside the sky was already glowing with the mix of yellow, red, and blue of the setting sun. Nightfall was quickly approaching. Warren and Will knew what all the rest of the survivors knew: the night belonged to the dead. You can't see them, and they can't see you, but they can hear you, and they seemed to have a supernatural ability to triangulate sounds to find you from surprising distances.

Saint George, UT

The firepit glowed, the wood popping and hissing. Chivo's big 50-caliber rifle lay propped up against his chair while he sipped on John's homebrew, a reward for such a successful day. Thanks to the horses, he and Angel were able to redirect the pursuing dead away from their path back to the compound. After testing the rifle, with Bexar sitting at the spotting scope to call out shot placements on targets, Chivo declared the optic sound and the rifle to be in proper working order. The only disappointment was the loss of one of the gear bags, but for such a bad wreck, overall the outcome was quite positive. Guillermo and the others not sitting watch duty finally left them alone after wanting to hear every detail of the day's action. Chivo didn't consider it a day of action at all, but when compared to living in a well-prepped fenced-off compound, he guessed it seem like an adventurous story.

"Like a slug-bug?"

"Yeah, but Baja style, off-road tires and cut-off fenders and such."

"Does it run?"

"Hell if I know, mano. I just saw it today, and we had to make up some shit to keep the dead from following us home like some lost fucking puppy."

"So what next?"

"Next, you get healed up and fast. While you're healing, I'm going to take care of Guillermo and Angel's problematic associates, and then we check the VW and bug out quick like."

"Wow, bug out? Really?"

Chivo smirked. "What, mano, like you wouldn't make that joke if you had the chance."

Bexar said nothing and raised his pint glass as acknowledgement.

CHAPTER 5

SSC, Ennis, TX
April 3, Year 1

Amanda dressed in the dark, putting on utility pants and a T-shirt, the typical uniform of the day at the SSC. Clint appeared to be sleeping in his bunk across the room. She looked at her dark bunk, the white sheets and wool blankets. They had shared a bed, pushing two of the bunks together. After shrugging into the smaller tactical carrier she used day-to-day and slinging her rifle over her shoulder, she looked across the room into the shadows and at the dark form of Clint's body.

I should kill him. If I killed him now, then he couldn't stop me . . . no.

Frowning, Amanda walked out of the bunkroom as quietly as she could. As angry as she was with Clint, she wouldn't kill him. The ugly honest truth pulsing through her thoughts was that she wasn't all that angry at Clint. She was angry at herself for acting so foolish.

That was the last time. Never again. I have a country to salvage . . . if there is one left.

Each quiet step through the corridors emboldened her mood, made her more confident that her choice was the only right choice and that she could succeed, would succeed. A few minutes later, she stood next to *her* MRAP. After she unplugged the block heater, Amanda shrugged out of her smaller tactical carrier and put the fatigue jacket on over her T-shirt. Then the heavier armor carrier that she left stashed in the truck went over that. The steam from her breath hung in the cold underground tunnel; each breath sounded thunderous, her heartbeat thumping so loudly in her ears that Amanda worried it would wake Clint. Shaking her head, Amanda climbed into the heavy MRAP and looked at the few cases of MREs, stacks of ammo in green metal cans, and water in the plastic jerry cans that she had cached since first forming her plan.

"Well, shit, here goes nothing."

Switches turned to the on/run selection, a push of a button, and the starter groaned to push the turbo diesel before it coughed to life, thunderously rattling in the tunnel.

Dear God, that's loud. He has to know now. He's going to . . . .

Amanda took a deep breath and rapped her knuckles against the driver's side window, which didn't make a sound. Heavily armored and powerful, as long as she didn't tip the truck over or seriously damage a tire, she thought she would be fine.

After pushing Drive, Amanda drove through the tunnel toward the exit, and her journey began with no sign of Clint.

SSC Command Center

Clint sipped the instant coffee, which had grown cold over the last two hours. A few keystrokes later, the closed-circuit monitor turned from greens and black hues to color, the lights in the bunkroom now illuminated. Amanda's bunk showed empty covers left askew. On his bunk, a pile of pillows lay under the covers. On another monitor, the MRAP drove slowly through the tunnel to the far north exit. He was fairly sure that Amanda didn't know where she was going to emerge on the surface, but Clint knew the exact spot and wished he still had overhead imagery so he could see what Amanda did when she didn't recognize the remnants of the old road. Parts of the steel bridges were still in the lake, which he was sure the fish loved, but the road was gone. Two turns and the country roads would run into the highway. Clint pulled a road atlas out of the bag next to him, trying to remember which highway it was.

Finding the lake and Highway 287, he traced the route he believed Amanda would take to get to Groom Lake and shook his head. Amanda had no idea how perilous the route was. If she was smart enough to stay off the Interstates, she might have a chance. With a small ruler, he traced the route to scale and made some notes.

The direct route takes some twenty-two hours of driving. She will have to refuel at least every three hundred miles, and if she stays off I-40, it could take an extra five hours . . . probably five days there and then five days back, plus layover—except there would be no return trip.

Clint flipped the pages in the big spiral bound atlas and traced another route, making notes.

Sixteen hours. No return, two days of driving, another day to enter and complete the objective.

A few clicks of the computer mouse and the daily planner calendar for his username appeared on the screen. Clint counted the days off, trying to fit his plan just perfectly.

Groom Lake, NV

Jessie sipped green flavored water. She wasn't sure what it really was or what it was supposed to taste like, but it was made with green-colored powder and tasted like nothing else. Sarah drank dark hot coffee, which Jessie really wanted, but she'd sworn off caffeine for the pregnancy. Erin walked to the table holding a tray; she set it in the middle of the table, three plates for the three of them.

Jessie tried not to smell the powdered eggs covered in processed cheese that Sarah began eating and instead focused on trying to nibble at the food on her plate and keep down some of her dry white toast. Erin ate buttered toast.

Jessie put her toast down and pushed the plate away from her. "Which way do we go today, Erin?"

"Sideways."

Jessie looked puzzled. "Sideways?"

"Yeah, Jason told me that there's supposed to be another bunker toward the north via some tunnels; the computers that run this place are in another room that way too."

Sarah glanced at her daughter and then Jessie, raising her eyebrows, before acting like she couldn't hear the conversation and continuing to blissfully eat.

"When did you see Jason?"

"Last night, after his shift ended."

"Where were we?"

"Uh, sleeping."

Jessie glanced at Sarah, who was still playing the role of a deaf-mute mother, before she directed the conversation back to the beginning.

"Do we know how to get to those tunnels?"

"Not exactly, but *we* might have an idea where a secret door is hidden."

Sarah finally decided to be a part of the conversation. "Why a hidden secret door? We're in a secret hidden facility under a secret base that isn't supposed to exist?"

"Aliens?"

They all had a good laugh, before Jessie stood up and announced she had to pee again and left.

Sarah bussed the table while Erin followed Jessie, beginning a conversation about birthing and what a newborn was like. Jessie stopped, suddenly aware of the connection.

"You're not sleeping with him, are you?"

Erin looked hurt. "No, and if I were, what does it matter?"

Jessie glanced across the room to where Sarah was standing talking to one of Jake's "mayor staff" and then back at Erin.

"I guess you're right. It doesn't matter. It only matters if you get pregnant. Do you want to bring a baby into this . . . this new life of ours?"

The lights cut out, the soft hiss of the air system being replaced with the capacitor sound of the emergency lighting flickering on.

"See, here we are in the safest place I've found and they can't even keep the fucking lights on."

The doorway's exit sign glowed red above them. Erin shook her head.

"I think about your baby every day, and it isn't even born yet. I don't know what you're going to do. We can't live here forever. Eventually we have to move topside, and we need to be able to hunt, farm, and gather what we need. We're in the fucking desert and . . . and that just won't work. And, no, I'm not sleeping with him; he's just a friend who misses his dead wife. Everyone we know dies, and now your baby is coming, and your husband isn't even here, so I have to be ready. What the fuck else am I supposed to do?"

Tears streamed down Jessie's face while she gave Erin a hug. "Thank you."

Erin nodded, trying to act like she wasn't wiping her eyes as well. The lights came back on as Sarah made her way to them.

"What was that about?"

"Nothing, Mom. Jessie, don't you still have to pee?"

"Oh, God, yes!" Jessie walked away quickly.

"Are you OK, Erin?"

"Yes, Mom. What did that chick want?"

"That was Marcia; she's looking for Brit, and apparently she hasn't been seen in a few days."

"Good, that bitch should be hiding for her worthlessness. She nearly got bit for being an idiot."

Sarah didn't respond, only sighed as she followed Erin down the passageway to wait for Jessie so they could begin their hunt for the hidden door.

Lost Bridge Village, AR

Mary followed Andrew and Oreo out the front door, her pink rifle at the ready, and the intense glare of her eyes betraying her fierce soul. Satisfied that they were currently free of the undead, with Oreo's agreement, the three walked to Andrew's parked aircraft at the top of the ramp.

"What can you do with such a small plane?"

"We can go just about anywhere. It's a Husky, and it's designed to be abused by pilots in the Alaskan brush country. There are no roads between villages there, so aircraft ferry people, food, supplies, and medicine."

"You can't carry much in that though."

"No, Mary, you can't. It's not like driving a pickup truck or something, but when I say this can land and take off just about anywhere, I'm not kidding. One guy even had a bear attack his plane in the bush once. A buddy flew out a box of duct tape and in a few hours he was flying back to home to complete a repair that would be more pleasing to someone with the FAA."

"What is the FAA?"

"They're . . . they were in charge of pilots and airplanes in the U.S. before all this went down. See the numbers and letters on the vertical stab—the tail fin?"

"Yeah."

"That's the N-number, like a license plate. The N means this plane is based in the United States."

"Is it hard to fly?"

"Not too hard, just takes practice."

"Can you teach me?"

Andrew looked at Mary, her eyes no longer showing the hard stare of before; her eyes glowed brightly with delightful curiosity.

"We'll have to talk to Warren and find more fuel, but, well, maybe we could start with just a test flight first."

It wasn't a yes, but it wasn't a no either, Andrew couldn't bear to disappoint someone who needed some hope, but airplanes were rotting into the tarmac in their tie-down spots, and who knew how many pilots were even left. The road atlas in his hand, Andrew patted his leg, and Oreo returned to his side from across the airfield. He reached down to pat his friend on the head only to see Oreo startle at the touch. Andrew looked across the field at the tree line and back up the road out of the small lakeside community. He didn't see anything, but he hadn't stayed alive this long by not trusting Oreo. He knew trouble was coming before trouble even knew where it was going.

Quartzsite, AZ

The last watch finished their sleep rotation, and the short-hop from the Yuma overnight spot, a tiny spec of a town on I-10, was complete. Aymond had no desire to drive through the night into the unknown. With the complete lack of air support causing serious problems for his men as seen in the previous battle, he gambled that they could stop even if only traveling a few hours away, even if the PLA may be giving chase. The sun was up, and sleep rotations for a team took longer than sleeping through the night would normally take, but it was essential to get everyone rest and still maintain security.

Aymond stood on top of the lead M-ATV, binoculars to his face, slowly scanning the area. He couldn't tell if the destruction and desolation was just how this town was or if the Zeds had caused it. Highway 95 North was the road they needed to be on, but they had to cross I-10 first, which lay about seven hundred meters to the north. No cars appeared to be on the bridge, which could be a good sign or could be bad, meaning the bridge was no longer there.

"Ready to roll, Chief!"

"Fuel?"

"Siphoned and served out of those big RVs across the way."

"Roger that, Snow, load it up and roll."

Aymond climbed off the roof and took the front passenger position, pulling the heavy armored door closed with a thud, noticing the new heavy-looking bags hanging on the rail outside of the rear bay, a rainbow of colors.

The convoy pulled onto the highway and rattled northbound. Clicking the comm-link push to talk, Aymond asked, "What's with the new fashionable-looking rucks hanging off our rigs?"

Snow, passenger in the second M-ATV, replied, "Found some useful shit in those RVs, Chief, thought we'd bring it along."

"Like what?"

"You know, Chief, a few gallons of milk, some yogurt, just about everything from the fridges that would survive and add to our morale."

Aymond didn't respond to the joke, the silence growing louder with each moment. Gonzo stopped the convoy. Aymond keyed again, "Bridge is out. Happy, Hammer, and funnyman Snow, dismount and see what's up."

Kirk turned the remote turret left and right, looking for any threats. Gonzo slowly rolled the lead truck to a slow walking pace, giving the dismounted Marines a place to take cover if needed. Snow stopped at the ragged edge and looked east and west along I-10 before keying, "Chief, the bridge is demo'ed, lots of Zeds crushed by it. All the cars on the I-10 are pushed to the ditches, like a huge dozer came through and destroyed everything."

Aymond thought for a moment. "Did the bridge seem to go east or west?"

"East . . . Chief, there's another bridge to the east and another bridge to the west; they're both demo'ed as well."

"Options, gentlemen?"

Happy keyed, "Yeah, Chief, what if we backtrack, hit one of those small roads, go west, and make our way to where the other bridge was. We could use the on- and off-ramps to get around all these damn fences."

Aymond didn't have to ask why he wanted to go west. Aymond wanted to go west, too; a group of Zeds powerful enough to destroy bridges is something they didn't need right now.

"All right boys, mount back up. Do it like Happy said."

Westward the convoy went, passing a trailer park and more RVs before reaching an intersection with a truck stop. What Aymond couldn't figure out was why no Zeds came out of the areas with homes or RVs as they passed.

"Snow, when you went shopping did you find any Zeds?"

"Just a few that were trapped in their coaches, didn't see any out in the wild."

"Guys, if a passing horde of Zeds goes by, do you think it was like the Pied Piper, taking all the walkers out of town?"

Kirk was the first to respond. "Maybe, but let's clear I-10 and then this shithole town before we verify any wild guesses."

Aymond knew Kirk had a point.

The convoy easily drove down the Interstate on-ramp, crossed the median at a spot that appeared to be for just such a purpose, and then drove up the off-ramp, turning right and pointing north once again.

The sign said "Main Saint," but there wasn't much to it while they traveled east. Reaching the original route, the convoy turned north again. More RV parks flanked either side of the roadway. For once, Aymond was glad to see abandoned cars in the road, even if they did have to drive around them. It was a blessing in disguise—they weren't on a motivated Zed route. A smattering of businesses passed by, but not a single Zed to be seen. The scene was eerie, and Aymond could feel that he wasn't the only one whose alarm bells were ringing.

Quickly the small town was behind the convoy, and the open desert bloomed before them with nothing but hard, parched asphalt beneath their tires and some mountains in the distance. Forty-five minutes later, the convoy stopped just south of Parker, Arizona. In the town ahead, they could see the dead meandering through the middle of town with no real direction or purpose.

Those were the dead that Aymond was used to seeing; the thought of them somehow teaming up to bring down concrete bridges wasn't one that he wanted to consider.

Ennis, TX

Shortly after the whine of the massive hydraulic and screw set began moving, a crack of light appeared, dirt and sand falling off the edge to the concrete ramp where Amanda sat comfortably in the big MRAP. The crack of light grew and slowly the large heavy door rose, her eyes protested the sudden glare of morning sunlight. Amanda squinted and drove the big armored truck up the ramp and onto the surface.

Her trip to the SSC from Little Rock had been perilous, even with her two specially trained agents. However, that was mostly due to their Gulfstream jet being destroyed and having to acquire civilian vehicles along the route, which were not able to stand up to the abuse of warlike conditions.

This war against the dead, how long will it last? How long will we have to fight? How will we win . . . what if we don't win?

Amanda had a rough idea where she should be by the general layout of the facility, as far as she understood it. At the gate she could go right or left. Left led to a dirt trail, right led to a small road, so her first decision was an easy one. The huge door to the secret world below closed slowly behind her. After taking a deep breath, her resolve solidified, and onto the road she drove.

Passing unkempt pasture, Amanda took the first road to the right that she came to and traveled in a mostly northern direction. The highway sign said 287. There wasn't a bridge or on-ramp, just a divided rural highway. Indifferent to the stop signs, Amanda crossed and turned left.

I need a road map, so I need a gas station or a truck stop.

With nothing but open country and farmland in her view, the roadmap would have to wait. In her memory of arrival, Amanda had a rough idea of what highways she would be immediately using, and she knew that Highway 287 was her first significant road. Alone with her supplies, with no music to play for the trip, Amanda drove in silence at a blistering forty-five mph, thinking, planning, and contemplating all that had transpired since late December.

The roadway had some disabled traffic and a handful of shuffling undead that she easily passed without incident. The plan was to stay away from the Interstates if at all possible. That had gotten them to the SSC from Little Rock, and it would serve her well here too.

The minutes ticked by, as did the miles covered. The highway carved around the top of Waxahachie, becoming a strange mix of rural and highly developed seemingly at once. The highway signs still stood, which was a help. The blue highway sign had the logos of some gas stations on it for the exit, so she took the exit.

On the frontage road, abandoned cars sat dead in place staggered back from the dark stoplight. As carefully as she could, fearful of getting stuck, she drove the MRAP into the grass between the frontage road and the highway, around the abandoned cars, before bouncing over the concrete island and into the intersection. Stopped momentarily in the intersection, Amanda looked at the gas station on the corner. Three cars were in view at the pumps. The windows were smashed out of the building, but the large green-and-white sign still stood triumphantly. The slap of rotting hands against the rear of the armored truck startled Amanda back into the reality of what she was trying to accomplish. Amanda turned and drove sharply away, heading north before threading the needle between more cars to drive into the driveway of the gas station.

Parked between the gas station and a Waffle House, Amanda left the MRAP running, its nose pointed to the exit onto the frontage road so she could continue. The dead she left in her wake at the intersection were making their way toward her, and more came around from the back of the Waffle House. Amanda knew she didn't have much time.

In a quick walk, Amanda held her M4 at a low ready, scanning the dark interior of the gas station for any signs of movement and then checking around her to keep track of how close the closest threats were. If possible, Amanda wanted to conserve her ammunition; she only had so much with her, and she only had herself, so fire discipline would be up to her alone.

She didn't see any movement in the shadows, but the smell coming from the gas station was horrible. All the food had rotted, the few cartons of milk and anything else in the cooler. The smell mixed with the smell of the corpses chasing her into the pungent smell of the new world. The door was locked, but the glass was broken out of it, so Amanda stepped through the hole where the glass had once been and into the convenience store. Flies inside the store dive-bombed her eyes and ears. Behind the counter, she found a handful of fold-out roadmaps, all sealed in plastic so people couldn't use them to figure out the directions they needed without purchasing one first.

The sound of something hitting the door and then hitting the ground with a hard, hollow thud helped motivate Amanda to speed up her scavenge mission. She grabbed one of each on the rack without paying attention as to what they were maps of. Turning around, she saw a body get up off the floor, pieces of broken glass stuck into the skin of his hands and face. A second corpse tried to step into the small convenience store and tripped over the bottom of the door, falling to the ground with a similar sound as the first, making no attempt to catch himself. Looking past her two new visitors, she saw a small welcoming party forming on the side of the gas station that she had come from. Deciding that discretion was the better part of valor, Amanda stepped through the door on the south side of the store, leaving her trail of undead friends to trip their way through two doors to follow.

Sitting safely in the MRAP once again, Amanda drove out of the driveway and onto the frontage road to resume her westward course. While driving, she looked at each one of the road maps that she had acquired. She had a map for New Mexico, Texas, and Oklahoma, plus specific maps for Dallas/Fort Worth and Houston. Houston and Oklahoma wouldn't be useful to her for this trip, but the maps would be kept, just in case.

Stopping in the middle of the highway next to a sign indicating how far away she was from Dallas and Fort Worth, Amanda tore open the Texas map and the DFW map. It took her a few moments to find Waxahachie on the Texas map; tracing her finger along the line for Highway 287, she turned her attention to the DFW map. She had to go near Fort Worth, but she didn't want to have to go through it.

Groom Lake, NV

"This is where Jason said it would be."

"Maybe Jason was wrong, honey."

"I don't know, Mom, maybe, but maybe we aren't looking at quite the right place."

Jessie listened to Sarah and Erin but stood in the hallway with the door to a janitor's closet standing open. The storage closet had the usual janitorial supplies one would expect, except that it seemed larger than it should be. Stepping past the shelves, she saw why.

"Erin, Sarah, in here."

Past the shelves was a large metal door painted in battleship gray. The little panel on the wall next to it contained a keypad and an RF reader. None of them knew what the numeric code could be, but the door clicked open with the card that Jake had given them.

"This place is spooky."

"After all we've seen and done, Jessie now decides that a secret door in a secret facility at a secret base is what makes it spooky," Sarah quipped with a smirk. Erin laughed.

"You know what? Fuck you both! Why don't one of you lead the way inside." Jessie stood aside and held her arm out like she was holding open the door to a restaurant. Erin stepped into the hallway, followed by Sarah and Jessie. The door closed behind them with a hiss and a heavy thud.

Erin turned around to look back at the door, "OK, now that was spooky."

"See, told you."

"Children, girls, cut it out. We have work to do."

Jessie and Erin both replied sarcastically, "Yes, Mommy."

Gray concrete walls matched the gray metal door at the entrance. The overhead lights were spaced just far enough apart that there were hard shadows on the floor between each of them. After what Erin estimated to be around one hundred feet, the trio reached another gray metal door, a recessed camera above it. This time, there were no handles or knobs, just a smooth flat door, but there was another RF chip reader on the wall, and the small LED turned from red to green after Jessie placed Jake's ID next to the reader. The door slid into the wall instead of swinging out or in to open. Beyond the door on the left side was a bland-looking office full of government furniture, some fake plants, and a fake window painted on the wall. To the right were showers that looked sterile and cold, all completed in sealed concrete. They didn't see any other doors in the office and decided to walk through the shower room to see if there was anything else.

An opening in the concrete snaked around a wall and to another room. This room looked like a smaller version of the supply warehouse in the main facility. As they walked through the facility, the lights flickered on automatically in each area they entered. At each transition to another room, the concrete was raised like a mini-wall about a foot high that they had to step over.

"Think this uses the same power as the main facility? Think this is safe from the rolling blackouts we experience?"

Jessie and Sarah gave noncommittal grunts in return to the questions. Beyond the storeroom was a bleak hallway with hotelesque signs pointing left or right for the bunkroom, dining hall, and common area. Meandering aimlessly and silently, they walked toward the bunkroom first. Appearing to have enough space for about fifty people, the bunkroom was outfitted with the same sort of beds and lockers as theirs was in the main facility. The restroom and showers looked the same, except that there was no obvious delineation for male or female in the bunkroom, restroom, or showers. The dining room was another, and again smaller, copy of the main facility, but the common room was something new. There was a large TV with rows of DVD cases filling shelving along the wall, a pool table that converted into a ping pong table, and a dart board.

Sarah broke the silence first. "Looks like a crappy bar or a low-grade frat house."

"Except that there's no bar to be seen. If I had to live here, I'd need a strong drink handy."

Erin shook her head. "No, don't you two get it? This is supposed to keep a special group of people alive if the first facility gets compromised. The designers expected the first facility to be vulnerable to something. The walls we had to step over? Probably to trip someone if they're not paying attention . . . this was designed as a refuge if there was an outbreak in the main facility. The little walls are to trip the dead, to slow them down so the survivors could kill them."

"Then why don't we have those in the main facility?"

"I don't know, Mom."

"What if it's because the zombies were too secret, like above top secret or whatever it is, so secret that even those who worked and lived in a secret underground facility at a secret base weren't to be trusted with the information?" Jessie said.

"Now that's damn creepy," Erin said, looking around the room. "If we've found all we can find, then I want to get back to the normal secret-alien-base shit."

Everyone agreed. They quickly finished checking for any more doors and retraced their steps until they were in the welcoming office with the showers. A small sign above the entrance to the showers stated "DECONTAMINATION," but they weren't sure who would be decontaminated from what. The next to last door opened to a dark hallway.

"Were these lights on or off before we stepped into the hall the first time?" Jessie shrugged. "I don't know, maybe off?"

Erin rolled her eyes, clicked on the weapon light on her rifle, and stepped into the darkness. The other two followed. The RF pad's LED wasn't lit green or red; it appeared to be off. Jessie tapped the ID against it a few times and got no response. Erin pushed on the door and was surprised to find it unsecured. The janitor's closet was dark, and the hallway seen through the open closet door was dark.

"Now *this* is spooky, Jessie." Erin cautiously stepped through the janitor's closet, Sarah and Jessie following.

"Maybe it's just a normal blackout, but we answered our own question. Past the camera door, it is on separate power; the hallway through to here is on this facility's power."

Everyone nodded in agreement with Jessie, not that they could be seen in the darkness.

From deep inside the main facility, they heard screams and rapid gunfire.

MSOT, Parker, AZ

The town seemed to consist completely of low-roofed strip-center shopping, gas stations, and palm trees. Zeds swarmed the convoy as they rolled through the middle of town, but they were too few to be an issue to the Marines. Soon they were crossing the Colorado River to take a left onto Route 62. The convoy climbed along the highway up the desert mountains, and any trace of civilization seemed to fall away. The convoy poked along at fifty mph in a part of Arizona so remote that it seemed even the wildlife commuted.

The minutes ticked by slowly, the hours following. Aymond checked his watch for the sixth time in as many minutes. Eventually they turned right onto Highway 95 and were pointed north again. In the back, the other Marines were sleeping.

"You going to be good to drive longer?"

"Yeah, Chief, no worries."

Aymond nodded and leaned against the door, falling asleep quickly.

It took a moment for his mind to snap back into place. "Chief, time to get up." Gonzo was shaking him.

"What, Gonzo?"

"Chief, we're in Needles, Arizona. The problem is that this highway jumps on Interstate 40 for a while."

"Is it overrun or has a herd of Zeds leveled everything?"

"Don't know yet, we're closing on it right now, wanted you awake for it."

Aymond nodded.

As they approached the overpass for I-40, it appeared to be intact. Gonzo drove under it and turned left, following the highway signs. Taking the ramp onto I-40, they saw that the cars on the Interstate were pushed from the center, but the damage wasn't as intense as they had seen on I-10.

"Same thing, just not as much. Maybe it was a smaller group of Zeds." Gonzo shrugged.

"Well, keep on going; we'll have to figure it out along the way."

Looking out the small bulletproof window, they could see that the town they were passing teemed with Zeds. Most of them didn't appear to notice the convoy passing by, but that could change in an instant. Quickly they were past the town and in the desert, and shortly after that Gonzo followed the signs and turned north on Highway 95. If Aymond was remembering correctly, they wouldn't hit another town until they were just outside of Las Vegas.

Lost Bridge Village, AR

"Bob said to be bringing the parts we got down to the comm'nity build'n before lunch. I'd bring your maps too. I think most everyone is going to be there, and they mean to hear about your travels."

Oreo followed Mary out of the kitchen and into the garage and then followed her back into the house as she carried the box of parts they had assembled the previous evening. It was their contribution to the radio. In the past day and a half, word had spread outside of the circle of Warren, Andrew, Mary, Bob, and Oreo to include the entire small community. Andrew hoped like hell the radio would work. These people were longing for something, anything positive to give them some hope. Now he regretted bringing up the massive herds of the dead, the destruction left in their wake. Nothing good could come from scaring these nice people with his stories. Looking down, Andrew saw Oreo sit at his feet.

They're not stories, it's the truth, guy.

I know, but the truth sucks, buddy.

The new world sucks.

The old world sucked.

OK, but Mary?

She'll be OK, she's more OK than you are.

Andrew looked away from Oreo's stare and at the wall, shaking his head, realizing he had just had a silent discussion with his dog in his mind.

"Warren, that's great. It will be nice to have some conversation with other people for a change." Andrew made a sideways glance at Oreo, who started wagging his tail.

Soon they were out the front door, ponytail and pink rifle leading the way, Oreo prancing along beside her, his ears erect and alert. The sun had begun chasing away the cool morning air, resulting in a beautiful day. In a blink, they were in the big multipurpose room, parts that Bob needed, many of which weren't on the broadcasted list, spread across a handful of folding tables. A few had brought hot Dutch ovens with a bit of a potluck lunch for everyone, and a few held watch by the windows that faced the road. Everyone was armed, and it was obvious that everyone knew one another.

The next few minutes were a bit of a blur, Andrew shaking hands with nearly three dozen men and women. A small group of children sat at a table away from all the frenzy to play a board game. Andrew noticed that all the older kids were also armed with a mix of pistols and small rifles. This wasn't the first group of survivors he'd met in which he encountered strict security rules, but this was one of the first times he wasn't so sure that everyone wasn't like this before the attack.

"How much fuel do you need?"

"Uh . . . the bladders can hold about fifty gallons, plus my can . . . fifty-five or so would completely fuel the aircraft, but I'll be thankful for whatever I might be able to trade for or have."

"Where are you from?"

"Have you met others?

"Are there any other close survivors?"

"Have you seen Little Rock? Is there anything left?"

"What about the military, seen any?"

The group of men and women swarmed him, questions flying. The whole scene was overwhelming, and Andrew had experienced it before. All the survivors wanted to hear news, good news especially, but anything from the outside was welcomed. Andrew tried to answer, but before he could even start answering a question another question was asked. The group was nearly shouting questions at him by the time Warren stepped into the middle.

"Now all y'all hold on just a minute. Andrew is our guest, and you all should be treat'n him better than this. Why don't we get the fold'n chairs out. We can all sit while Andrew is nice enough to tell his story and give us any news he can remember. Once he's done, then maybe your questions will have answers."

A handful of muffled sorries were heard as the group released its crushing weight from around the pilot, and were replaced by the sounds of metal folding chairs coming out of the storage room and being set up.

Andrew looked around the room a little bewildered before finding Oreo lying at Mary's feet while she played the board game with the other children, eyes closed but ears up and twitching. *You little bastard, what about me?* Oreo peeked at Andrew with one eye open before letting it droop closed again. Shaking his head slightly, Andrew walked to the chair Warren offered.

"Thank you, Warren . . . thank all of you for your kindness. Well, let me start by saying things are both better and worse than you think they are out there."

Andrew continued his meandering talk for close to an hour, turning the pages of his atlas to show his notes and marks, describing the other survivor groups, the massive herds of the dead, and every detail he could think to talk about. The group remained silent and quite motionless the entire time, all eyes focused on Andrew and his atlas. After Andrew finished, everyone remained silent. He expected a lot of questions, not this uncomfortable silence, which was thankfully interrupted by Bob.

"I think we're ready to string the wire for the antenna."

Most everyone stood and went outside to see what Bob was going to do for the antenna. Two wooden electric transmission poles stood about one hundred and fifty feet apart from the main driveway down to the edge of the parking lot. The lines weren't live; just like all the electrical lines in the U.S. that Andrew had seen, they had no electricity flowing through them. Bob directed two men on ladders leaning against the poles and another who was on a ladder under the middle of the wire between the poles as they hung the smaller cable Bob was using for the antenna. After about thirty minutes the work was done, and a wire snaked across the parking lot into the building. One of the older kids, a young teenager, was already on the bicycle made into a generator and pedaling in a steady rhythm, shifting gears as the rear wheel spun in a blur. The small bank of car batteries connected together had a lone voltmeter wired at the end, the needle slowly climbing off the zero pin. Bob sat down at the table. The radio looked like something in the background of a mad scientist's lab in a movie, but Bob seemed confident that it wouldn't shock him and would work.

Once the needle reached the mark Bob had drawn on the dial, the battery bank's voltage was high enough to power the radio properly. Bob made sure the power switch was off and counted the coils wired on the stand next to the main box, moving alligator clips to the desired spacing. The group all seemed to hold their breath as Bob arranged his pencil, notebook, and the odd-looking device that he called the "key." Once settled, Bob flipped the switch on the radio.

Nothing happened, and the group stood silent for a moment before starting to grumble, having expected immediate communication to start pouring in, like turning on a car's FM radio. Bob waved his hand dismissively at the grumbles and tapped the key lightly; the wire strung between the insulated ends of spark plugs from his truck buzzed with a visible spark of electricity popping across the gap. A couple people gasped, and a few laughed.

"That's why it's called a *spark-gap* transmitter, folks." Bob smiled and began slowly tapping out a message, using a handwritten chart next to him with markings for each letter. Finished with the short message, Bob waited and repeated the transmission with no response.

"Warren, did you bring the shortwave?"

"Ye'sir, like you asked."

Warren handed Bob the hand-cranked shortwave radio. After cranking the radio for a couple of minutes, Bob turned it on and tuned it to the original transmission frequency from Groom Lake. Only static was heard. Bob tuned the radio up and down the shortwave bands, but there was nothing but static around the frequencies that Groom Lake had been heard on previously.

"Well, they're a few hours behind us. Maybe they're not up yet. We can try again this evening."

"Maybe they're dead," an anonymous voice called out from the back of the crowd.

"Maybe they are, but even if they are, maybe there are others like us who made a radio. This radio is a wonderful idea; we're not going to give up on it yet."

As the afternoon continued, different children and a few adults took turns on the bicycle to generate power as asked by Bob. Slowly and piece by piece, the crowd left to walk to their homes. By dinner time, the only people who remained were Bob, who continued to transmit and wait patiently, Mary, who napped in the corner with Oreo curled up against her, Warren, and Andrew, who sat quietly, exhausting the topics of conversation of the day.

"Bob, are you going to work into the night, or are you going to actually get some sleep?"

"Andrew, why don't you take Mary and Warren back up to their house. I'm going to keep at it for a while."

Andrew nodded, stood up, and stretched, snacking on the remaining potluck lunch, which substituted for dinner. Warren scooped Mary off the floor and held her in one arm, still sleeping, her head on his shoulder, and picked up her rifle with the other hand. Andrew was a little surprised; Warren was stronger than he appeared. Oreo yawned and plodded along next to them as they sauntered up the hill to Warren's house, slowly racing the setting sun. Both of them knew that Bob would probably stay up all night trying to make contact. They would have to check on him in the morning.

Highway 67, TX

The large MRAP sat idling in the middle of Highway 67 just on the edge of Stephenville, Texas. The start of Amanda's journey, which should have taken no more than a few hours, had taken the entire day. The sun hung low against the horizon. Large dark clouds approaching in the northern sky glowed purple and green, lightning causing the clouds to flash and glow like lightning bugs in a field. The sky above her was clear, but Amanda was confident that her night would be spent being rocked by the looming storm. The atlas she had open in her lap didn't have much detail for the city of Stephenville, but, so far, the map hadn't much detail for any of the towns she had seen roll by her windshield. She had successfully avoided Fort Worth and the surrounding large cities of the DFW Metroplex, but the cost was an entire travel day and being a little lost. Across the field to her right was the end of a runway; a small municipal airport in a small Texas town. The highway, small with only two lanes and shoulders, provided no answer as to what was ahead of her. She knew that another town was near as the yellow sign warned of a reduced speed limit ahead, but she still wasn't exactly sure where she was and what she could do for the night.

The airport would have been Clint's choice – large, open areas, hangers with possible Avgas or gasoline to be found – except that her new ride didn't run on gasoline, it needed diesel, and Amanda wasn't sure that being in a metal building/hangar would be the safest choice for the night with the taunting storm approaching. She had no meteorological schooling on any professional level outside of what she'd read as the SecAg and what life experience had given her growing up in Arkansas. Spring storms were nothing new; lightning was nothing new, but Amanda knew for sure that an approaching storm with emerald-green clouds meant she would probably get some hail fairly soon and maybe see some tornados in the area. As awesome as the big armored MRAP was, tornado proof it was not, although she assumed that it would handle hail just as well if not better than it was supposed to handle small arms fire.

Driving forward, Amanda passed another intersecting small highway and a rather large BBQ joint on the side of the road. This was the heart of Texas cattle country; she assumed that the BBQ had probably been good back when such things still existed. Vague memories of eating BBQ in small shack restaurants while on official visits to Texas felt like a previous life; the smell of smoked brisket seemed to be a ghost of a whiff on the air. She was feeling more discouraged than she'd felt that morning, as fat rain drops started to hit the windshield hard. Muffled by the heavy armor, the sudden impact snapped Amanda out of her daydream and back to the reality she was in, driving slowly on US-67. On her left and right, every structure she saw seemed to be made of a metal building, as if the townspeople expected a tornado to rip the town off the face of Texas and they wanted to have an easy time rebuilding.

The sky turned ominously dark overhead, blotting out the remaining sunlight and requiring her to switch on her headlights and bright auxiliary lights.

Amanda rolled through the stop sign, turning left onto Highway 377. The wind gusted, rocking the heavy truck, the trees around her moving back and forth in protest to the increasing wind strength. Dust and debris gusted across the road, and the rainfall increased, falling with hard angry drops and defeating the windshield wipers in their attempt to keep up. Amanda kept driving, slowly. Lightning streaked across the sky, illuminating the road ahead with the ghostly figures of people walking onto the road. Amanda blinked fast, trying to reset her limited vision from the assault of light, the macabre vision imprinted on the back of her mind. Squinting, she tried to see past the edge of the heavy rain that seemed to stop her headlights just past the front bumper. Another streak of lightning, and the hard clap of thunder vibrated through the armor plating almost immediately. The silhouette of an obese man shown in relief against the rain just as the headlights flashed against his mangled face and a split second before she heard the dull thud of his body being slapped to the ground by the heavy front bumper.

Another flash of lightning provided a snapshot of the growing horde of reanimated dead straggling out of the neighborhood on Amanda's left. Steering to the right-hand side of the road, Amanda drove over a highway sign while trying to dodge the next body, but it bounced under the truck and under the left side tires. Sweating, she wasn't sure what she could do except stop, wait, and hope for the best or speed up and do the same. Not one for inaction, Amanda stomped the accelerator to the floor and the big diesel roared, the turbo screaming as the heavy beast of a truck rocked and began to gain momentum.

Bodies bounced off the truck to the left, some falling under the truck, some being caught under the tires, but Amanda had no other options that she could see. If this truck failed, she would find another; if nothing else, she would walk. This was just like the arduous journey to the SSC in the first place, except now her mission was clearer in her mind. She had her own choices, she had her own mission, and no one would lord over her any longer.

Hail hit and bounced off the hood, the windshield, and the roof. The rain kept getting heavier and heavier. Another streak of lightning, and the dark Wal-Mart sign flashed by on her right side, along with an image of hundreds of dead swarming in the parking lot like a frightened herd stampeding on the prairie. Calm washed over her body as she realized that the storm was her ally. The lightning, the hail, the thunder, it confused the dead; they paid no attention to the truck passing by. The businesses and buildings tapered off, and the storm continued to rage, but as Amanda drove past the other side of town the amount of dead she saw went from much too many to nearly none, leaving only the occasional abandoned car or truck on the highway to cause her problems now.

Free from most of the danger from the dead and now trying to get back to finding shelter from the storm, she slowed down. With the next flash of lightning, Amanda saw some sort of church on the right. The wide concrete driveway bore a sign with the name of the Catholic church, but Amanda only saw "Catholic" and assumed the rest. The parking lot was empty, but the gate on the entrance of the drive was open, so entry was fair game for any who passed.

Amanda pulled to the edge of the V-shaped parking lot furthest away from the building, careful to stay on the concrete. She didn't want to chance getting the heavy truck stuck in the mud the storm was surely making. After switching off the wipers and the lights, Amanda turned the switch next to the steering wheel to the OFF position. The truck hissed and groaned as it shut off, but the vibration and the noise were soon replaced by the sound of rain and small hail bouncing off the armored glass and roof. Lightning flashed in a jarred rhythm with seemingly no end. She climbed over the center console to the back area, where instead of troops, gear and supplies occupied the spaces and the seats. Amanda moved a few of the boxes, retrieved an MRE and tore into the sealed package anxiously. It was nearly impossible to see anything but the flashing sky from where she sat, but eventually the hail ceased, the rain turned from squall to steady, and the thunder rolled away with the light show that had brought it. Her first day on the road found her in central Texas, alone and exhausted. Amanda was thankful that she was full, dry, and more comfortable than she had been on her first journey after the attack. Confidence in herself and her plan grew as she drifted into a light sleep.

Groom Lake, NV

The lights flickered on and off, staying on for what felt like only seconds and off for what felt like hours. In reality, the lights were cycling off and on every few minutes. Erin was the first to notice that the cycle was rhythmic, as if deliberate, like a child playing with a light switch. As a team they moved as quickly as they dared, forming a three-man active-shooter response team, just as Bexar had taught Jessie, and Jessie had taught both Sarah and Erin. The small handful of Groom Lake survivors who had attended the training courses thus far were taught the movements too; Jessie hoped that they would find some of those few individuals so they could add to their beleaguered team of tactical women.

With purpose, but not rushing to the detriment of their safety, the trio made their way up decks to where the main "towns" were housed. Each had rightly sheltered in place, keeping the doors locked. The safety protocol that Jake enforced, which had been in place before Jessie and her girls had arrived, appeared to be working. At each of the doors, Erin and Sarah would take a defensive position in the hall while Jessie knocked on the door. An easy and quick passphrase exchange would result in the door opening. Jessie would ask the number accounted for and the number missing and remind the "town" of the lockdown procedure while she made quick notes on the notebook she carried in her pocket.

Once lockdown started, those sheltered in place were supposed to light the emergency lighting in their bunk rooms, if needed, and begin a systematic strip search of everyone to look for any bites or other signs of injury that could be infected with Yama. Two of the towns had completed the procedure; three hadn't, but promised to begin immediately. The goal was to lock down the facility and prevent an outbreak from killing everyone. If one town was killed then at least the rest of the facility would survive. It was also left up to the town to put down any infected in their midst. The needs of the many outweighed the needs of the soon-to-be-dead.

Sarah and Jessie formed the front of the formation as it moved up the hallway. Sarah walked backwards, her rifle hanging on the sling, her pistol out and held with one hand, her free hand holding onto Jessie's belt, giving movement, direction, and speed through feel like the hard leash of a service dog. Their weapon lights shone in the darkness and stayed on when the lights came on, as the lights went off just as suddenly and any moment of blindness could result in their death by a stealthy corpse, reanimated and waiting silently as they passed. The dozen bodies on the ground that they had to step over or around so far all had dark holes in their skulls and bite marks on their arms and necks. Some had no bite marks at all that they could see. Jessie realized that an outbreak would be a perfect opportunity to kill someone without cause or consequence, just for a grudge or past slight. Only a handful of reanimated corpses had appeared in their path with just a couple more towns to check before the "time-out" portion of the lockdown could begin. Another failsafe was that, once swept, the facility would remain in lockdown for another twelve hours until the all-clear could be sounded.

Those cycles were supposed to be announced over the PA system, but with the power cycling in and out, it seemed unlikely that this would be very organized. It might be the end of the facility if something couldn't be done to stop the system madness.

After a quick and hushed conversation, the three of them were left with only the cafeteria, Jake's offices, and the radio shack to clear, at least of the known facility. Jessie felt confident that they had only begun to unlock the bare surface of secrets to be found here. Sarah and Jessie threw the double doors open. The three-man formation they'd used to move through the confined space of the hallways no longer needed for a large area like the cafeteria, all three of them entered and closed the doors behind them. They would have to clear the hallway again before they left, but that would help prevent someone, dead or alive, from sneaking up on them through the open doors.

Beams of light from the powerful weapon lights they each had pierced the darkness, as they methodically swept the room, moving slowly and purposefully along the walls, away from the fatal funnel of the doorway and staying away from the open center where cover could elude them. The tactics were meant for police officers responding to an active shooter in a school or a building, and seemed a little strange for the risen dead, but they couldn't be sure that there wasn't a shooter lying in wait for them. Tables and chairs were scattered and knocked over. Blood smears on the walls and floor gave off a warning; the lack of any bodies on the floor gave an even stronger one. Jessie bumped an unopened can of Rip-It on the floor. She stopped and paused for a moment. Erin, a few yards behind her, did the same. Momentarily, Sarah, who was across the room, detected that the other lights had stopped moving and stopped as well, sweeping her light across the cafeteria and askew tables. Jessie held the can in front of her weapon light to show Sarah, then threw it into the dark opening of the center serving line.

The loud crash of large serving trays and plastic plates was the result, which was followed immediately by a handful of gurgling moans and more crashing as reanimated survivors of Groom Lake straggled out to meet their end. Erin put each person down one by one until she saw a hand with a red knit mitten appear from the darkness. Waiting, a wry smile stretched across her lips as she saw her favorite of the Groom Lake residents appear. Brit looked bad. It was obvious she had been dead longer than the rest. One gentle squeeze of the trigger and Erin sent the back of Brit's skull and brain matter across the white tile floor, Brit's reanimated body crumpling in place. Jessie wasn't sure, but she thought she heard a faint "fuck you" just as Erin's rifle coughed the last shot.

The rest of the cafeteria was cleared. They found Major Wright outside his office near the radio shack, his throat torn from his neck and blood soaking his uniform as he staggered toward the women down the hall. Jessie put the major down. Jake was locked in his office, as he was supposed to be. Bill and the airmen were found in the radio shack, all the radios unplugged due to the surges of the power switching on and off. All told, nearly three dozen people were dead due to Brit's arrogance and incompetence. Something that Jake felt responsible for after setting everything in motion by entertaining Brit's grudge against Jessie, Sarah, and Erin.

Bill had a quick conversation with Jake followed by Jessie before he led the way to the server farm deep in the bedrock. One by one, they disconnected he network switches from anything that did not appear to be an internal intranet-only connection. This was a drastic measure, one that Bill hadn't wanted to attempt because no one knew what would happen. The facility could be rendered completely dead, nothing could happen, or the madness might be stopped; no one knew for sure.

Once disconnected, the servers were hard-powered with fingers crossed that they would reboot without issue or concern, since neither Jake nor Bill had anyway to log in as a user with any amount of privilege to fix any issues. Slowly the servers appeared to reboot, but there was no way to tell for sure for a few more minutes. After all the activity settled in the server rooms, Bill, Jessie, Sarah, and Erin left for the radio shack. They would either need to start the evacuation process to the top side, retrieving as much gear as they could while establishing safe areas on the surface, or cleanup would begin in the facility. Jessie had no idea what time it was on the surface or what time it was at all, but she knew that it would take them a long time to accomplish a full evacuation. People might die if they moved too fast, and people might die if they moved too slowly.

Eventually, the facility lights came back on, the air system's faint hiss returned, and the lights stayed on, though each of them expected the lights to fail at any moment. Growing more anxious with each passing minute, by the time that Jake announced the all clear they no longer expected the lights to go out. They grew to hope the lights wouldn't.

Exhausted, Jessie, Sarah, and Erin retired to the bunkroom to clean weapons, top off magazines, shower, and sleep. Persons assigned to the cleaning crew were tasked to move the bodies to the service elevator and to the main hanger for disposal by burning by the yet-to -be-formed burn crew. Bill, tired but excitedly awake from the events, returned to the radio shack and began transmitting in the blind on the electronic radio he'd modified to receive and transmit on the correct frequencies to match the radios that might be built if anyone took the shortwave transmissions seriously. The remaining airmen started up the shortwave broadcasts again, along with the other radio equipment.

Bill still used the old Races call sign, his own personal HAM geek humor for the end of the world, but he wasn't sure if anyone was left that would get it. Headphones on, a blank legal pad of paper and a pen sat at the ready while Bill leaned back in the large desk chair with his eyes closed. Faint and scratchy, the first dah and dit of a weak transmission took Bill a second to realize what he heard, but he shot up, pen in hand, and began writing out the letters of the slow transmission.

Waving eagerly, the airmen gathered around Bill to see what the excitement was all about. All the external speakers turned off on all the other radios, Bill set his headphones on the table and turned up his own speaker. The faint scratched transmission of other survivors came across slowly. Bill quickly wrote a note on another sheet of paper and handed it to an airman, who left immediately, note in hand. At the end of the transmission, Bill took an excited breath. It was the same sense of excitement that he'd had the first time he'd made contact with another HAM radio operator on the other side of the world, or like the first time he'd made contact with an astronaut on the space station. Bill's heart raced, and he had to concentrate not to key in the reply too fast. The survivor on the other end of the radio didn't seem like a seasoned CW operator, but there were only a few HAMS before the end of the world.

Back and forth the short messages were sent. Bill also resisted the urge to use the shorthand that was common amongst other HAM radio operators for fear of confusing the person on the other end. By the time Jake arrived in the radio shack, Bill had a short conversation written down. It was only a page long, but it told an incredible story.

Lost Bridge Village, AR

Bob's heavy eyes snapped wide open at the buzzing sound of the received transmission. Instead of the usual dit and dah of a modern CW transmission, the buzzing spark-gap receiver took a little getting used to. Just before he could begin to key a response, a faint transmission responded. Now very awake, heart pounding, Bob wrote down the conversation that ensued from the back and forth transmission. One side was the operator in Groom Lake; the other side was an operator who claimed to be in Montana. Bob had no reason to believe otherwise; this was a momentous day, a momentous week. Not only had Andrew swooped down from the sky to open their small world to the idea of other survivors all across the country, but after building the radio, another group of survivors in another state far away were also alive and transmitting. Bob's heart raced, and he wished he could tell Warren, or Andrew, or anyone, but everyone was long gone, the sun setting hours ago.

Once the bulk of the back and forth of transmissions had slacked off, Bob keyed in his call sign followed by the shorthand "AR" keyed quickly as a single word. Across the country, Bob didn't hear Bill as he yelled with excitement, but the return transmission was fast, clear, and the sort of thing that old HAMs would be excited about, which Bob was, and he assumed that the operator using an old Races-style call sign in Groom Lake was too. Twenty minutes later, and Bob had his contact logged, along with the questions he had answered. Keying his station's signoff from the frequency for the night, Bob left the Groom Lake operator calling himself "Bill" to chat with others, which Bob listened to and transposed to show the others in Lost Bridge Village in the morning. Any chance of going home to sleep was wiped away, Bob being much too excited to even attempt it.

CHAPTER 6

Saint George, UT
April 4, Year 1

The eastern horizon glowed yellow in the morning twilight. At the kitchen table, Bexar chatted with Gary, who wrote quick notes of the conversation that he would transcribe later. After the initial surprise from the group members wanting to know their story, Gary spoke with Bexar about recording the story of who he was and what had happened after the EMP and after the dead rose to hunt the living. Bexar realized he was sincere and genuinely interested, and for the first time in his life while sober the chains fell free of the locks, the doors opened, and Bexar spoke openly of his time as a Texas peace officer. He talked about all the plans, prepping, and training that went into the group's bug-out plans, the cache site, all the details good and bad: Malachi's death, the attack in The Basin, burying Keeley, his own retaliation and attempt to rescue Jessie. Tears streamed down his face as he spoke nearly in a whisper as all the guilt, remorse, and anguish of being one of the lucky few to live through the past few months washed over him. Gary's soft eyes and gentle words, both encouraging and caring, helped Bexar talk about all the memories and feelings that he was running from.

Guillermo stepped out of the kitchen and set a fresh cup of coffee down on the table before quietly ushering the remaining group members out of the kitchen to give the two some privacy. Gary was a special member of their group, a bit of a misfit crew; Gary's self-imposed title was the "Chief of Good Morale." Professionally, Gary was a licensed therapist, gentle and caring, supportive, not the stereotype of a person most people picture when they think of a therapist. Gary was an avid outdoorsman, hunter, shooting enthusiast, and general fitness nut. Long multiday hikes across terrain that most wouldn't want to even fly over was where Gary found his solace. In nature, be it hiking, running, cycling, shooting on a range, or hunting, Gary would have fun no matter what the activity as long as he could be outside. He was one of the last members added to the group, long after John and Brian helped form the original cell, after Heath and Coach joined, after Merylin and Frances began all the intensive food prep, after the other group split off into their own faction, joining just before Jennifer and Doc.

Walking outside, Guillermo found Stan and Chivo readying the horses for another journey, this one an attempt to salvage an old and wayward VW Beetle. Stan, the group mechanic and systems guy, was the obvious choice for Chivo to take. Angel wanted to return with him for tactical reasons, or maybe Angel thought Chivo was cute; Guillermo wasn't sure, but Stan would be more useful in an attempt to resurrect an old car after the end of the world as we know it.

Stan used the solar array to charge a small car battery that was used with some of the equipment. A roll pouch of tools, some lunch, some water, weapons, ammo, a small can of treated gasoline, a can of starter fluid, and the will to succeed were tied onto the horses, and, just after sunrise, the pair left. Walking across the yard and into the open side door of the shop, Guillermo found Heath with an electric motor disassembled on his workbench. Without a word, Guillermo walked up to him and stood, watching the process.

"Hey, Willy, aerator's acting up."

"The what?"

"Aerator. It's the motor that keeps the septic churning to help the biological processes break down all the waste. The spare unit is in place for now, but I'm rebuilding this one so I can place it in storage as the spare. Without it we would need to be on the hunt for another."

"What happens if it all fails completely?"

"Then we're literally up shit creek."

"Heh, OK, Heath, good work, buddy, and thank you for what you do."

Heath smiled and went back to work, Guillermo leaving him be.

The rest of the group was fast at work with their daily chores. Guillermo's chores for the morning were complete. Kitchen rotation was one of his favorites because he got to cook. He had to clean, too, but he didn't have to do any of the harder outdoor chores or sit safety watch at night. Walking back into the house, he found Gary and Bexar still chatting, now sitting on the sofas in the living room. Gary motioned to the rocking chair and nodded, so Guillermo sat.

"You've not just survived, you've battled, fought, scratched, and just flat-out forced yourself to survive damn the odds. It is easy to dismiss things as circumstance or luck, but luck favors the ready, and the ready don't favor luck. You aren't lucky, you're ready. I have no doubt that you will succeed, that you'll rejoin your wife, and your child will survive. I strongly suspect that no matter what could possibly happen your family will be whole, and you'll make sure that child lives to see us reclaim this world for the living."

Guillermo smiled. Gary was really animated, genuinely excited, and he meant what he said. Missing out on the majority of the previous talk, he would have to read the story after Gary transcribed it and wrote it out, with Bexar's approval of course, but something about the gimped survivor cop from Texas really had Gary fired up. This was going to be a good day. It had already started well, and in a few hours Guillermo would start cooking dinner.

I need to ask Merylin and Frances for something they can spare from the cache; a special day today means tonight should have a special meal.

Smiling, Guillermo excused himself. Gary and Bexar were laughing and, if John wandered in at some point, they might start pouring beer even though it wasn't even past eight in the morning.

Stephenville, TX

Stretching her neck, Amanda sat up. The bed of boxes and troop carrier seats wasn't exactly what her weary body needed, but uncomfortable sleep that is relatively safe is better than no sleep at all. Another storm had ripped through the area during the night. The wind had rocked the heavy truck hard enough to cause concern, but all the stress of the previous day left Amanda so weary that she couldn't keep her eyes open for just a little bit of weather. She figured that if the MRAP tipped over she would wake up and deal with it then, but as sturdy as the truck was she would probably be OK inside if that happened.

After snacking on the crackers left over from the previous night's MRE dinner and downing a half-liter of water, Amanda stood to look out the windows. She needed to pee; preferably she could squat against a tire, but if it wasn't safe, she wasn't above hanging her ass over the edge of the turret and peeing on the roof while the dead world watched from below.

The scene outside the heavy bullet-resistant windows was surreal. Half of the church building to the south was gone, and debris filled the parking lot. The metal church buildings at the back of the parking lot were leveled, which was probably the source of much of the debris. Bodies littered the ground. Most of them appeared to be reanimates that were thrown by the storm and hit by debris. Some were mangled, still twitching with movement, the virus holding onto the last vestiges of ability from the destroyed bones and flesh.

"Oh my God."

Amanda released the hatch for the turret, climbed up the slung nylon step and pulled herself onto the roof. Standing on the roof and in the cool air, she turned slowly, looking at the scene around her. It appeared that a tornado had come through or had been close enough to destroy the buildings. Trees had been uprooted and overturned. The few cars and trucks she had seen on the highway were tossed aside like discarded toys. She counted seventeen dead in the parking lot.

I can't fathom being caught in a storm and being struck by a flying reanimated body like a fucked-up remake of The Birds.

The thought caused Amanda to shiver before she grunted, frowning at the destruction. It didn't matter; the seventeen in the parking lot were seventeen that no one would have to deal with in the future after she got the country back on its feet. Holding onto the edge of the turret, Amanda hung her ass over the edge of the truck to pee. There were few moments that she envied men, but being able to stand up and direct pee at will was something she envied at this very moment.

"Fuck it," was all she said after pulling her pants up and tightening her belt. Climbing back into the cab, she pulled the heavy roof latch closed, dogging it in place. Rotating the switch to RUN, Amanda waited for the gauges to come online and for the motor to be ready. She pushed the momentary button for the starter and the turbo diesel belched to life, ready for another day in the modern world of combat against the dead. The fuel gauge showed a half-tank left, so the day could start, but she would need to fuel at the first opportunity so things wouldn't turn into an emergency. After consulting with her road maps, Amanda drove to the end of the driveway and turned right onto the highway. Driving south on Highway 377, the route seemed wrong, but the map showed her connection, Highway 6, would be after the next town, and that would point her back in the right direction. To avoid a direct route involving an Interstate sometimes meant that the wrong direction had to be traveled on a small highway.

Amanda wanted to see Dublin, Texas to see if it had any Irish pubs, but the highway split and routed her away from the city, which was fine since it still intersected Highway 6. Another right turn and into the countryside she went. Instead of a gas station, Amanda was watching for a construction site or farm with a fuel tank on a raised platform. She had a universal key, also known as bolt cutters, in the MRAP, so a padlocked gravity-fed tank of diesel for tractors or road equipment would be even easier to get into than an electrically powered tank of diesel for trucks.

The storm damage in the area along the new highway wasn't as severe as the path of destruction that had been carved out next to her overnight spot. *God smiles on children, drunks, and idiots.*

Smirking for her dumb luck in parking near the future path of a tornado and then surviving without any damage, Amanda figured she must be a favored idiot; she had too many gray hairs to be a child, and a glass of wine felt like an ancient dream. The Texas countryside rolled by her windshield; small homes were carved out between pastures and farmland, and wooded areas dotted the landscape.

The sign said De Leon, home to a celebrated peach and melon festival, with slightly over two thousand residents, but Amanda had to take its word for it because she had never heard of the town. Passing a cattle trailer pulled by a large dually pickup that sat abandoned in the road in the opposite lane, she stopped the truck. In the bed of the truck was a diamond-plate toolbox, but there was also a tank of fuel with a fuel spout. It was common for farmers and ranchers to have up to about a fifty-gallon tank of fuel for farm equipment on a farm truck; they usually all ran on diesel. Most of the pumps were electrically operated with a simple DC-electric motor, which could be a problem, or it could still work. Most of the ranchers wired the pump up themselves by running a hot wire directly to the battery, so it could be possible to run it off the MRAP's battery too. Amanda wasn't sure if the MRAP's system was twelve volt, twenty-four volt, or something else that she couldn't fathom, but she figured the worst that could happen was that it wouldn't work.

Or you catch it all on fire while trying to fuel.

Amanda shook her head and hoped for God's continued providence on her idiot ways. Idling in the middle of the road, she climbed down from the driver's side of her big truck and cleared the immediate area. No dead were seen; nothing seemed to be reacting to the sound of her truck's loud motor. The cap on the auxiliary fuel tank in the bed of the truck was locked with a padlock, as was the nozzle. Returning with the bolt cutters, she quickly relieved the locks of their duty. Unscrewing the cap, she was happy to see the tank was nearly three-quarters full. The placard stated that the tank did hold fifty gallons, so she might net approximately thirty-five gallons. The pump was electric, and it was held in place with worn electrical tape. The pickup was unlocked and unattended; Amanda pulled the release inside the cab and walked to the front to open the hood. The battery connections were a rat's nest of extra wires, a fine example of cheap redneck engineering on an expensive farm truck. The toolbox in the bed of the pickup did not have any jumper cables, but it did have a small spool of thin red electrical wire and a roll of duct tape. The battery for the MRAP was on the wrong side of the truck for an easy connect, so Amanda decided to siphon the fuel out of the unscrewed cap. Ten minutes later, the MRAP was buttoned back up. Amanda drank water in an attempt to get the taste of diesel out of her mouth, but no dead had come to investigate, and the fuel gauge was nearly full.

"Life is good; today will be a wonderful day."

By the time she was in the town, she was exiting it again. Overall, the town looked quiet, as if everyone was on vacation; there wasn't much visible damage to the buildings or anything that she could see. If most of small-town America had survived this well, Amanda held hope for the future chances of the country.

More open country rolled by through the heavy windows. Barely any cars were left on the highway. Only a handful of dead roamed along the deserted Texas highway, nothing of interest appeared, and the town of Gorman scrolled past without incident, as did the next small town. Lulled into a bored sense of safety, Amanda felt like she was nearly standing still, but her map showed progress, progress and I-20 approaching.

Stopping abreast a lonely, small truck stop where Highway 6 crossed I-20, Amanda studied her map. She had two routes marked on her atlas. The first and presumably faster route took I-20 west through Abilene, turning on Highway 84. The second crossed I-20 and stayed on Highway 6 until catching Highway 180. The two routes met again near Snyder, Texas, and the safer route

- 1- 1- 1- 1-

would be to stay off the Interstate, but Amanda couldn't put aside the desire to save a little time.

Ahead of her a semi-truck and trailer lay on the berm of the overpass, appearing to have been knocked off the Interstate. A car lay on Highway 6 below the bridge; it also appeared to have been pushed off the bridge. Amanda hadn't seen damage like this before, but it would match what was described weeks ago as damage from one of the massive roaming herds of the dead. Clint said they amassed along the Interstates; his theory was that the dead ended up attracting each other by the sounds of their movement. The larger the group, the louder they were, the more dead would be attracted. Interstates went through large cities, and large cities had lots of people, so it all snowballed together. Like wandering cattle, nothing and no one was in charge, just the herd following the herd in an infinite loop of meandering destruction.

Amanda didn't have the desire or the need to see more or to encounter a herd. She knew it wasn't here right now; she had no idea if it was heading east or west and if she would catch up to it or run into another one. Her choice to take a faster route was immediately removed; the back roads and smaller highways would remain her choice. She drove around the crumpled car, under the overpass, and toward Eastland, Texas.

Lost Bridge Village, AR

Andrew woke up to Oreo nudging him. The room was dark from the heavy blankets over the windows, but the kettle sat on the hearth of the fireplace, and the breakfast fire was already reduced to white coals. Somehow he had slept late, but if he was lucky there was coffee still left in the kettle. He had no idea what time it was, but after checking the house, he found himself alone.

At least they trust me enough to let me sleep unattended; that's nice.

The kettle had coffee. It was a little stale from sitting next to the fire for too long, but as little coffee as Andrew had been able to enjoy over the past few months, any coffee was better than no coffee. Relaxing with Oreo on the couch, sipping the coffee, Andrew looked for his atlas, which was missing. Assuming he'd left it at the community building, Andrew didn't worry about it. This group didn't seem like the type that would steal from him. Another warm sip of the bitter coffee and Andrew felt more relaxed than he had at most of the other survivor camps. Others were better armed, better staffed, and better protected, but this group had better people. Or this group had kinder people at least;

they were quite pleasant. The potluck lunch yesterday had been a treat, even if Bob's radio was unsuccessful. At least he'd tried. Some groups wouldn't have even tried; most wouldn't have for lack of a shortwave radio that still worked. Andrew made a mental note to tell others about Groom Lake and the shortwave broadcasts. Even if Bob's radio didn't work, the shortwave broadcasts might be a way to get some new information. He leaned his head back, held his mug in one hand, absentmindedly petted Oreo with the other, and closed his eyes, visualizing the map in his head, trying to decide where to fly next.

Groom Lake?

"What do you say, Oreo, want to fly to Nevada?"

The dog lazily opened his eyes before shutting them again.

"I know, but I want to go to Area 51. That's where that facility is supposed to be. If not, we can look for aliens. That sound fun?"

Oreo gave no response. Andrew tried to remember where Area 51 was located. He thought that it was near Las Vegas because he remembered a *Popular Mechanics* article years ago about people commuting via a private airline from Las Vegas to work in Area 51. He would have to look at his atlas, except that he was sure a top-secret government base wouldn't be marked on it.

Maybe Bob would know. Well, if I am going near Las Vegas, I could roughly follow I-40 west for navigation, stop where I can along the way for fuel, maybe meet more survivors . . . I need to get fueled up and flying. We've been here for too long, even if they are really nice.

"Hey, Oreo, we could visit the Grand Canyon along the way. That would be cool. See the Hoover Dam. Maybe there are people living near that who have working electricity from the dam. That would be incredible."

Oreo's head snapped up just before Andrew heard the doorknob of the front door rattle. Andrew looked at Oreo, who climbed down and waited with his tail wagging. He figured if Oreo was happy, then he didn't have to worry. Andrew was correct, as Warren and Mary came through the door, Warren carrying his atlas.

Mary gave Oreo a hug and excitedly blurted out, "Bob made contact with Groom Lake and listened to the radio guy there talk to a guy in Montana and another in Minnesota."

"Wow. What did they say?"

Warren had a piece of paper that he had scribbled the notes on. "The one in Minnesota has an odd name and has a small community of survivors right near

Minneapolis. Some town called Winnebago or something. The one in Montana is named Dorsey and is near Great Falls. He's saying that it's been bad with the snow'n all. Most of them survivors have been starved. Some drank themselves to death, and others just killed themselves off. He also said they don't be hav'n many of the dead either. Supposed the cold weather is makin'em stiff, and they can't move. He done bugged out to one of them missile silos up there, could you believe it, living below ground like that."

"Really! Hadn't thought of that. Not much of a harsh winter in my part of Florida; the worst is when we have a late frost, and we lose a bunch of oranges."

"This'n guy Dorsey was talking about getting close to six feet of snow this year, hoping to thaw out by July."

"Damn, six feet? Six inches of snow would shut Deland down for a week!"

"No joke, we get snow here, but nuth'n like that, nuth'n even close."

"Warren," Andrew glanced at Mary and back, "do you think I've earned my keep well enough to get some fuel? Oreo and I want to attempt flying out to Groom Lake to that facility."

"What'n for?"

"Well, I've got a bunch of information marked in my atlas, and I'm sure I'll gather more while en route. I'm sure they could use that, and besides I'm curious. I want to see what is left of our government. I want to see if they have a plan, if we have a chance."

"That's fair, and I'm suppose'n we owe some gratitude for giving us the link to the outside world. It was like hell getting Bob to get off the radio and rest. Most of the town is down there; others are taking shifts on the radio, sending messages and listening to others. It's slow'n work, little buzzes here and there that you've got to be writ'n down and such, but it be better than nuth'n. Well, come on down with us again. We can ask the town. Between everyone, we might scrape up enough fuel to get you headed out the right way."

Andrew was grinning from ear to ear as they all headed back down to the community building. If yesterday was a fun get-together, what Andrew found today was an all-out party. It was like the town had won the lotto. An hour later, Andrew's plane was topped off, and his little spare fuel can was full. Half the town watched as Andrew taxied into position and completed a preflight run-up on the ramp. Happy that the magnetos should work and the engine probably wouldn't fail on takeoff, Andrew pushed the power button, and the little aircraft raced down the runway. The tail wheel popped off the ground first before the yellow aircraft floated lazily into the sky, banking right to fly westbound.

Once the sound of the engine was gone, Mary wiped her eyes, sad to see Oreo leave and sad that she didn't get to go flying.

"Grandpa Warren, I want to learn how to fly."

"I'm sorry, baby girl, maybe you'll be hav'n a chance in the future when all this mess is behind us."

Warren picked up Mary and carried her across the road to their house. The brave new world was a sad place, no place for his little princess, and it broke Warren's heart to know that the future was more bleak than the past could have ever imagined.

Saint George, UT

Stan and Chivo rode in silence, the soft clops of the horses' hooves along the desert the only noise besides the occasional snort or fart from the horses. Following the same path that he and Angel had used, the pair eventually arrived at the neighborhood near the truck wreck where Chivo had spied the VW previously. Chivo's rifle sat across his legs so the muzzle wouldn't poke the horse and possibly spur him, the sling across his body keeping it from falling to the ground. He held the reins loosely in his left hand, his right hand gripping the stock of the M4. The last go around he'd had in this area nearly turned south on him. The plan was to clear the house, get the horses and the car into the garage, shut the garage door, and work in relative safety. The houses had practically no backyards, so they couldn't secure the horses in a backyard. The front yards had no fences, so the horses could be attacked by the dead if they were tied up in the front yard. Stan commented that they should bring the horses into the living room and let them rest there. Chivo wasn't opposed to the idea; he just wasn't sure that the horses would fit through the front door very well. Besides, all they needed was a horse to get injured tripping over a sofa or something. Chivo figured that in the worst case they could clear another house and secure them in its garage while they worked in the first. Since the homes were set a bit like duplexes with paired side-by-side driveways, it wouldn't be that hard to do. It would only add a little bit of time. Time in the new world was a strange beast; they had both too much time and not enough time. It all depended on a slight change in circumstance.

The neighborhood was quiet; a few dead thumped against the front windows of homes. Only a couple reanimates were seen out roaming the streets. They weren't worth killing and alerting the area that someone was scavenging from the sound of rifle fire. The second street on his right and five houses down was the Bug. Reaching the driveway, Stan remained in the saddle as mounted security. Chivo tied his reins to the tube bumper of the Baja-beetle and knocked on the front door. A few moments later a wet thump hit the back of the door. Chivo shook his head as the reanimated corpse on the other side of the door continued to step into the shut door with a loud thud each time. Checking the door, he found it locked. After retrieving a lava rock from the desert-style landscaping in the front yard, Chivo threw it through the large front window with a sharp crash. The thumping against the door ended, and a few moments later the reanimated corpse crashed through the broken front window and onto the lawn. As it struggled to get up, Chivo drove his knife through the back of the undead woman's skull. After wiggling the knife to get it loose, Chivo looked at the rotted nude body, the sagging gray flesh, and stepped to the window to clean the blade on the curtains before replacing it in the sheath.

Chivo looked back at Stan, who sat on his horse looking a little wide-eyed. Chivo gave him a wink and stepped into the dark home. In only a few minutes, Stan heard the garage-door latch release before it rolled up to show a garage full of junk.

Stan guided his horse near the edge of the garage, and Chivo appeared behind a mountain of random boxes and a ping pong table holding a silver car key in his hand. "What do you say? Should we try a different garage or not use the garage? What do you think, Chivo?"

"Naw, mano, this is fine, just time for a fucking yard sale . . . maybe some napalm."

"What?"

"I'm kidding. Give me a hand, and let's push all this shit out into the fucking yard."

Stan climbed off his horse, tied it next to the other one, and helped with the garage reorganization, unceremoniously tossing boxes of Halloween decorations, old clothes, dishes, and everything else imaginable onto the lawn and driveway next door. Fifteen minutes later, a few dead had straggled near, and the garage was empty.

"Stan, there's a little side yard that's paved and there should be room for the horses. I'll take care of these assholes if you move the horses. When you get back, we can push the Bug into the garage and get to fucking work."

Nodding, Stan took the horses around the far side of the house; Chivo unsheathed his knife and jogged toward the closest walking corpse. Stopping in front of the reanimated dead, Chivo took a side step and tripped the old man lunging for him. Once on the ground, the knife plunge was repeated. Rocking the knife back and forth, Chivo couldn't get it to come loose from the man's skull. Frowning, he worked harder as the other two dead came closer and closer, but the knife wouldn't budge.

"Pendejo!" Chivo spun in his crouched position while pulling his pistol clear of the holster and fired twice in rapid succession, each shot striking a zombie in the forehead. He kicked the handle of his knife, which caused the knife to pop loose from the skull. He jogged to where it had skidded to a stop on the asphalt, retrieved it, and headed back to Stan and the Bug. Stan was already trying to push it into the garage. Around them the sound of the dead slamming against doors and windows crescendoed. Once the Bug was in the garage, they shut the door behind them and latched it closed, just as dozens of approaching dead marched up the driveway. The sound of the dead banging against the thin sheet metal garage door rattled the frame.

"Well, mano, hopefully out of sight out of mind for a little while and they'll give it up before they knock the door down."

Stan lit a match, and the darkness of the closed garage pushed against the small flame until it slid behind the glass globe of a camp lantern. The gentle hiss of white gas followed by the poof of the flame catching preceded the warm glow of the dual mantel lamp that Stan hung from the garage door opener on the ceiling.

"At least we don't have to take the deck lid off or worry about jamming our hands into tight places around that tiny motor."

The rear bodywork of the Beetle had been cut away, replaced with a classic-style tube bumper and short-cut rear fenders, with the engine hanging from the transmission in the open air. Stan popped off the cap of the distributor, inspected the rotor, and used a shim to check the gap in the points.

Chivo opened the passenger door and replaced the old car battery under the back seat with the freshly charged battery that they'd brought. Assuming they could drain the tank if it didn't work, Chivo raised the hood and poured about one of the two gallons of gas they'd brought with them into the metal tank, saving the rest in case they actually did need to drain the tank.

One by one, Stan removed each of the four spark plugs and inspected them in the light, checking the spark gap and verifying that they appeared to be in good working order. The oil was dark and used, but Stan didn't see any evidence of water or contamination; if water was in the oil, this entire enterprise would have been for naught. After removing the valve covers, and while using a large crescent wrench, Stan turned the crank via the bolt on the crankshaft pulley, stopping at top dead center and bottom dead center with each turn to check the valve adjustment for each of the four cylinders. None of the valves needed adjustment. While Stan checked the engine and mechanicals, Chivo used two cans of Fix-A-Flat to fill the four small tires. The foaming can of glue wasn't the best choice, but it was a field-expedient choice when you had no other way.

"It looks like ass, but, so far, whoever kept this old Bug kept it in apparent almost-good working order."

Chivo nodded. Even if it wasn't in good working order, the old Bugs were so robust that they would just run anyway. People always said that they were easy to work on. Growing up poor, he'd learned that they were just as hard to work on as anything else, but the design was so good that they would run while forgiving egregious mechanical mistakes on the part of the homegrown mechanic.

After checking that the bowl and float were clean, Stan reassembled the carburetor and pulled out a test light to static test the ignition timing. Once complete, the pair packed up the tools in preparation for starting the car and leaving once everything became really noisy. Both of them knew that the Baja-style stinger exhaust would be really loud since it was just a straight pipe with a flared trumpet end that made the exhaust even louder.

Chivo sat in the driver's seat, a cheap fiberglass bucket seat, pushed in the clutch, turned the key, and gave the gas pedal a quick pump. All they heard was the click of the starter. Chivo tried again, and the motor didn't turn over; again, all they heard was the click of the starter.

"Chivo, flip on the headlights for a sec."

Chivo did as instructed and was surprised to see that even in the darkness of the garage, the headlights were very weak.

"Shit. Let me swap out with the old battery, maybe we'll get lucky."

Stan made quick work of swapping the battery connections. "Try the headlights again."

This time nothing shone at all.

"OK, let me switch them back. I think it'll run, but we might have to push start it."

"It's like I'm back in the old neighborhood, mano, except we never took this long to steal a fucking car."

Stan grunted. He didn't see it as stealing and missed that Chivo's comment was a joke. In his mind, it was salvaging for the good of the group, and it was righteous, not dirty and uncomely like theft. The moral line that was a hard, sharp one in his mind was wide and light gray for Chivo, who was surprised by the sudden appearance of all the tools being tossed into the passenger seat.

"OK, Specialist Hood-rat, I'm going to open the garage door and push you out backwards, so put the tranny in reverse and pop the clutch when I say to."

Chivo glared at Stan, mumbling, "Hood-rat? I'll fucking put your tranny in reverse, fucking mang."

"What?"

"I said it's a great plan, Stan-the-man, fucking outstanding, quit dicking around and let's get your wonderful plan in action."

Stan took down the lantern, turned the gas off, and set the still glowing and hot light on the floorboard of the passenger's side. After pulling the release, he lifted the garage door and let the latch hold it open; it had been some time since they'd heard any reanimated dead banging against the metal.

Some dead shambled down the darkening street. Chivo hadn't realized how long they had been in the garage, but apparently it was more than the couple of hours that it felt like. The sun had already set, and they needed to haul ass back to the compound or setup for the night.

Chivo turned the key to the on position, pushed down on the gear shift, selected reverse, released the parking brake, and held the clutch pedal to the floor. Stan began pushing as hard as he could, the little car gaining speed as it reached the end of the driveway. Chivo didn't wait, it was now or not, so he released the clutch and began pumping the gas pedal. The car lurched against the transmission before roaring to life. Chivo shifted to neutral and yelled at Stan, "We'll come back for the horses tomorrow; there are too many dead fucking about! Get in and let's get home!"

Stan climbed in on top of the tools piled in the passenger seat; Chivo shifted to first and drove away from the assembling welcome party of death, the obnoxiously loud exhaust echoing off the houses. As they passed the far side of the house, Chivo caught a glimpse of one of the horses on the ground, two dead feeding on it, and blood running into the street. The other horse was missing. Shaking his head, Chivo wasn't sure what he would tell Angel. It wasn't like they could replace the horses before they left for Groom Lake.

The Compound, Saint George, UT

Bexar put his beer in the cup holder of the camp chair and pulled himself onto his good foot. Gingerly, he began putting some weight on the cast, steadying himself by holding onto the chair. He wasn't quite ready yet, but the leg would hold his weight, if unsteadily.

In the morning, I've got to get Guillermo to cut this cast off. I'm sitting around getting drunk and fat when I should be training for survival, for my family's survival.

Out of the corner of his eye, Bexar saw the ghost of a faint streak of light in the sky. Before he could turn his head, the concussion thumped into Bexar's chest with the force of a sledge hammer. Ears ringing, the world came to focus slowly; in view were flames, movement, the moving shadows of people running as seen only by firelight.

The shop . . . oh God, the shop is on fire!

The Beetle

"What the fuck is that?"

Chivo looked up and right to where Stan was pointing. In the distance, flames licked the night sky. The slow roll of an explosion rumbled through the small car.

"Shit, mano, that's the fucking compound!"

Chivo focused forward; the headlights' faint glow on the roadway made it feel like he was driving by candlelight. Going as fast as he dared, Chivo carefully threaded through the thickening mass of the dead, dodging left and right. The nimble, loud, air-cooled car drove as commanded. All that Chivo and Stan saw of the dead were the backs of their heads, as each pair of dead eyes in the area were pointed toward the beacon calling them home to feed.

The Compound, Saint George, UT

Bexar stood, adrenaline coursing through his veins, ears ringing. He couldn't hear the screaming. Two people lay motionless on the driveway. Angel ran to the first, heavy med bag over his shoulder, and pointed toward the shop. Bexar couldn't hear him, but he saw the shop was well on its way to being fully engulfed.

The flames danced across the lunar landscape of the desert night. Movement caught his eye; spinning quickly toward the movement, Bexar raised his rifle. Three people outside the fence were running toward the gate. The tip of the red triangle in the optic tracked just ahead of the leader. Two smooth pulls on the trigger, and the first person fell; the second person tripped over the body. Bexar drove the rifle to the person at the rear, who stopped and turned to run away. Another two shots and the rounds pierced his back, blood erupting out of his chest where the rounds exited, the man crumpling to the ground in mid-stride. The remaining person of the assaulting force stood, arms raised. An odd-looking tube was slung across his body; it looked vaguely familiar to Bexar, but he wasn't sure why. Anger pierced the air between them. A fraction of a second passed, but for Bexar it felt like ten minutes. Through the reticle all he saw were the eyes and the hatred they held. A single squeeze of the trigger and the back of the attacker's skull exploded in a shower of bone and brain matter. Bexar scanned left and right. Nothing else moved; no other threats arrived.

Bexar could hear yelling. Guillermo was attacking the growing flames of the shop with a fire extinguisher. Years of being a cop didn't make one a firefighter, but it gave Bexar a feel for fires and response. Guillermo was fighting a losing battle. Finally understanding what Angel was yelling, Bexar let his rifle hang on the sling and ran as fast as the cast would let him, the massive adrenaline dump of the attack and battle blocking any pain that he'd had just moments before. As he charged into the open door, thick black smoke poured through, choking him, the heat searing his lungs with each breath. Bexar didn't stop. The light on his rifle shone dimly in the smoke, but he still couldn't see anything but smoke and flame. Bexar stumbled to the floor; looking back, he realized he'd tripped over Heath's body, burned and blackened. Standing and grabbing Heath under his arms, Bexar walked backwards, dragging with all his strength, struggling against the cast on his leg. He made it into the courtyard before collapsing, choking and coughing on smoke and soot. The last thing he saw was Guillermo tackling him with a heavy wool blanket.

The Beetle

Chivo followed Stan's excited instructions and turned onto Twin Lakes. Reaching the long driveway felt like a half hour for Stan; the forty-five miles per hour Chivo drove seemed like a walking pace when it was obvious that the compound was on fire. The main gate was intact. Stan made quick work of the combination lock and chain, opening the gate for Chivo before closing and locking it behind the VW. Chivo didn't wait, but sped off to the end of the drive and towards the fire. Anger flushed through Stan before he realized that Chivo had the training and could probably help immediately with whatever had gone wrong. Stan locked the gate and began running up the long driveway.

Chivo slid to a stop in the courtyard. The shop was fully engulfed and would have to burn itself out. He looked at the fire and the embers floating in the wind. Thankfully the wind was out of the north and was pushing the flames and embers away from the house. Four bodies lay in the courtyard; one was very badly burned, another had an obvious life-ending head wound, and the other's neck lay at an unnatural angle. Ignoring the obvious casualties, Chivo ran to the only remaining patient and found Bexar.

Covered in black soot and unconscious, Bexar lay there, his rifle next to him, the sling removed, and the tactical carrier badly damaged and cut off him. His clothes were in a ruined heap, also expediently removed by a pair of EMS shears. Guillermo knelt over Bexar, latex gloves on, working methodically and quickly, an IV already started. Jennifer stood nearby holding the IV bag above Bexar. Angel ran up to Chivo.

"What the fuck happened, Angel?"

"They attacked again, that's what happened. They blew up the shop, and I think they somehow rigged the propane tanks."

Chivo doubted they could have rigged anything without getting inside the wire, which someone would have noticed.

"Did you mount a patrol, a security sweep?"

"No."

Chivo cursed, "Get me Coach and Brian. We'll do it."

"Coach is dead."

"Fuck, mano. Fine! Just get me Brian. We're going out the side gate to make a sweep. Make sure those fucking bodies don't get up again, and get Bexar and everyone else the fuck inside in case there's another attack!"

Angel turned and yelled for Brian, quickly executing the instructions Chivo gave him. This was not the time to argue, and Angel knew he was right.

Brian hustled over, visibly shaken.

"Brian, I need you to focus, mano. We're going to need to do this the right way or more people might die. I can't babysit you while we do this, and it would help me for you to come along. Can you handle your shit?"

Slowly nodding, Brian turned, looked at the shop, and saw Angel standing over Heath's badly burned body before firing a single shot into the skull. His eyes narrowed as anger burned deep in his soul.

"Yeah, Chivo, fuck'em all! Let's roll."

The pair jogged to the side gate next to the garage. Brian worked the combination lock, and the pair were outside the wire. Chivo began moving west, quickly putting distance between the fence line and the compound and themselves. Brian followed about a dozen yards behind him, and they each moved methodically and quietly. Brian tried to match Chivo's movement, but Chivo was less than a ghost; he seemed to absorb light and sound, a dark quietness in the desert that was reserved only for master hunters. Halfway to the road, Chivo turned and began moving south. A few moments later, he stopped and melted into a crouched position. Brian stopped and crouched, unable to detect whatever it was that Chivo saw. The moon barely gave enough light to create shadows on the low vegetation. The light of the burning shop a few hundred yards away danced across the desert, and his ears pounded with a heartbeat so loud that he was sure Chivo could hear it.

Movement. Someone was crawling through the desert, coming from the direction of the compound, almost on a straight course for Chivo. Brian froze, holding his breath, trying to be a shadow of a hole in the ground while moving only his eyes back and forth, looking for more movement besides the single person. He didn't see any, and he couldn't even see Chivo's form anymore.

The crawler reached the area where Brian remembered Chivo had been. Waiting, anticipating a rifle shot, all Brian saw was some fast movement before seeing Chivo's hand sticking up and motioning him to come close.

Face down on the ground was a man whose hands and feet were bound with flex cuffs. Chivo's shemagh was wrapped around his eyes and tied, the ends stuffed into his mouth.

"He said that he's the only survivor of the raiding party, that the other three were killed by someone inside the compound after the RPG attack."

The sound of the dead crashing through the desert behind them to the west became more apparent, growing in intensity and size. Chivo was confident that they were about to have a serious problem with all the undead moths heading to the flame. It was still hours until sunrise; once the sun was up, the fire wouldn't be as obvious. Chivo knew that they needed to act quickly or be overrun. The fence would eventually fail, just like the bridge that killed Apollo.

"OK, mano, let's get this fucker back to the compound. We'll tag him and bag him, and then I've got to unfuck the march of the dead."

Chivo stood and pulled the bound man into a sitting position, drew his pistol, and struck the man across the face. His body went limp. Chivo then squatted and pulled the prisoner over his shoulder into a modified fireman's carry. Moving carefully but swiftly, they made their way back to the side gate, passing the three bodies of the remaining raider party.

The Compound, Saint George, UT

Bexar gasped awake. It took him a moment, but he realized that he was lying on the kitchen table; Guillermo was standing next to him, as were Frances and Jennifer. Another moment passed, and then he realized that he was nude and the cast on his leg was gone. Bexar didn't know why he kept waking up nude in strange places, but he was sure it wasn't from being an alcoholic.

"Frances, if you wanted to see me naked, you could have just asked."

Guillermo laughed.

"Honey, if I want to see a dick, Merylin has a whole drawer of them."

Bexar began laughing, which quickly started a coughing fit.

Brian walked into the room. "Guillermo, Chivo caught one of the attackers. He's chained to the flagpole outside."

"Where's Chivo?"

Stan ran into the room. "Chivo left, tore ass out of here in that Beetle we got."

Angel replied, "You got it, good job. What about the horses?"

"I think the horses are a loss. I'm sorry."

Angel scowled, shaking his head.

"I'm sorry, buddy; we were overrun and couldn't get them as we left. On the way back we felt the blast and saw the flames. What the hell happened?"

"They somehow got the shop to catch fire, and I think the propane tanks exploded."

Brian interrupted, "No, the captive said it was an RPG attack. Three of his party were killed. One of them had a launch tube, at least that's what Chivo called it."

To Bexar, the attack felt like a bad dream, lingering after waking up. "I killed three of them before going into the shop."

Angel patted his shoulder.

"As much fun as this is, Guillermo, I don't feel like I'm hurt. Do you have anything I could wear? I want to get up."

Guillermo laid a towel over Bexar's midsection and groin. "The towel will have to do for a few minutes. You aren't hurting because I shot you up with morphine, guy. Heath is about your size, and Jennifer can fix up something to fit tomorrow if it's not quite right. I also gave you some antibiotics in the mix. That's about all we can do for you right now."

"What all is wrong with me then?"

"We'll have to wait and see about your leg. The cast was damaged in the aftermath, so it came off. You have some pretty good burns on your arms and chest. Your gear and your clothes were burned and ruined. I think your rifle is OK. We washed most of the soot off and cleaned the burns. It'll all probably hurt like a son of a bitch tomorrow."

"Such optimism."

"That's easy for you to say, Bexar; you're the one flying on the morphine rocket."

Jennifer walked down the hall and returned a few minutes later with some underwear, a pair of socks, a T-shirt, some heavy-duty work pants, and a pair of work boots. Guillermo helped Bexar sit up. The IV bag hung from the light fixture over his head. Jennifer and Guillermo carefully helped Bexar get into the shirt and underwear before helping him to his room and his bed to rest.

The Beetle

Chivo stopped in the middle of the road at the end of the compound's long driveway, revving the obnoxiously loud engine and honking the horn. The smashed-out tail lights and turn signals kept the vehicle dark, except for the headlights, which Chivo had switched to bright. The dead slowly began shambling toward the loud air-cooled car, and Chivo began slowly threading his way through the undead on the road, making his way down the hillside and back toward the Interstate. He didn't know the area away from the compound at all; the surface streets were a mystery to him, and anything he couldn't see from the powerful optic of his big 50BMG Barrett rifle was unknown. Frank, the captured raider, wouldn't tell him anything about his group's location either—yet. Chivo would take care of that first thing in the morning. He had left Brian with specific instructions to cut off the man's clothes, chain him to the flagpole, and spray him with the hose until he regained consciousness. Once he was awake, Brian was to make sure he didn't fall asleep. Chivo needed the man shaken, cold, tired, and disorientated.

Slowly, Chivo made his way to the frontage road. He took a right and found a tanker semi-truck abandoned on the road, a car wedged under the middle of the tank, the top of the car crushed from the crash. Chivo pulled alongside the tanker, rolled down his window, and fired a half-dozen times into the aluminum side of the tank with his pistol. He wasn't sure what the tanker held, but the red hazard placard told him what was in the tanker was combustible. Liquid spewed out of the tanker, covering the crashed car. Chivo pulled forward and turned around, the dead continuing to swarm to his obnoxiously loud car. The camp lantern from the garage where the VW had been kept still sat on the passenger floorboard. A few moments were all it took to get the dual mantels lit and burning. Chivo stopped next to the tanker and the crashed car to roll down his window again; the air stank of the dead and raw fuel. Smiling, he threw the lantern onto the fuel-slicked roof of the crashed car, which whooshed into flames. Chivo accelerated as hard and fast as the VW would go, dodging the dead the best he could while resisting the urge to watch in the rear-view mirror. The air around him glowed bright orange, shadows of the dead approaching the flames dancing against the hillside; the hard thump of an explosion seemed to propel the car even faster. The tires squealed as he made the left turn to go back up the hill toward the compound and the burning shop, and Chivo was glad to see that the fuel truck burned much more brightly than the burning shop. It appeared that the small strip center near the semi-tanker had also caught fire. Together it might as well have been a bug zapper for the dead. The mass of the dead shifted. Chivo saw more macabre faces shambling down the hill than the backs of heads this time coming up it.

Yup, Bexar, one piece at a time.

CHAPTER 7

Outside of Boulder City, Nevada
April 5, Year 1

The air churned and buzzed with the sounds of flies. Aymond lay on the ground high upon the rocky mound with binoculars to his eyes, scanning the curved roadway; marked units sat idle and abandoned at each end, the police officers who'd placed them long missing.

The rest of the team knelt in a loose defensive position around the M-ATVs and the PLA radar truck. The dome was up and ready to run, but since the device was unknown and the Chinese seemed to purposely keep from walking in front of it, they would only activate the dome if Zeds appeared on the bridge.

Aymond, reasonably sure they were alone, or at least that the PLA or Koreans weren't around yet, stood and began hiking down the south side to where the rest of the team was waiting. As he reached them, the team gathered close enough to hear but remained facing outward in a defensive posture.

"Completely overrun. There are police vehicles on either end, but obviously they appear abandoned. There are no signs of survivors; I have no idea if some are sheltering in the facility below."

"What about the generators?" Happy asked the question that everyone was thinking.

"I have no idea, but some of the exterior lights are on, though the fuses on the transmission lines appear disconnected or blown. We'd have to get a Corps of Engineers team in here to really know, unless one of you dickheads knows anything about electricity."

"I fucked a stripper called White Lightning once."

Muffled smirks and coughing erupted from the group.

"Outstanding, Gonzo, your mom would be so proud."

"That *was* his mom!"

Aymond tried to ignore Hammer, but the whole team was straining, trying not to laugh.

"OK, gentlemen, and you too, Gonzo, saddle up. This is a wash. Time to point north to Nellis."

The convoy lurched out of their spot on Highway 93 near the Hoover Dam, turning right on Lakeshore Road. The route that Snow had mapped out on a civilian road atlas was a meandering, indirect one, but it kept the team from driving through Henderson and it would drop them near Ellis Air Force Base without having to drive through the heart of Las Vegas. Aymond had no idea what they would find in Vegas, but he assumed it wouldn't be magic shows and gambling.

The road loosely followed the far edge of the shore of Lake Mead, passing a few RV parks and establishments along the way. December was apparently high time for the area. The RV parks looked full, a handful of Zeds shambling through the mass of expensive-looking mobile homes, but the convoy passed far enough away that by the time the Zeds turned to follow them, the rising dust was all they caught. They took Lakeshore to Northshore Road, a narrower two-lane roadway with open desert sprinkled with vacationers, which led to Lake Mead Boulevard. The drive with a sports car or a motorcycle would probably have been enjoyable, but lumbering along in an armored truck, even one as advanced as the M-ATV, wasn't exactly deserving of a hot lap on *Top Gear*.

As they exited the mountains, the roadway abruptly crashed into the eastern edge of Las Vegas. Snow stopped and glanced at Aymond in the front passenger seat, holding the civilian road map.

Aymond pointed out of his side window. "Take a right. If we go through open country, we'll run into the southern edge of the base."

Snow nodded and radioed the following trucks with the plan before turning the wheel and crunching onto the rocky desert floor. A few hundred yards later, the convoy bounced across a small paved road and continued northward across the desert, the edge of civilization's rotting City of Light out their left-side windows. Without GPS, an overland route required orienteering skills that the team members possessed, with compasses they had in their kits, but they needed better maps to be accurate. Dead reckoning was all they really needed, just as long as they kept the edge of the city in sight. Much like early explorers sailing down the coast of Africa, they could get home as long as they kept land in view. Little league fields required a minor course correction, as did the gravel quarry, but the fenced-off edge of the air base stopped them in their tracks. Happy made quick work of the fence with his bolt cutters before removing the cross beams to make room for the trucks. The convoy drove slowly onto the tarmac of the runways. A row of angry-looking A-10s sat on the ramp with flat tires. A few members of the team had trained with the PJs at Nellis before and had a good idea where they would be found; the runways and taxiways would lead them right to their doorstep like the yellow brick road.

Aymond scanned the flightline across the acres of concrete and desert. "There's a whole bunch of Zeds on that side, Snow. Keep us over here as long as you can." This didn't look good to Aymond.

Snow didn't speak, but he felt the same disappointment, that this base was like the others that they had visited. He drove to the north end of the runways and across the taxiways to the long ramp leading to where the PJs' helicopters should be tied down. On the tarmac were numerous Zeds who had been killed; they lay motionless, baked by the sun and completely untouched by the buzzards or other wildlife.

"Well someone's been here, Chief, and they were fucking pipe hitters!"

"Let's hope they're still here."

The convoy drove to the edge of the ramp where the PJ facility stood, windows dark. Aymond keyed the radio. "Set a defensive position, and use the radar truck. Chuck, Davis, Gonzo, and Hammer, sweep the two buildings fast, but keep your asses from getting bit."

No one responded verbally, but the flurry of activity was enough to know that the message was received and well understood. The M-ATVs parked in a loose V-formation with the radar truck at the tip, the inside of the protective V being toward the buildings. Jones had the radar truck's dome up and on before the armored war wagons had even turned their motors off. All they could do was standby, hoping that the search team found some friendlies.

Snyder, Texas

The second night away in her MRAP-turned-motorhome was much less eventful than the first. There were no tornados, no driving rain, no dead lit by lightning's flash. The morning had been looking up until now. The fuel gauge meant that Amanda wasn't comfortable moving on until she could top off the heavy truck; the semi-tanker parked at the truck stop was the first choice. What was contained in the still-shiny aluminum tanker trailer was anyone's guess. Amanda wasn't willing to chance accidently putting gasoline or cooking oil or who knows what else into the fuel tank of her rig. She assumed that the placards and numbers on the rig explained what the load was, but Amanda had no knowledge of them and no idea where to find the information in this post-Internet era.

She knew the big saddle-tanks on the semi-truck held diesel fuel and many gallons of it. The trusty length of rubber hose could be her pipeline to success. Across the large parking lot from her chosen truck stop was a squat three-story hotel; no large semi-trucks in the parking lot there, although there was a propane delivery truck with a large tank on the back parked next to the building. None of this mattered, as teeming through the parking lot were the dead, dozens of them converging on the rattling exhaust of her diesel engine. They were beginning to slap against the armored hull. Amanda wasn't worried about her safety yet, and she could slowly drive through the massing swarm, nudging the bodies out of her way and hopefully away from her tires. A spare tire was on the truck, but she had no idea how to get it down or how to jack up the truck, so the spare might as well have been a birthday cake for all the good it would do if she got a flat tire.

She did not have a surplus of fuel, and she had no outside help; the one thing she had at the moment was time. Time to think through the problem piece by piece. If the dead would act like her dogs and chase something she threw, life would be a lot easier. She could throw a stick, the dead would trace the stick in the air as it flew, and follow obediently. After all, they acted like moths to the flame.

Flame . . . fire!

Familiar as Amanda was with her M4, the big M2 machine gun on the turret was something she had only fired once, the day of the library raid. The hotel and the propane tanker truck loomed large in her windshield. From the highway, she estimated the truck to be about six hundred feet away, and that guess would have to do because there was no way she was going to get outside to pace it off.

If I do nothing, I have to drive off and find other fuel. Worst case I blow everything up, and I have to drive off and find other fuel. Amanda shrugged to herself, ignoring the fact that the worst case would be her vehicle being disabled. She opened the roof hatch and climbed up the sling into the turret. Walking herself through a mental checklist, she pulled the charging handle hard to the rear and let go, switched the safety, moved the big rifle in the mount a little to get the muzzle pointed in the propane truck's general direction, and pushed the make-it-loud button. The air ripped open from the assault of automatic weapons fire. Windows shattered, and pieces of the hotel's façade broke away and fell in chunks. An obese person, long dead, shambled out of his hotel room, falling through the broken window to the parking lot three stories below and into a crumpled heap.

Amanda quickly pushed on the handles, arcing a rain of steel toward the propane truck, squinting in anticipation and ducking behind the armored glass of the turret. The large holes walked up the cab of the truck and the 50-caliber rounds pierced the heavy tank like a laser. Immediately, the propane tank ruptured, venting the pressurized propane—and nothing happened. Instead, every pair of milky-white eyes stared at her as the dead shambled toward the enormous eruption of sound of the M2 ripping the air apart.

"Fuck, that always worked in the damn movies . . . I need fuel. Fuck!"

She climbed back into the interior of the MRAP, and the roof hatch thunked closed. After dogging the latch and sitting in the driver's seat, Amanda drove across the worn grass median and next to the semi-truck. The side of the MRAP rubbed against the semi-truck, knocking both trucks' side mirrors off. Amanda could get the driver's door open, but it wouldn't open far enough for her to get out. Angry at the dead, angry that a propane truck wouldn't blow up like she'd thought it would, and angry at herself for believing that it would in the first place, Amanda slammed her door closed. After unlatching the roof hatch, Amanda grabbed her hose and climbed out onto the roof again.

Standing on the roof, she could see the situation that she'd created, and it wasn't good, not good at all. More dead streamed from behind the hotel, from across the street, from the fields, and from the highway. Wrapping the hose around her shoulders, Amanda climbed down the side of her armored truck into the small gap between it and the semi. As luck would have it, she'd been able to stop with the fuel filler cap on her tank quite close to the filler cap on the tank of the semi. With no gap between the trucks the dead didn't appear to be able to get to her, so Amanda got to work. She unscrewed her cap and let it hang on the safety chain; she went to unscrew the cap of the semi's saddle tank and found it locked, needing a key to release it. She banged on the driver's door window of the semi and got no response. Trying the door, she found it too was locked.

"Fucking hell."

Angry, Amanda drew her pistol and fired twice into the thin glass of the semi's door window, breaking the glass. After pushing the shattered safety glass window out of the way and unlocking the truck from the inside, she opened the door and squeezed inside. The cab of the truck was disgusting, some unknown goo was in the driver's seat, and the interior smelled worse than it looked, which was saying something. Coughing, Amanda tried the cubby holes and storage areas around the driver's door before finding a single silver key on a cheap truck-stop keychain. Outside the truck, she tried the key in the gas cap and was happy to find it worked.

With the cap now off, one end of the hose went into the semi's fuel tank; she took a few breaths, wrapped her lips around the hose, and pulled with all she had. Spitting fuel out of her mouth, she cursed as diesel splashed on her pants and boots before she got the end of the hose in her tank. Now she waited.

Tucumcari Municipal Airport, NM

Andrew walked across the tarmac. His home for the previous night had been in one of the short rows of hangers. It had felt like a real home for all the time he'd spent in his hanger over the years. Oreo plodded along next to him, happy, alert, and ready, just like always. The two big tanks of aviation fuel for the field had Jet-A and Avgas. The Jet-A was of no use to him, but the Avgas was exactly what he needed for the Husky. For a field in the middle of BFE New Mexico, one of the runways was surprisingly long, and the fuel-delivery system was much more complex than it needed to be, which also meant that the system depended on electric pumps . . . electric pumps that no longer worked. Although if the tanks worked like the others he had used before, Andrew's guess was that he might still be able to fuel from the tank. The short grip of a pair of bolt cutters stuck out of the top of his backpack, and, after the short walk from the hanger, he and Oreo stood inspecting the fuel tanks.

The tanks were idiot-marked with big bold letters labeling which tank held which fuel. For all the problems of filling a diesel truck with gasoline, fueling a turbine aircraft with Avgas was more annoying and more problematic. Pilots never being ones to trust a guy on the flight line, they liked big markings that they could see from the cockpit to help them feel safe in the knowledge that the correct fuel tank was being used. The filling connection and the output hose were of no use; the output would flow too fast and dump fuel all over everything, not exactly Andrew's first choice. The two vents on top of the tank didn't seem promising either, but small tank access in the middle of the tank on the top was their best bet. This wasn't exactly a gamble; this exact sequence had played out with similar tanks all across the United States during the past few weeks. After cutting the two locks off the cap, an adjustable crescent wrench made quick work of the cap's bolts, and Andrew was able to peer down the small hole into the tank; it smelled like Avgas and not Jet-A, and he could see tiny rays of sunlight shimmering off the fuel surface.

"We're in business, buddy."

Andrew climbed down to where Oreo sat dutifully waiting; the pair walked back to the hanger, started the Husky, and taxied off the tarmac, across the dusty desert ground, and right up next to the tank. After shutting off the engine, Andrew climbed out, loosened the fuel caps, and began siphoning fuel, filling the aircraft's bladders and his small gas can.

"I bet we only have six more months of flying before the fuel all goes bad. Thank God there's no damn ethanol in aviation fuel or we'd be going up shit creek already!"

Oreo yawned; he had heard the same thing repeated at every fuel stop. After sumping his tanks for water, Andrew walked the aircraft for a fast preflight check, climbed in, and taxied back onto the tarmac. The windsock hung limp. With no wind, there was no need to taxi to take off into the wind. Andrew conducted his run-up and magneto checks on the flightline in front of the small airfield's FBO. Once the engine reached a reasonable operating temperature and the final checks were complete, Andrew pushed power and began his take-off roll, bounding across the flightline and taxiway, eschewing the runways all together. Before the fall of society, such foolhardy actions would have left him with some explaining to do to an agency known far and wide for their complete lack of a sense of humor, but now Andrew simply didn't care.

Rolling out toward the west, he flew over the small town of Tucumcari, New Mexico. Keeping his altitude low, Andrew scanned the town with his binoculars for any signs of survivors. An entire section of the town appeared to be ruined by fire; the main drag appeared to be owned by the dead. Andrew didn't see any signs of survivors. If there were any down there, they were alone and on their own. Only desert stretched across the landscape in every direction that he could see. After retrieving the road atlas from his bag and scratching Oreo between the ears, Andrew flipped pages until he found what he needed, making pencil marks and notes along the route and of what the town held. I-40 snaked westward, and he followed it, taking a straighter and faster route overhead than the roadway below could give.

"We should be over Albuquerque in a bit!" Andrew yelled over the engine and wind noise to his K-9 companion. Smiling, Andrew let the yellow aircraft gain altitude and airspeed.

Saint George, UT

To say he felt sore was an understatement; Bexar had a headache and felt hungover. The skin on his arms hurt. Looking in the mirror on the dresser, he saw the burns and scratches. Black soot was still smeared on his face. His leg ached, but he could walk on it, sort of, limping a bit because the leg was tender. Folded neatly on the dresser were more pairs of underwear, socks, a T-shirt, and thick brown work pants with cargo pockets; the tag indicated that some place called Duluth Trading made them. Bexar stared at himself in the mirror, at the injuries, the scars, cuts, and bruises he'd earned since December.

"What is it with me and getting fucking blown up?"

His reflection had no answer. Moving slower than usual, Bexar bent over to put on his new pants and proceeded to get dressed. The pants were a little long and a bit loose, but beggars couldn't be choosers in the brave new world of the dead. The T-shirt fit well. A worn pair of work boots sat on the ground. A belt was on the dresser, along with his pistol, rifle, magazines, and his beloved custom CM Forge knife. The tactical gear was gone, the carrier, mag pouches, all of it. The holster for the pistol wasn't the same one he'd had before, but it fit the weapon and seemed to function.

Bexar press checked the pistol; it was still loaded, as was his rifle. His rifle was filthy and needed to be cleaned. The spare magazines went into the cargo pockets on his pants for now; perhaps Angel had some spare mag pouches, or maybe Jennifer could whip up something with her badass seamstress skills.

In the living room, he found Guillermo and Chivo standing close and speaking in hushed tones. Chivo looked up and waved him over.

"One chair, a cheese cloth or light dish towel, or worse case a T-shirt, a bucket, a hose, and my man Bexar here is all I need to gather the intel that we need to rectify this problem."

Guillermo's eyes were puffy. He was filthy, covered in dirt and soaked in sweat, and he looked exhausted and emotionally defeated, giving only a weak smile for a greeting to Bexar.

"OK. I'll tell the others to stay away."

"Good. Let them know that they don't want to be a part of this."

Guillermo looked up from the floor and at Bexar again. "But I do."

Chivo put his hand on Guillermo's shoulder. "Are you sure?"

"They . . . " tears rolled down his cheeks, streaking through the dirt, "they did this to us, and I want retribution."

"Retribution will come. Today is only about making sure we can get it."

Guillermo nodded and walked out of the room.

"What happened?"

Chivo looked at Bexar. "You don't remember last night?"

"I remember the shop exploded and burned."

"You pulled Heath out of the shop after it exploded. You don't remember that?"

"Vaguely, like a bad dream."

"Mixing adventures with morphine will do that. Heath died, but you did the right thing."

Bexar's expression didn't change, "Anyone else?"

"Yeah, mano, Gary and Coach got it too."

Bexar shook his head. "So tell me how we're going to fix this."

"We have a prisoner; you and I are going to interview him in an hour or so."

"Bad cop, bad cop again?"

"Something like that, buddy."

Groom Lake, NV

A general assembly, the first full assembly since the Groom Lake survivors had met to see Amanda Lampton sworn in as President, sat noisily in the assembly hall. Some of the residents hadn't been here for the swearing-in ceremony, arriving after the surprise and missing the festivities. The celebration had been vibrant and happy with so many people releasing the fear and anger of the previous months. The only thing that Jake found missing was an open bar, the facility being poorly stocked on spirits, wine, or beer, but some people told him that they were glad about that because this was the longest they had been sober, and they felt like they had new lives. Jake wasn't one to disagree and decided against the previous plans of trying to distill some liquor out of the stored grains.

Jessie, Sarah, and Erin stood in the back of the hall, along with Jason and a handful of the shooters who had completed the first, and thus far only, Alien's Home Tactical Training Academy, as one of the participants had named the basic tactical shooting course.

Jake took the stage to a round of applause. "Thank you, thank all of you. Every single day we live is a day we are winners, winning the war against the onslaught of the dead and the Yama Strain. All of you here today were instrumental in the containment of the outbreak. If it hadn't been for your quick action and adherence to the lockdown rules we have in place, I am confident that more of us would have been taken by Yama."

The crowd applauded for themselves, Jake smiling at the interruption, happy for the positive outlook the residents had.

"We live and learn, just as all of us have done since the attack on December 26th of this past year. We have learned what caused the outbreak, and we have a theory as to why the lights and systems were turning on and off. First the outbreak: Brit Sanchez was aboveground without good reason. She was attacked by a reanimate and was bitten. She failed to follow the rules of safety and further failed by concealing a bite wound from all of us. Her selfishness killed our fellow residents. Her selfishness also resulted in the death of our military commander, Major Jeffery Wright."

An audible gasp was heard, and whispering began immediately. Jake held up his hands.

"This won't happen again. We have a future plan to prevent another outbreak, but before we get to that, we need to talk about the systems. This facility is more complex than we had realized. I know all of you are surprised to hear that a secret underground base at Area 51 is a complex and advanced place, but you'll have to believe me."

Jake winked at the crowd, which chuckled politely in return.

"The systems are all computer controlled. Those computers are connected to other, similar facilities around the United States. Of all those facilities, this one and the one in Texas are the only two that have survived and have survivors living in them. We believe that the Chinese and Koreans were attempting to hack this facility via that network. We physically disconnected the servers from any outside connection. The servers all rebooted and are running. We don't know how all the systems in the facility work, but thankfully the issues with the lights, air systems and everything else have become reliable. That is why we think the systems came back online and why we believe they will remain online for the foreseeable future. Until we find a survivor that has an idea as to how the computers control the facility, we'll work hard to keep the status quo and keep us all safe."

The crowd clapped.

"Now, the new procedures so we don't have another Yama Strain Sanchez infecting our protected survivors. All aboveground working parties will be strip-searched by selected persons before they are allowed re-entry. Just as we quarantine our new friends before they're allowed to take up residence here, we will check each of us for our protection. No one is exempt. Any time an aboveground party returns, a male and a female will conduct physical examinations on the returning members, of the same gender, of course, before they are allowed entry back into the facility."

The applause was slower than before but still there.

"I know some of you have no desire to return topside. I understand and respect that decision. Others are happy to go topside any chance they get; I understand and respect that decision as well. We have many jobs and a place for everyone here, and we are committed to helping you. Today, though, we need twenty volunteers for a special detail, an important detail of honor to help in the respectful cremation of our fallen citizens, our fellow residents and friends."

Hands were raised around the room.

"Thank you all so much for volunteering. Check in with Sarah in the back of the room for the details. In a few minutes, I ask all of you who are not assisting with the detail to join us in the cafeteria. The kitchen staff has prepared a special lunch in remembrance of our fallen friends. Thank you."

Jake gave a curt nod and walked off the stage, the crowd applauding shortly before the room erupted in conversation and movement. The volunteers made their way to the back of the room as instructed. Their day was just beginning, and it wouldn't involve the bland sheet cake that the rest of the residents were going to eat.

As the hall cleared, Sarah addressed the volunteers, thirty in all. "Thank you for volunteering. The task is honorable work, but the work is going to be hard. The victims' bodies have already been moved to the blast door, and we need help carrying them outside. Once outside the hangar, we have a location to the west of the hangar chosen where some of the detail will dig a shallow mass grave. We have acquired some jet fuel from the tanks and have some other material that we'll be using to start the funeral pyre in that grave."

Much to Jessie and Sarah's surprise, none of the volunteers balked at the task, the plan, or asked to be excused. All of them were resolute in the need for the work to be done.

Jessie spoke up. "Don't forget that we will all be strip-searched upon returning. Some privacy partitions are already in place in the hangar constructed out of the office cubicles, and we will do our best to have some small portion of modesty."

"What if someone is bit?"

The question that no one in the assembly had asked, but everyone had thought, was finally said out loud. Erin replied first. "Then that person will be put down."

No one spoke for a few moments. The comment was cold and without feeling, but they knew it was the only answer. A few months before, such a concept would have been outrageous to the point of lunacy. In this new world owned by the dead, it was expected.

Work Party, Groom Lake, NV

"East of the hangar, between the taxiway and runways we'll start by digging a shallow grave. I have to apologize, but all we have are these folding army shovels. I wish we had a backhoe or even full-sized shovels, but this is it, so this is what we'll use. According to the number of bodies that we have, we're guessing that a hole about ten foot by ten foot will work if it's about three feet deep. The rules are simple; everyone digs. When you're on break, you really aren't on break. You can sit and rest, but your rifle will be in your hands, you'll be facing outwards, and you'll call out for any zombies you see. We're not going to have another damn Typhoid Mary here."

Erin interrupted Jessie, "Brit the bitch!"

Jessie glanced at Erin and continued. "Once the hole is dug, we'll douse the bodies with the fuel and light it."

No one else spoke. Some in the small group nodded; others were now a bit annoyed at what they had volunteered for, but now that they stood in the hangar next to the stack of their dead friends, it would be impossible for them to shirk their duties at this point.

"I have no idea how hot the fire has to be to burn bone, but we'll try. When we're done burning the bodies, we'll all take turns shoveling the dirt back into the hole and finishing the burial. Any questions?"

A middle-aged man who appeared to have lost a lot of weight recently spoke up. "Who's going to be checking us before we go back inside? Are we checking one another?"

Sarah spoke up for the answer. "Good question and, no, our greeter guards are in a meeting right now discussing the procedures for the searches. By the time we're done, they should be ready for us."

"If there's nothing else, everyone grab a shovel," Jessie said. "I'll be right behind you with my FJ, water, and snacks, and we'll meet over at the worksite. Sarah is going to mark off the edges, and then we can all get to work. The faster we get started, the sooner we'll be done."

General grumbling faded behind her as Jessie walked to the FJ, loading two blue jugs of water and a box of protein bars from the storeroom.

Nellis Air Force Base, NV

"Chief, no one is here. It appears that there were some survivors, but they're gone now."

Aymond nodded. "Thanks, Hammer. What about supplies?"

"That they've got. It looks like they raided half the base. Damn near a pallet of XM193, like fifty cases of MREs, various M4s, magazines, those massive trauma bags the PJs take on their helicopters, and some other random stuff. Chuck is taking an inventory. We're clear to move inside though."

"Roger that, Hammer. Not many Zeds coming our way, which is surprising. You tell the others to lock it down and head inside, I'm going to check with Chuck and take a look around. Tell the others team meeting in thirty mikes."

Hammer didn't respond. He just walked off to complete his task. Five minutes later, the entire team crowded into the conference room that the PJs had been using as a supply cache, each of them digging through bags and crates of gear, turning on electronics, night-vision goggles, and tactical lights to see if they still worked, and making notes along the way to help Chuck with the full inventory. They didn't have the complete mission-profile load-out containers that the SEAL teams had in California, but this was better than what they'd had on their trucks.

"Hey, Chief, check this out. It's a shortwave radio. My dad used to play with one when I was a kid. You could pick up broadcasts from Europe sometimes. This one has a hand crank to power it up."

"Does it work, Gonzo?"

"Not as hard as his mom's crank works," was called out from the back of the room.

"Fuck you, Chuck! How many sailors did your sister fuck before the clap became applause?"

The rest of the room laughed as Gonzo spun the handle on the radio until it lit up, static coming out of the speakers. "Whoa, everyone, shut the fuck up."

This time he wasn't joking. Everyone got quiet, and radio static filled the room as Gonzo slowly rolled the tuning dial across the bands.

". . . secured underground facility, food, shelter, clean water. All survivors are welcome at Groom Lake, Nevada. You can make a radio out of parts from disabled cars, tune . . . ."

The radio transmission faded out to static.

"Get it back, Gonzo!" Chuck was no longer lobbing insults at his teammate's mother; genuine excitement filled his voice.

Gonzo slowly spun the dial, as he paced around the room, trying to find a spot to regain the signal. After a few minutes, the static faded, and the limited energy from turning the handle had been used.

Aymond nodded. "That's like what we heard on the HF weeks ago. I thought it was bullshit. Any of you been to Groom Lake?"

"Do you think we'll find aliens, Chief?"

"No, Happy, I doubt it, but I don't think we're too far away from it. OK, Gonzo, you, Chuck, and Happy finish up with this inventory. First we recon the rest of Nellis, and then it's time we visit a top-secret base."

Snyder, TX

Amanda left the fuel cap on the half-full saddle tank of the semi-truck open. Using one of her spare T-shirts from the supplies, she soaked it in diesel and stuffed it into the tank. The fuel tank of her MRAP was topped off and the cap back on. Dead surrounded the trucks, all of them pawing at the metal sides, trying to get to a fresh meal. The flies were like nothing Amanda had ever experienced. Her shemagh was wrapped tightly around her head and face, sunglasses pushed tight against her eyes, but the flies still found their way into her ears and mouth. Between the diesel fumes and the flies, she could barely breathe. She tossed the hose on top of her MRAP and used some 550-cord to tie it onto the turret handle. She didn't want it in the vehicle stinking up the interior with diesel fumes, although she still had to deal with the fuel spilled on her clothes, which burned against her skin as she sweated. Climbing between the vehicles one last time, Amanda lit the soaked T-shirt sticking out of the semi-truck's saddle tank with her lighter and quickly pulled herself up the side of her truck and into the cab, leaving the turret hatch open, hoping to air it out a little. She would have to change pants soon, but now was not the time. The MRAP in gear, she drove forward, nudging away the dead clawing at her vehicle, some falling under the bumper, others knocked to the ground. She had no time to waste.

Frustrated, Amanda drove faster, running over the dead as she did so, u-turning out of the parking lot to go west before turning north on Highway 84. The mass of the dead were near the semi, so she accelerated quickly, watching in the rearview as the gas tank on the semi-truck spewed flames out of the open filler neck. The dead appeared to ignore her as they zeroed in on the fire like moths to a bug zapper.

They like fire. I like fire. I like that they like fire.

The Compound, Saint George, UT

The group members had been warned that they might not want to watch, but that if they did watch, they would have to be perfectly quiet. The captured attacker from the previous night lay on a folding table completely nude, shivering in the cool air, his hands and feet tied and also tied to the table. The end of the table was propped up on the edge of the fire pit, which had the prisoner laying with his head low at a modest angle and his feet above his head. He writhed against the restraints. A rope around his waist kept him from raising his hips off the table. A black T-shirt served as a blindfold. Chivo had two buckets of water, a dish towel soaking in the cold water of one. Bexar had a hose that was fed from the rain cistern, which had surprisingly good water pressure. Chivo gave

Bexar very specific instructions; he was to help hold the towels tight and be quick to refill the water buckets.

Guillermo and a couple others watched from about ten yards away. The group's medical bag sat at Guillermo's feet, his presence and the bag standing by at Chivo's request.

"OK, Frank, this is your first and only chance. What is your group leader's name?"

"Fuck you, spic!"

Chivo's face showed no change, and with absolutely no emotional reaction, he gave a single curt nod to Bexar. Bexar pulled the soaking wet towel out of the bucket and placed it across Frank's mouth, nose, and face. Chivo, bucket in hand, began pouring water on the towel.

"What is your group leader's name, Frank. You can make this stop at any time, but only you can make it stop. What is his name? Just one name will make it stop."

Frank's body writhed against the restraints, his head jerking unsuccessfully back and forth, trying to escape the water. Chivo stopped the flow of water. "The name. Frank, only a name."

Frank's coughs gurgled. "Fuck you."

Chivo nodded to Bexar and began slowly pouring water across Frank's face, mouth, and nose again. Frank struggled, coughing. Chivo stopped, "You can end this, Frank. Only you can end this, and I want you to end this."

"Fuck your mother!"

Chivo's face was completely devoid of any expression. The insults didn't matter, the torture didn't matter; the only thing that mattered to Chivo was obtaining the objective. He poured water on Frank's covered face.

"There is no end until you decide, Frank."

Gasping against the towel, Frank called out, "Dan!"

"See, Frank, that wasn't so hard, was it? Just a simple answer, and you could breathe again. Where is your hideout?"

"No, I can't!"

Chivo nodded to Bexar, and the process began again, Frank struggling and gurgling. The waterboarding interrogation only took thirty minutes, but Chivo learned that the group's hideout was less than a mile as the crow flies to the southwest. There were only four of them left, and they were in dire straits. Nearly out of water, nearly out of food, the only thing they did have was a serious amount of weapons and ammo, as the RPG attack the previous night had shown. Chivo left Frank tied to the table outside in the cool air, where he shivered more in fear than from the cool air. Walking over to Guillermo, he saw that the others had left, unable to watch Chivo's enhanced interrogation techniques.

"OK, Willy, they're close to here; they're very well-armed, and they're almost out of water and food. This is your firebase on an exposed hill, so it's your choice. Do we kill them, or do we save them?"

Guillermo shook his head, his cheeks wet with tears from what he had watched. "It isn't my choice. This requires a group vote."

"Why don't you make it snappy, I either need to get us geared up for an op or geared up for a peace offering between your tribes. Either one you choose, I need to get Frank up and work on becoming his best bud for either plan to work."

Guillermo nodded and walked inside. Chivo gestured with his head, and Bexar followed to where Frank was tied to the table.

"You did good, Frank; you did really good, but understand you're not out of the woods yet. I'm going to take you off this table and let you get dressed, but if you even think about attempting to fight or escape, my man here will kill you before your 50cc brain can even finish the thought. Do you understand?"

A very weak "Yes, sir," was the response. Chivo looked at Bexar, who understood he was to provide hard cover. Like a bizarre felony traffic stop, Bexar pointed his rifle at Frank while Chivo cut him loose, handed him his clothes, and let him dress. Once dressed, Chivo zip-tied Frank's hands behind his back and also to his belt to keep him from being able to move.

Brian walked out of the house alone and headed straight to Chivo, leaned into his ear and whispered, "No peace. Fuck them. They killed . . . those friends were our family; every person in this group is my family."

Chivo nodded. Brian walked back inside the house. The burned-out shell of what was the workshop still smoked and smoldered a few yards away. First Chivo looked at Bexar and then to Frank. In one fluid motion, Chivo rotated, striking Frank on the side of the neck with the back of his arm, on the common peroneal. Frank collapsed, dazed.

"Help me tie this fucker to the flagpole again; you and I need to chat, and I've got to leave to take care of something before we go take the fight to Frank's group."

Five thousand feet AGL, NM

Andrew descended and banked over the heart of Albuquerque. Massive destruction was all he could see with the naked eye. Using the binoculars, Andrew saw that some bridges had collapsed, but he saw no signs of any survivors. The dead owned the city. Not wanting to waste any more time, he and Oreo continued westward, loosely following I-20 so as to not get lost. Without proper pilot charts, there was no way for Andrew to know where all the airports were located and, just as important, where the tallest radio and communication towers stood. So for his safety, he tried to eyeball it and keep around five thousand feet above ground level.

Before the attack, his Garmin unit would give him the correct altitude above the ground, the altimeter on the dash set to mean sea level. At least he was still able to verify or reset that altimeter at most of the airports that he landed in as they had small signs near the runway with the field elevation. Finding those fields was more difficult than he would have liked, but keeping to his rule to only fly during daylight, Andrew scanned for landing strips. Not that he needed one at any given minute, but if something happened, he would rather land at an airport or private strip than on a highway or in a field. At an airport there was a chance he could scavenge parts from other aircraft to get flying again. On the dash, the indicated airspeed still worked, but without his Garmin, Andrew had no idea what his ground speed was; he didn't even know how far he had flown except for making rough estimates with a road atlas. His Husky could climb, slowly, as high as twenty thousand feet, but Andrew had no supplemental oxygen nor any reason to fly that high. More importantly, the aircraft had a listed range of around eight hundred miles. That wasn't a number he wanted to chance, so when he was roughly half full of fuel, Andrew was on the hunt for a landing strip in hopes of scoring some Avgas.

In this part of the country, the airports were often roughly an "A" shape with long runways from being leftover auxiliary airports for military pilot training, so they weren't too hard to spot from the moderate altitude that he tried to keep.

Andrew located one of the big A-shaped airfields. It had old-looking surfaces with a big "X" on each end of the runways signifying that the runway was out of service, so the dark black tarmac of the primary runway was the obvious choice.

Taxiing near the fuel pumps, Andrew could see that the sign on the FBO said "Winslow." Flipping through the pages of the big spiral-bound atlas, Andrew saw that he was nearing Flagstaff, Arizona. The sun was well past being directly overhead, nearly halfway down the sky toward the horizon. Andrew decided that Winslow was a wonderful place to sleep but decided to fuel his plane first today, unlike the day before.

Today, the roadway scene on I-40 was weird, something like Andrew hadn't yet seen. All the cars were pushed off the roadway, and signs were knocked down. It looked as if a giant bulldozer had come through and destroyed all that was in its path. Andrew's mind flashed back to a favorite childhood movie, remembering that to stop the Nothing, he would have to name the princess.

"Of course, it couldn't be that simple, Oreo."

Oreo cocked his head, as dogs do.

After the fuel tanks were topped off, Andrew eschewed the couple of hangars available on the airport and taxied to the far south end on the unused runway. After walking Oreo for his much-needed break, they sat under the shade of the wings and ate a light dinner while watching the desert sunset. Then they both climbed back into the Husky and secured the door and windows to sleep in the plane. Andrew felt better being as far away from I-40 as he could be after seeing the destruction that day.

Groom Lake, NV

The day was one of hard work; Jessie was exhausted and nauseated, and the memories of her first pregnancy, carrying Keeley, began to come back: the hardships, the sickness, the pain, and the constant need to urinate. As those experiences returned with this pregnancy, she felt a sense of wonderment as to how her mind could forget all the bad parts of pregnancy when she held her little girl in her arms for the first time. Tears streamed down her cheeks, streaking through the dirt and soot from the horrible fire they had to tend, but the day was done. Soon she could shower, send these clothes to the laundry service, and then attempt to eat and sleep. Her back hurt, and she was beginning to really show the pregnancy, which meant that the others in the work party kept taking her shovel away. She wanted to help, but for all the work she attempted, Jessie spent most of her time sitting on the roof rack of the FJ with her rifle in hand watching for threats.

The new facility policy, one that she, Sarah, and Erin had helped Jake write, meant that even though not a single undead menace had appeared for the day, each and every one of them would still have to submit to a complete strip search for bite marks.

After parking the FJ back in the hangar, Jessie walked over to the women's line. She thought it strange that for a work party of their number, the vast majority of the volunteers were women. Just like public restrooms before the end of the world, the women's line was a half-dozen women deep and taking longer than it probably should. Safely hidden from the men behind the row of partitions, they all stood in the nude, waiting, holding their clothes in one arm, their rifles slung across their nude breasts, but none of them felt embarrassed or all that uncomfortable. It would seem that the new world order had given rise to the end of modesty.

"Fuck this," was all Jessie heard; by the time she turned to look, Erin had walked away from the back of the women's line and headed left toward the men's line.

The men's line had a single man currently being searched; neither he nor Jason, who was conducting the search, noticed her waiting for her turn. Soon the man headed to the exit area where he could dress, once again in private and still separated from the women's dressing area.

Jason's face flushed red at the sight of Erin standing in front of him completely nude, clothes tucked under her left arm and holding her rifle in her right hand. He stared at the floor. "Um, Erin, uh . . . you aren't supposed to be here."

"The women's line was taking too long, and I want to go shower and eat, so here I am."

"I can't do this. I have to check everywhere. I can't . . . you can't. It's not right . . . uh, I . . . ."

Erin cut him off, "Just check me! Man the fuck up about it!"

The tension between the two of them was more than this situation; a growing history between them exponentially increased Jason's awkwardness.

"I heard you were the hero of Cortez, so what is your problem with this?"

"My, it, this . . . no, it isn't this. You know what it is."

"I do, and what's your deal?"

"I . . . we can't."

"But I know you love me, so why's it such a problem?"

Jason frowned. "I'm nineteen, I'm, you . . . we . . . Erin, you're too young."

"I won't be too young forever. Now inspect me for zombie bites so we can all go inside."

Radio Hut, Groom Lake, NV

"Whoa, what the fuck was that?" The airman ripped the headphones from his head and pushed back in his chair. Bill sat at his spark-gap radio, waiting to see if anyone else would transmit; so far he'd had contact with seven different groups or people from all across the United States. It was the best news that they'd had in weeks. People were alive and fighting to survive, but something had to be done quickly or none of them, including him, would survive.

"What was it, Jeremy?"

"Some sort of broadband wave of noise; it's hard to describe."

"Did you get a sound grab of it?"

"Yeah."

"Play it over the external speaker so I can hear it."

Jeremy did as instructed, and the room filled with five seconds of loud broadband sound, like some sound effect from a sci-fi movie.

"That sounds like an encrypted transmission."

Jeremy shook his head. "Doesn't sound like anything I've heard. The digitally encrypted stuff pixelates from the digital encoding."

Bill nodded. "Sure, but this wasn't digital. It was probably made using an old analog trick. Long before you were born and after WWII, agents had recordings, like actual records, not tapes or CDs obviously, that they carried. The record was of random radio-wave spectrum noise from space emitted by the suns and stars, completely random. Copies of that record were kept and sent out to agents in the field. With some basic work that the radio transmission recorded, it was phased with the record, and the agent receiving it would have to reverse the process. Damn near impossible to break, unless the Soviets got their vodka-soaked hands on one of the recordings. Some of the hardest encryption to crack, securing open air transmissions from interception, amazing technology really."

"Did they ever?"

"I think so, but I'm no secret squirrel like you, gents. I'm just an old man who likes playing with radios."

The other airmen laughed.

"Jeremy, play it again, please."

SSC, Ennis, TX

Clint sat at the computer terminal. The one-time cipher wasn't too terribly difficult to remember, but the thumb drive he had carried for six months had to be used with a computer. The thumb drive held more than just text documents or music, although both were present in case someone got suspicious, but no one had ever suspected, none of his teammates, not his boss, not his agency, and his reward would be coming soon.

The radio signal received earlier was encoded and encrypted. Password-protected secret memory sectors on the thumb drive were devoted to radio signals. First, Clint had to run the program from the thumb drive, and then in the program he could apply the MP3 that the jump drive carried. Once those two things were lined up, the message would be easy to read.

A few minutes later, Clint had the message decoded.

Nevada go dark disconnected. Enemy present on West Coast. New mission. Destroy San Diego and enemy.

Although Clint tried to practice, his Korean was rusty and quite subpar for what he needed. However, even if he didn't understand the message correctly, the message was sent simply enough so he knew that the righteous invaders were suffering losses.

The interface of the software only allowed so many characters, so Clint found himself writing poorly and shortly as if he was on Twitter, hashtag-doubleagent.

Targetto Nevada, five days.

Five days was longer than it would have taken Clint to reach Groom Lake, but he assumed that Amanda wouldn't have much of a chance in the wild rangeland of the dead, except that Clint had helped to teach her how to survive. With the message encoded, Clint could now wait for his communist brothers and sister to arrive. He would hand over the entire northwestern ICBM field and the best the government had to offer at the SSC.

Radio Hut, Groom Lake, NV

Bill insisted that the radio remain open to scan all the amateur radio bands, which was hard for the changes between the high-frequency frequencies and the seventy-centimeter frequencies. Without warning, a similar sound as before erupted from the studio speakers.

"What the fuck do you think that is?"

"I don't know what they're saying Jeremy, but it's the same kind of transmission. What's the transmission power like?"

"Damn, Bill, it's like ten times as strong."

"So we can assume that either the first was a weak radio or it was a radio that was very far away. The second was a strong radio or one that was much closer than the other. I'd bet money that the first was far away, and the second was much closer."

"Like how far or how close?"

"That I don't know, Mike, but on those frequency ranges it could be China or it could be somewhere else on the continent; the other could have been from next door or a few states over."

"So it was a strong signal, so what."

"So what? So it sounded like a message broadcast on an open channel that was encrypted by adding some type of random noise that can only be decoded by another who has the same random noise sample."

"Who the hell would be sending encrypted signals?"

"The Chinese, the Koreans . . . I doubt it would be a random survivor community or we would have probably heard it before now."

"Why now?"

"No idea. I'm going to get Jake. This could mean nothing or it could mean something. With the cyber-attack on the facility, I'm leaning toward it means something, and that something isn't good."

Saint George, UT

Bexar sat hunched in the back seat of the tiny VW that Chivo drove. Frank sat next to Chivo, his hands and feet free. Frank had begun to believe that Chivo was his newfound best friend. Bexar held his pistol in his hand, the muzzle against the back of Frank's seat, where it would be harder to miss his target than holding it against his head and much easier to conceal. The last thing they needed was for Frank to understand his precarious situation in remaining amongst the living.

Chivo had explained his plan to Bexar before they left; it wasn't a grandiose plan, just simple and effective. They had no reason to believe that Frank was a strong enough person to lie effectively. After witnessing Chivo's enhanced interrogation techniques, Bexar was sure that he would have quickly given in after helping and watching the process. It was not for the faint of heart.

The undead were a bit sparser in the area; they weren't headed for the Interstate, just down the drive, south on Old Dump Road for a few hundred yards, where they turned into a loose industrial park. After turning onto Red Rock Road, Chivo deftly misshifted and caused the car to lurch and die.

"Shit, mano, looks like we have to walk from here. These old fucking cars. I bet the gas is already bad. Fucking ethanol goes bad in a couple of months, and it's been over three."

Frank was a bit wide-eyed. "Um, yeah, well, we're less than a half-mile away if we walk straight there."

Chivo climbed out of the car. Frank joined him, and Bexar holstered his pistol as he climbed out on the driver's side so Frank wouldn't see him do it. Chivo and Bexar retrieved their rifles from the back seat, the car being too small to climb out holding one without getting caught up on everything. The car sat next to the worn caliche drive of a trucking company.

"You guys just going to leave the car here?"

Bexar looked at Chivo. "What do you think? Frank's got a point."

"Hey, mano, you two head up. I'll catch up in a minute. I'll try to get it started. If it's dead for good, I'll leave it and join you in a few."

Frank nodded, Bexar gave thumbs up, and they began walking down Red Rock Road before climbing down a retaining wall and taking the direct route to the hideaway. Once out of sight, Chivo turned south and began sprinting through the trucking company's lot and up the hill on the far end. The top of the hill was a ridge and was flattened, the trucking company using it for storage. He only had a few hundred yards to go, but he had to get there fast, much faster than it would take Bexar and Frank to make the short walk.

Bexar stopped and tied his boot, asking Frank to watch for any approaching dead. A few shambled by in the distance, aimlessly, but none of them appeared close enough to be a threat. Frank stood nervously, shifting from side to side while Bexar was knelt down. When Bexar had silently counted to thirty, slowly tying his boot as he did, he stood and continued the walk. The hardest part of the walk wasn't slowing the pace down. Bexar exaggerated his limp, explaining that his leg had been broken and describing the truck crash. The hardest part of the walk was resisting the urge to look over his shoulder. It would have been pointless. Bexar knew that even if he did look, there was no way he would have been able to see Chivo anyway.

. 116 .

"We're almost there. Once we're safe in the fence line, you can sit and rest for a while."

"Thanks, Frank." Bexar paused. "So why the shop and not the house?"

"We watched everyone for a few days and knew the shop was just a shop, the food was all stored somewhere in the home. We needed the food."

"Why not just ask for it?"

"What if they said no?"

"What if they had said yes, Frank. Then some good people would still be amongst the living."

"Why chance it?"

This parking lot was paved. There were numerous semi-trucks and trailers parked and abandoned, all of them appearing to have been opened and rummaged through. Ahead of them was the storage lot; the tight compound had a u-shape of storage buildings on the north side, a central building, a short fence, and another building on the south side. It was tight, secure, and secluded. If not for the two men standing on the roof of the outer ring of storage buildings, Bexar might not have noticed that it was occupied. Walking out of the parking lot onto the road, Frank stopped and waved to the two men standing guard. Bexar recognized the rifle that one man carried as some sort of AR-15; the other man carried an RPG. The only real experience Bexar had with that was from watching classic action movies from the 1980s, news reports from the wars in the Middle East, and the man he'd killed the night of the attack on the compound. Luckily, when he was still a cop, in his part of Texas most of the turds were armed with ghetto blasters, not explosive rocket-propelled weapons of war.

"We thought you were dead, Frank."

"I did too, Dan."

"Where are the others?"

"They did die."

"You know the rules about outsiders; you just signed this man's death warrant by bringing him here."

"No, you don't understand . . . ."

The RPG carrier's head exploded in a red mist and his body crumpling to the ground, interrupting Frank. Dan, the man with the rifle, turned his head, trying to comprehend what had just happened. His head vanished in a spray of red, blood spewing from his neck as he fell off the roof to the ground below. Frank, shocked and frozen in place, didn't see Bexar unholster his pistol. A single shot to the side of his head, and Frank fell to the ground. The heavy sound of Chivo's 50-caliber rifle echoed off the buildings.

So far Chivo's plan was following the script. Bexar ran as quickly as he could to crouch against the outer wall of the storage units. He stayed still and waited. If Chivo was four for four, then the remaining member would appear quickly. Against the north wall, Bexar was in Chivo's view and the most out of view for the remaining member of Frank's group. One last heavy rifle shot echoed through the area, and Bexar knew they were in the clear, assuming that Frank hadn't lied about the number of people in his group.

Bexar stood and swung his rifle over his back on the sling before taking a few steps back to gain some running room, as much as he could run. A few quick steps and Bexar leapt, using his good leg, his hands grasping the rooftop. Bexar pulled himself up and flopped onto the roof. It wasn't as graceful as he had hoped, but he'd accomplished his goal. While lying prone, he pulled himself to the inside edge of the roof, took out his pistol, and scanned the small courtyard. There was no movement, and no other people appeared. Three bodies lay near him, motionless, thick pools of blood congealing on the roof, some dripping off the edge to the dusty ground below. Each of them was missing the most important piece of anatomy required to reanimate. Bexar wasn't worried about them rising to attack him. His focus was toward any new threats that might appear. Soon the sound of the VW reached his ears as it backfired back to life, the sound of the obnoxious muffler growing closer. It shut off, and Chivo soon joined Bexar on the roof.

"A bunch of dead are making their way toward us, so we shouldn't take too long. Hold cover, I'll go first." Chivo didn't wait for an answer; he slid off the roof, rotating gracefully as he did, silently falling to the ground below. Soon in view, he signaled for Bexar to join him. Bexar fell loudly to the ground with a curse.

"Smooth, esé."

Bexar shrugged. They moved forward as a team, first clearing the large main building and then the second large building. The storage units were last. They were all closed and, at a quick glance, appeared to be latched.

Twenty minutes later, the compound was cleared and deemed safe. Frank had been right, very little food, water, or any other supplies besides crates of stolen military weapons were found. They had thousands of rounds of 5.56, a dozen crates of RPGs, another three cases of hand grenades. This group was loaded for war, and Guillermo's group would have been killed off if not for the crime of being prepared. Chivo didn't blame either group; he could see Frank's group's desperation and Guillermo's group's grievance. If Frank, Dan, and the rest of the group had approached Guillermo for help peacefully they might have had a chance, but they didn't.

"Like the fucking bikers, man."

"At least nothing exploded this time, mano."

"The shop did, and I'm getting really damn tired of being knocked the fuck out by shit exploding."

Chivo smirked. "How're we going to get all this hardware back up the hill?"

"Why don't we let Angel and them figure that out; we did our piece. Except we should take what we want first off the top. We're done here, we're leaving, we need to arm up. In this fucking world, the dead are the easy ones; the living, shit, Chivo, the living are the worst."

"Yeah, mano, it's always people, desperate people who make really desperate choices. Your life, no one's life matters except to provide for their own."

Bexar nodded. "So, are you going to show me how to use these RPGs?"

"Dude, I've taught people who couldn't read or write how to effectively deploy an RPG. You can at least figure out a pop-up book, so you're already a step ahead."

Bexar flipped Chivo off, but he only laughed as he stacked case after case of 5.56 on the ground to take to the car. They needed a full-ton truck. What they had was a car that was light enough to sit in the bed of one.

Groom Lake, NV

"What can we do about it, Bill? I mean, we're not exactly a standing army; we're deep below ground. All we can do is shut the blast door and let it blow over."

"I don't know, Jake, it's just, well . . . those transmissions really creeped me out. First, one of the numbers stations came back online, then another, and now this. Something is going on, and I don't like it."

"How many different survivors have you made contact with so far?"

"What?" Bill was caught off guard by the sudden change of subject.

"With your radio, what is your count up to now?"

"Between the open HAM radio channels and the spark-gap radio, we've made contact and plotted over a hundred survivors and groups."

"Where are they located?"

"All over. You should come down and see our growing map. All the pins are something to get excited about."

"OK, then reach out to those groups, tell them that you . . . tell them that *we* believe something is afoot. They can be our early warning system, our NORAD for an impending attack of some sort. Any of them military units?"

"No, a bunch of former military though."

"Well that's a start. If one of our survivors, one of our modern Paul Reveres sounds the alarm, we have to devise a response, some way to get help, to send help, or to be of help. Otherwise, it does us no good."

"I'll make contact, but there just isn't anyway, I mean, what can they do; they're going to ask."

"We'll figure something out. For now, tell them to report anything suspicious."

"See something, say something."

"Heh, yeah, sort of like that, Bill."

Bill looked worried, but he left to do his job. Jake leaned back in his office chair and put his feet on the desk and closed his eyes, concentrating. *Cliff would have known what to do; he always had a plan. He always had a simple plan . . . simple. We need a simple plan, but I don't have any idea where to even start. We had almost lost the survivors here. If it hadn't been for a high-school-style lockdown drill followed by Jessie and Sarah cleaning house with their rifles, we would have all been dead. We fought our asses off against the damn homegrown cult and still had to be saved in Colorado. Cliff rescued us, and that was against some low-grade assholes, not a trained invading military force.*

Jake shook his head and sat up. He needed to go for a walk and think; for once he was at a complete loss as to what to do or say.

Post, TX

Amanda's map didn't show more than a small speck in the middle of nowhere Texas for Post, but she knew that this was where the turn onto Highway 380 would be located. That much she had marked on her map, but first she had to drive through the town. The sun was beginning to set on the western horizon. She could stop or go, and the smart option would be to stop, even though Amanda was anxious to cover more ground, log more miles, and get another step closer to Groom Lake.

A small lake on her right glistened in the orange glow of the ending day, making her decision for her; a scenic spot would be a nice change. Amanda turned and drove into the small parking lot for the park. American and Texas flags hung, tattered, on the flagpole outside of an old wooden building that had a sign for WIC services on it. Driving over the curb, Amanda parked in a small grove of trees just because she felt slightly safer than sitting out in the open. The nose of the big truck pointed toward the exit; the side windows glowed orange on the left and she could see the lake on the right. Scanning the area, it appeared that she was free from any meandering dead. After turning off the engine and grabbing her rifle and a crushed roll of toilet paper, Amanda climbed out of the truck and stretched before choosing a low brick wall that doubled as a bench as her spot for now.

Finished and feeling relieved, Amanda left it all uncovered; she didn't feel it necessary to bury it or even deal with it. With so few living people left, it really didn't seem like it would matter. A short walk to the lake gave her cool water to rinse her hands off. She hadn't exercised since she'd left, not more than a few pushups in the back of the MRAP. Checking that the area was still clear and safe from the dead, Amanda set her rifle on the ground and started with some light stretching before completing a series of eight-count body builders, which were finished off with some burpees and a few sprints back and forth; she was careful not to wander too far from the MRAP or her rifle.

Sweaty, steam rising off her skin in the cool air, satisfied, and feeling better about her day, she noticed that darkness crept across the ground, the shadows growing faint as the last light of the day fell from view. Amanda retrieved her rifle and climbed into the armored truck to her dinner of a cold MRE and water.

If Groom Lake has real food, any kind of real food, I think I will feel like I've died and gone to heaven.

CHAPTER 8

S4
April 6, Year 1

   The commander studied the computer screen with the latest satellite images displayed, and he used the electronic tools to measure the distances. Thirty-five kilometers if they could drive the four-wheeled APC straight over the mountains. Although Groom Lake was a secret facility, the entire area had been used for more than just aircraft development; other secret projects and not-so-secret nuclear weapons tests had been conducted, all contained within the Nevada Test Site. Numerous roads traversed the area, connecting all the different facilities to the nuclear test sites, to the landing fields, and all the other items the corrupt imperialist government demanded. Ironically, the easiest and fastest way for the recon element to get there was to drive on a paved road through the field of craters from all the bomb testing, turning off to a dirt road that would put the team at a good position on the mountain ridge to the southwest of their target. Still approximately five kilometers away from the heart of the complex, they would be close enough to establish the sort of eyes-on-the-ground information that he needed. He needed to know what sort of movement and resistance they could expect. They planned biological-warfare sabotage in a simple form, as they wanted to take everything intact, just as the other complex would be; if they weren't successful, another crater would be added to the numerous others passing by the armored windshield.

Saint George, UT

The compound was a flurry of activity, and the sun was only just now above the horizon. The horses killed by the dead and any chance of fabricating a cart or something else useful destroyed by the RPG attack on the shop, a meeting was held and improvisation was running rampant, just for a single idea. The group meeting the previous evening, after Chivo and Bexar had returned, was one of excitement and lament. The chance to significantly increase the group's weapons, ammo, and general arsenal was alluring. But the difficulty in transporting so many heavy items using an old, worn-out Beetle with an exhaust so loud that more dead would come just for the car show was a problem they couldn't grasp for an outcome. That was until John talked about the steel works and large fabrication shop near Frank's storage-area compound. The fabrication shop had an enormous forklift that ran on diesel, or that was what he assumed, doubting that one that large would run on propane. Regardless, now that morning was upon them, the group opted to send a scavenger party outside the wire and into the wilds of the industrial park for a forklift that may or may not work; if it didn't work, their plan was to search, improvise, and find a solution.

Chivo smiled. These sorts of by-the-seat-of-your-pants operations happened more often than not in the Special Forces world; despite all the training and planning, sometimes the guys would have to head out, hunt for bad guys, and break stuff.

Bexar wore a new chest rig to hold his pistol and rifle magazines. Jennifer had done a wonderful job with the supplies she had on hand. Black and basic, it fit well and seemed to function just as it should. In heavy-duty work pants, work boots, and a T-shirt, Bexar felt more like himself than he had wearing all the high-speed tactical gear that Chivo still wore. For all his days in training, courses, and department in-services, Bexar was still just a cop, not some tactic-cool SWAT guy.

The morning was perfect, with clear skies, cool but not cold. Bexar was ready to get the party started. Brian and Stan were joining the expedition to adventure. Each person carried a small day pack that held water, some snacks, and some medical supplies, all matching; a group standard item. The bags belonging to their lost friends were given to Chivo and Bexar. The VW sat in the courtyard, a small oil drip under the rear of the car staining the concrete, and there it would sit until Chivo and Bexar left for Groom Lake. The one thing they did take was the battery out of the Bug. No one in the group knew anything about forklifts but they all assumed that it probably required a battery to start and run.

After the walk down the long driveway, the jokes and talking came to an end. The seriousness of exiting the relative safety of the fenced compound now became paramount. The gate was opened and then closed behind them and locked. The threat of Frank's group was eliminated, but after some discussion, Chivo convinced them that others might spring up when they least expected it.

The walk down Old Dump Road didn't take long. With a set of borrowed binoculars, Chivo could see movement on the Interstate further down the road, but so far, they hadn't encountered any of the dead face to face. Chivo had a shortcut planned, the layout committed to his memory from his recon and sniper skills the previous day. Cutting through a dirt parking lot, climbing down a short retaining wall, walking through another parking lot of yet another business housed in a dirty metal building, the team of four stood at the chain-link fence of the steel-fabrication business. Large sections of steel pipe, bars, beams, and other pieces of steel sat rusty in the yard.

A whispered discussion as to whether they should split up or move as a team was quickly ended with Chivo's not so tactful statement that they stay together, move together, and work as a team. Quick work with a pair of bolt cutters and Stan had the group inside the fence line. The main fabrication shop, a massive metal building, stood to their right. In a covered area to their left sat an oil-stained, greasy, and dirty forklift larger than some cars.

"Well, John, there's your forklift, mano. Get to work."

John looked at Chivo and then at Stan. Stan shrugged and walked to the forklift. Under faded yellow paint, obscured by rust and dirt, "CATERPILLAR" could barely be discerned on the back of the beast. A large rusted muffler stood erect on the side of the roll cage of an operator's cab. The engine compartment was under a vented cover behind the driver's seat. Stan lifted the engine cover and inspected what they'd found.

"Uh, I have no idea guys . . . maybe we should just try it first. If that doesn't work, we'll have to figure out where the battery is and swap ours in. Which one of you knows how to run this thing?"

No one spoke; Bexar shrugged. "Can't be too hard, can it? I mean you drive it, and the forks go up and down. Guess I'll try."

After climbing into the operator's position, Bexar was met with three long handles, another on the side of the steering column, a small handful of gauges, and one key sticking out of the dash. If any of the controls had been labeled when the forklift was made, the labels were long gone. With a pedal on the left of the steering column, another on the right, and another long one that looked universally like an accelerator pedal, the big machine was intimidating, more so than Bexar realized before he'd volunteered to be *that* guy.

Holding his breath, Bexar turned the key. A clicking sound came from the engine behind him, which then belched to life, black smoke pouring out of the exhaust stack. If the VW was a problem because it was loud, this massive forklift was a serious problem because it was even louder! After a few moments, the engine settled down into an idle that shook the whole beast. Turning the steering wheel back and forth, Bexar realized that the hydraulic system pushed the rear wheels left and right; the dual front tires were rigidly mounted. Testing each lever, Bexar found that one slid the huge fork assembly left and right, another tilted the whole lifting tower forward and back, and the third raised and lowered the forks.

Bexar yelled over the engine, "Hop on; we need to get our shit and get home before we attract a crowd with this big yellow bastard!"

Chivo stood next to Bexar in the large open cab, steadying himself by holding onto the protective cage over the cab. John and Stan stood on the steps on either side of the cab, holding onto the handles used to climb into the cab. Like a low-budget zombie-killing A-Team, Bexar raised the forks off the ground and drove forward slowly, trying to get the hang of the rear-axle steering. More than once, he had to stop and reverse, getting caught driving into the large pieces of steel in the facility. Amazingly, the forklift turned tightly, almost like a zero-turn lawn mower.

An off-road vehicle it was not, so after driving out of the fabrication facility, Bexar stuck to the paved road, taking the long way around to the south and cutting through a paved parking lot to travel north on Red Rock Road. Every couple of minutes, one of them would have to take a few shots at the approaching dead. The loud old diesel forklift was Saint George's Pied Piper of the living dead. Finally reaching the storage unit and fenced-off compound, Bexar drove the forks into the section of chain-link fence by the parking lot, tilted the forks back and raised them, ripping the fence off the posts and out of the ground. There wasn't room to drive the forklift inside the compound, so Bexar spun it to the left to point toward the road home. Chivo and John pulled the fence off the forks, and Bexar lowered them to the ground and shut off the engine. The sudden silence was unsettling, but not as unsettling as the growing moans of the approaching dead.

"OK, we better make this quick. John, you and Stan are a team. Start grabbing the wooden crates and stack them on the forks, and Bexar and I will do the same. If things go sideways, we can get on the roof and thin the herd if we need to, but I think if we work fast enough, it won't be that big of a problem."

John and Stan didn't have to be told twice. They trotted into the compound, grabbing the first wooden crate they found, carrying it as a team back toward the forklift.

"Won't be a big problem? You had to fucking say it out loud, didn't you?"

"Bexar, it either is or isn't, you superstitious dick. Now get your white ass moving so we can get the fuck out of here before the big problem arrives."

Bexar grunted, walked into the compound, and team-carried one of the crates with RPGs back to the forklift. After the first two loads, each of the two teams was having to put down one of the dead that was getting too close. The sun marched across the sky and was nearly overhead when the last crate was loaded. They had a pile of crates that reached the end of the long forks and was piled high enough that all of them had to team up to lift the last few over their heads to reach the top of the stack. Dozens of the dead lay in crumpled heaps in the parking lot; many more were approaching, slowly shambling with singular focus.

"Fucking pop smoke, mano! Time to roll."

Chivo didn't have say it twice. Everyone climbed aboard the forklift. Bexar couldn't see past the load, and all of them were glad that the engine coughed to life once again. After tilting the lift rearward, Bexar slowly raised the forks until he could see under the stack of wooden crates. Somehow they'd been able to fit every single one of the crates holding weapons, ammo, explosives and who knows what else onto the forklift. Moving slowly, Bexar guided the forklift out of the parking lot, making a right turn onto the road to head for home. Their pace riding the giant old forklift was slower than the group's pace walking down the hill that morning, but it was slightly faster than the growing number of followers. Chivo turned around to face the rear, kneeling on the metal floor, and held his rifle against the driver's cage to steady his aim. One by one, he took careful shots to put down the closest of the following dead. None of them spoke, the loud diesel engine making it annoying trying to yell and hear one another.

What felt like hours later, the forklift turned off Old Dump Road and onto the long asphalt driveway leading to the compound. Stan jumped off the side of the forklift and jogged ahead, not having to run very quickly to outpace the slow-moving beast. With each bump and bounce Bexar held his breath, worried about the teetering load high above the ground, the solid rubber tires offering nothing in the way of any dampening. This forklift wasn't meant to be driven down a road like this, but the dead weren't meant to rise to hunt the living either.

Reaching the gate, Stan stood at the ready, the gate open. The rest of the group members stood just inside the gate, rifles ready. Once the back of the forklift cleared, Stan shut the gate and locked the chain holding it secure. Angel, Guillermo, and rest of the group stood at the fence, shooting down the dead who stumbled up the drive following the loud yellow beacon.

Parking next to the Beetle, Bexar carefully lowered the forks and set them flat on the ground before shutting off the loud motor. One by one, the rest of the group members came back up the driveway with wide-eyed excitement like kids on Christmas. For preppers and survivors, large quantities of free ammo, rifles, explosives, and uncommon items like some RPGs made for a present that was worth three Christmases and a birthday all rolled into one!

Las Vegas, NV

Aymond sat in the big meeting room the Pararescue Jumpers had in their building. None of them were sure where the PJs had gone; some had obviously been killed, as indicated by the small makeshift memorials they found, but the cache of stored goods was fairly complete: ammo, MREs, water, extra gear, and even some small camping stoves and fuel, which Aymond promptly used this morning to make some instant coffee from the MRE he ate for breakfast.

The shortwave radio broadcast the previous night changed everything. It also really concerned him. If they had picked it up, the PLA might have picked it up too, and they might come looking for whomever was broadcasting it. It wasn't good OpSec on the part of the people in Groom Lake, which was surprising for how secretive the facility had historically been. Even with his top-secret clearance, Aymond had no idea what he would find when they arrived.

It could be alien technology or singlewide trailers, he didn't know, and after all they had been through since December, he wouldn't be surprised by either one.

The team's sleep and security rotation would be complete in about two more hours. It was important that all his men got a full night's rest when they could because when the shit hit the fan again, they might have to go days without sleeping. They needed to be rested, well, and strong to face that and come out on top. Happy and Kirk sifted through the stored cache of gear, picking and choosing what they could carry on the M-ATVs along with what they needed. Jones and Gonzo were exploring the hangars close by for any parts or equipment that Jones needed for the trucks or that they could use. Aymond believed in cross-training, but he also believed in letting someone who was highly experienced in a field of knowledge do what they knew best. Jones was an experienced mechanic, better than any of Aymond's men, so it was best he do the job. Gonzo was along to carry anything heavy and to provide extra security.

Absentmindedly, Aymond flipped through the past November's issue of *Popular Mechanics*. It all felt surreal, the way things felt in some sort of dream, and the future felt completely uncertain. There was only one thing that Aymond knew for sure. If they didn't find more people and more help, the United States would fall to either the Chinese or the Zeds. There was no way to win either war by themselves. Aymond tossed the magazine on the table and stood, slinging his rifle and taking his coffee with him. He wanted to check on Jones' and Gonzo's progress.

Jones and Gonzo returned before Aymond could make it past the protective ring of the M-ATVs and the radar truck. They were unsuccessful in finding any useful spare parts, except for a set of tools that Jones said he needed, so the minor excursion was a waste of time. Now that the final sleep rotation was coming to an end, it was time for a team meeting to plan the day. Nellis appeared to be abandoned and left to the Zeds, but Aymond wanted to know for sure. If there were any survivors they would need them. What they needed was an army, or at least a few more Marines, if they were going to have any chance against the PLA.

S4

Twenty-five miles southwest of Groom Lake was another dry lake bed in the large sectioned-off piece of government-controlled land; bomb craters large and small to the north spoke to the area's past life as a test facility. However, marked off on the edge of the dry lakebed was a ten-thousand-foot-long runway; next to the same was a newly constructed five-thousand-foot-long paved runway with a handful of newly built hangars, including a large clamshell-opening hangar that harkened back to the days of lighter than air travel.

The big Y-20 seemed to hang in the sky. Flying low and from the southwest, the big cargo plane banked gently to line up for the final approach over the dry lakebed. Since it was heavily loaded, the pilot didn't dare use the shorter paved runway, opting to trust in the rugged design of the new aircraft and the supposed ability to land on unimproved surfaces.

There was discussion about conducting a low-level air drop, but the satellite intelligence suggested that the area was secure, either ignored by or unknown to the rogue group in the underground facility to the northeast. So the safer option of simply landing to offload the vehicles and men was taken.

Soldiers, members of the elite PLA Siberian Tiger unit, quickly exited the tail ramp of their aircraft, forming a defensive line as the first anti-Yama radar truck was released from the tie downs and driven to a position to provide sweeping coverage.

Nearing sunset, the two Chinese APCs drove across the lakebed to the hangars by the paved runway, which would be their command post for the upcoming operation. The radar truck set a position on the southwestern side, the side not shielded by the mountains. Their plan was underway.

In the MRAP, TX

The towns of Brownfield and Plains, Texas may not have had many people living in them before the attacks, but Amanda was sure that there weren't any people living in them now, at least from what she could see. Rumbling along US-380, Amanda dodged only the occasional car and some semi-trucks and was amazed at how flat and open this part of Texas was.

Flatter than flat; someone could watch their dog runaway for three days out here and never lose sight of him.

Abandoned homes and farms dotted the flat landscape; most of them appeared to have been left to rot back into the dirt long before the attack happened. If not for the small sign, Amanda wouldn't have known that after a slight bump in the pavement she was now in New Mexico. She was bored; no music, no one to talk to, nothing to do but listen to the droning diesel engine as she bounced and jarred along a lonesome highway in a part of the country that defined what it was to be in BFE.

The wire fences along the highway still stood. It almost appeared as if nothing was wrong, that the attack had never occurred and the dead weren't stumbling around trying to bite the few who remained amongst the living in the rest of the country. No, if this town had electricity, it would probably be carrying on just fine, minus deliveries for food and other provisions.

If this country has a chance, if the United States can survive, it will be due to the survivors we can find out in the rural areas, hard-scrabble people used to making a life out of desolate areas and through desperate times.

The highway widened from two lanes to four lanes, and the signs warned of a lower speed limit, not that Amanda really cared. The sparse landscape became slightly more cluttered with metal buildings and older homes. Staring out of the driver's side window, Amanda drifted left and right, not really paying attention to the road. She watched for signs of life, chimney smoke, if the homes even had chimneys, anything to give her hope. Movement out of the corner of her eye caught her attention, and she instinctively slammed on the brakes. The heavy armored truck lurching forward snapped Amanda's head forward with it, and she saw a child riding a bicycle in the middle of the road waving at her.

"Holy shit!"

Sitting in the MRAP, now sitting stationary, Amanda stared at the child.

I've lost it. I've only made it to the fourth month after the attack, and I've completely lost my mind.

Squinting, waiting for the child to vanish or to see that it was actually a walking corpse of a child, Amanda waited, holding her breath. The child waved again and rode away, pedaling as fast as he could. Amanda followed slowly, trying not to spook the kid. Quickly the boy took a left, and Amanda wasn't sure if he was trying to get away, just going somewhere, or trying to get her to follow. Curiosity won the argument in her thoughts, so she slowly followed, trying her best to drive casually in a large tan armored military vehicle with a machine gun on top. She drove close enough to keep the boy in sight but without getting so close as to be a threat to anyone watching, if that were even possible.

At the second cross street, the boy rode into the yard of a white house, dropped the bike, and ran into the home. Not sure what to do, Amanda stopped in the middle of the intersection and waited, watching the house. If this was an ambush, she would probably be OK in the truck against whatever small arms the people had, and she could just drive away. But it didn't feel like an ambush should feel, which confused Amanda because she really had no training in any of this stuff. Before she'd just relied on Clint for his expert take on tactical situations. Now it was up to her and her limited experience. The curtains moved behind an open window on the second floor.

If someone were going to ambush travelers, why would they use a kid to lead them to a house? Why wouldn't they just stage it out on the highway?

A woman appeared from the front door holding some sort of rifle that Amanda didn't recognize, except that it had wooden stock and a scope on it. Amanda drove in front of the house, stopped in the middle of the street, and turned the truck off. Waiting, she and the woman stared at each other through the thick glass. Not able to roll down a window, Amanda wasn't sure what to do. The woman didn't move, but she appeared to be trying to talk to her. Amanda nodded and climbed into the back of the truck, stepped up, released the top hatch and climbed into the turret, leaving the M2 pointed away from the woman. She smiled.

"Are you with the Army?"

"No, not exactly."

"Where did ya get that thing?"

"From a base in Texas. What town is this?"

"Tatum. Where are you headed? Is there help coming? Do you have any food or water you could spare? What the hell happened, and why is it taking so long for us to get help?"

Amanda felt like the woman was sincere. "I have some. I'm headed to Nevada. Are there many of you left besides you and the boy?"

"Of course there are."

The blunt answer was given in such a way that it was obvious the woman thought it to be a stupid question. Why would there not be a lot of people left in the little town of Tatum, New Mexico.

Amanda smiled. "Give me a minute to climb down. Would you mind if we sat down and spoke for a while?"

"If you have some food to spare and can tell us when FEMA is going to get off their asses to come help, you're welcome to come inside."

The boy appeared behind the woman, smiling. "James, go get your daddy and tell him we have a visitor. Then go tell Mr. Finch. He's going to want to come by as well."

The boy ran into the yard, jumped on his bicycle, and rode off as fast as he could. After opening the back hatch, Amanda grabbed a case of MREs and climbed down, closing up the MRAP behind her. If she had known that there would be others, Amanda would have packed the entire back of the truck with cases of MREs, but as it was she didn't and hadn't made that plan. She walked into the home, her mind spinning with the thought of how to get some of the supplies stockpiled at the SSC to this town. Then she thought of all the other small towns she had simply driven through. She should have taken the time to explore each of them to look for other survivors, but she didn't. Back and forth the argument went in her mind; she was heartbroken for the people she might have been able to find and help but didn't, too anxious to get to Groom Lake to complete the mission she set out to do in the first place.

Flying Above New Mexico

Andrew trimmed the aircraft and let it fly. The road atlas in his lap, he flipped pages, holding a ruler over one page and then the next. The mountains were passing safely below him, and the sprawling mass of Albuquerque could be seen in the distance. He closed the atlas and stuffed it into the open bag in the back seat, Oreo nudging him again as always. Amazingly, Andrew didn't have to clean much dog waste out of the aircraft, his friend somehow keeping it together for hours at a time, but this was the first time he was actually trying to make a destination quickly. Before he would have lazily followed the Interstates and searched for more survivors and, hopefully, answers to this whole mess, landing where he pleased when it was safe to do so, but now he wanted to get to Area 51 as fast as he could. There was a chance he could make it in a single hop, but without knowing the winds aloft, Andrew had no way to plan his route, to know which altitudes would give him the better winds for speed and efficiency. All of the tools that modern pilots were used to were gone, pushing him back into the stick-and-rudder barn-storming days of aviation history long past.

He adjusted the trim slightly and the small aircraft tilted forward slightly, slowly descending toward the big New Mexico city. So far, every large city that he had flown near appeared to be completely dead and overrun by zombies, but even in this strange new world in which he lived, Andrew still held hope.

The Interstate near the city was completely clear of vehicles; the ones he could see were pushed into the ditches. Descending lower, Andrew banked right and then left, looking out each side window, trying to see as much detail as he could. Shaking his head, Andrew knew that sort of destruction was from a massive horde of the dead. If one came through Albuquerque, then he doubted anyone could have survived; even some of the bridges had collapsed. Flying a northwesterly route over the heart of the city, thick black fog blocked his view, but Andrew knew that it wasn't fog and that hundreds or thousands of the reanimated dead were below the veil of black flies.

Oreo whimpered a little as Andrew began slowly climbing and gaining altitude.

"I know buddy, but we can't stop yet, not there. Try to hold it. I'll stop soon."

Saint George, UT

Each of the wooden crates stood open, and all the new toys of war were spread out in the courtyard. There were rows of green metal cans of ammunition, mostly 5.56 XM193, but larger cans of 7.62 and 50-caliber as well; two crates labeled "30 GRENADE HAND FRAG DELAY M67" stood by themselves, the lids removed. The new gear seemed overwhelming and endless, and it was dangerous to let it sit out in the open. Chivo checked each item, explaining it to Angel and Guillermo, who was writing down what each was, what it was for and how much of it they now had. The hard work of unpacking each of the crates complete, Stan and John went inside to prepare the group's lunch. Merylin and Frances held security positions, standing at the edge of the courtyard near the driveway, their rifles in hand, and Brian sat on the roof of the house with binoculars scanning for any threats. Jennifer was the only one of the group not out in the courtyard. After sitting security during the night, she'd opted to sleep; she was content to find out what all the new toys were later.

The inventory complete, Angel held the yellow pad of paper and clipboard in his hand, reviewing his notes, meticulously checking to make sure he hadn't missed a single detail.

"What are we going to do with RPGs and grenades? I can't imagine those would be all that effective against the zombies?"

Chivo shrugged. "Who knows, Guillermo. They might be, but I know they would be really effective against the living."

"But you took care of that for us."

Bexar shook his head. "Everywhere I've been, I keep finding turds, wolves preying on other survivors. Fuck, I wish I had all this when we were in Big Bend. Things might have gone much differently."

"We don't even know how to use half this stuff. The M-16s sure, but I've never seen a real grenade in person much less used one."

Chivo smiled. "First of all, if you try to pull the cotter pin out with your teeth, you won't have many teeth left, but I'll show everyone this afternoon. If Angel continues to take notes, then you can review them later, practice, and train. This sort of hardware is hard to come by, and you might be thankful to have it at some point."

Guillermo nodded, looking at the pile of arms that made their prepper compound look like a terrorist commune, and then back at Bexar.

"What about you? Do you know about all this?"

"Nope, but I'm going to pay attention this afternoon. That's for sure!"

Bexar glanced at Chivo, who nodded slightly. Taking his cue, Bexar continued. "With you guys safe, our plan is to leave in the morning."

Angel looked up from his notes and looked at Guillermo, who tilted his head. "That's too bad. The group voted, and you're both welcome to stay. We want you to stay."

"Thank you, but I made a promise to my friend here, and I'm going to make good on it. It's time to finally return him to his pregnant wife."

Groom Lake, NV

Jake, Bill, representatives from each of the different "towns" of Groom Lake, Sarah, and Jessie sat at the conference table. Erin flat out told her mother she wasn't going to "some stupid meeting," and Sarah had half a mind to join her in not attending, but Jessie was going so she felt like she needed to go to give support. Jake smiled and tapped his knuckles on the table. The conversations in the room slowly died off until all eyes were on him.

"Good afternoon, and thank you all for coming. First of all, I wanted to thank Jessie and Sarah again for their help. They may be new members of our community, but they have really made their mark in a short amount of time."

The group clapped politely before Jake continued. "With his new radio setup, Bill has made contact with more survivors. Some have expressed interest in attempting to come join us; others are content to continue to shelter in place, but all have expressed a strong need for help, which I can imagine surprises no one here. However, that is not why I asked all of you to this meeting. We have two issues that may become serious problems if we don't address them. First of all, we have lost all contact with the Texas facility; we haven't heard from Clint or President Lampton in a few days, and we are hoping that they are only experiencing technical difficulties. I would ask that we keep that information only between us. I'm afraid that rumors may get out of hand if we make that public knowledge.

"Second, we intercepted two radio broadcasts that by themselves would be concerning, but in the context of losing communication with Texas, the apparent cyber-attacks on our facility, and some previous radio broadcasts that we've heard, we are quite concerned. Bill?"

Bill fidgeted in his seat and looked at his notes. "At least one numbers station appeared briefly recently, broadcasting for two days, two different messages on two different frequencies."

One woman raised her hand; most of the others looked puzzled.

"Right, umm, *numbers stations* is a generic term for radio stations that began around World War One but really became prevalent during the Cold War. They would broadcast random numbers or letters, sometimes with different tones or other sounds. There were a few conspiracy theories about them. As we sit here in Area 51, I would tend to assume that the theories may have been right; regardless, it was generally assumed by those of us in amateur radio that the stations were broadcasting secret messages to spies or agents. Since the stations were broadcast on the shortwave bands, the recipient could have been just about anywhere. Back in the height of all these stations some other ham-radio operators began DF'ing, or locating the broadcast locations, or at least where the broadcasting antenna was located. Sorry, direction finding or triangulating the locations. Anyways, the numbers stations that appeared recently are now gone; we have no idea who broadcast it, who received it, or what it meant. That alone isn't too big of a deal. I mean, we know that Clint and Cliff are out there. It is possible that others are out there too, trying to do the right thing, but two really strange radio broadcasts really makes me concerned about the numbers stations too. The best way to describe the two other broadcasts are that they were broad spectrum noise on HF, the high-frequency bands, like the radio broadcast equivalent of someone hitting a large gong. One of the broadcasts appeared to have been sent from some distance away, and the other was much closer."

Bill took a drink of water, holding up his hands in response to the questions that started immediately.

"Most likely those were encrypted messages, one being sent and the other being a reply. We have no way of knowing what the messages were. We don't know where they came from exactly, but HF broadcasts, depending on propagation, could have come from nearly anywhere in the world. The one guess I'm willing to take is that the reply message came from within North America, possibly somewhere fairly close to here."

All the representatives from the different Groom Lake cities began asking questions, talking over each other, nearly shouting to be heard. Jake stood and held up his hands to get their attention; once everyone had calmed down, he sat again.

"My concerns aren't really about those radio broadcasts; my concerns are specifically about our underground city surviving. I broke all of this down into bite-sized bits of information so I could understand it better. If Cliff were here, he would have a plan of action, but he isn't, and we can't reach him, so all we have are one another."

Jake stood and walked to the dry-erase board on the wall and began writing. "Some of this most of you probably know; however, a lot of what I'm about to tell you hasn't been told to anyone but myself by Cliff. After this meeting, after we have a plan of action, we will have another full assembly, and I will explain all of what I'm about to tell you to all of our fellow survivors and residents."

All eyes were glued on Jake; the room felt as if it were collectively holding its breath.

"Number one, we know that the Chinese and North Koreans teamed up to attack the United States with an EMP strike followed by overflights that sprayed what we know now to be called the Yama Strain. The name doesn't really matter, all that matters is that it is a tool of mass genocide, a way to kill off an entire country with little damage of war. Cliff assumed that since the attack happened, the Chinese had devised a way to counter Yama. He didn't know if it was a way to stop it or a way to inoculate others from it, but he was confident that the dead would remain the dead. Even the infected dead couldn't be brought back to life; they could only be destroyed. In the depths of this very facility, a group of scientists were working on a solution. The United States government knew about all of this and expected the attack; the problem is that they thought there was more time before it came. Cliff was originally in a facility in Denver under the airport when the attack came. That facility was overrun and went dark, but he somehow escaped and came here, this being the closest backup facility. Besides Texas, there were many other facilities, but

Cliff said they were destroyed, except for Texas, as far as we know. Basically, the whole plan that the U.S. government had for what they felt to be an eventuality fell apart; the entire safety net failed, and here we are. Cliff found this facility overrun but lit and operational, unlike the one in Denver, which had completely failed. Systematically, he cleared the entire facility of zombies, the evidence of which can still be seen on the floors and walls in some areas. There was one lone survivor here, Lance, a young scientist still trying to find a solution, an end to Yama. Lance died; Cliff didn't really go into detail about it, but said that with Lance's death any chance to scientifically combat Yama died with him.

"If the attack was the prelude to invasion that we think it could be, then we may be in store for actual war, more attacks. We've done well to save so many people and to provide a safe place to survive and live, but the Chinese must know that we're here by now."

Some gasped, and others shook their heads.

"We have a few ideas and are welcome to any other ideas that any of you have, but as we see it, our options are to continue as we are and hope we're wrong, lock down the blast doors, turn off the radios, and go dark, or train for war with the weapons and gear we have on the fifth level."

"What about the others, all the people out there that have made contact with us, the ones who can't or won't come here, what about them?" someone called out.

The room erupted in conversation, growing louder with each passing second. Jessie stood abruptly, and her chair hit the wall behind her and tipped over with a crash. Everyone turned to look at her in silence.

"We have to tell them. We fucking tell them everything. There is no choice but to tell them the entire story, the history, and the fears. Let them prepare. Let them know. Bill, where are all these people located?"

"Uh, all over. We have a map in the radio hut with pins showing each contact we've made."

"Tell them all, Jake, tell them everything you just told us. Keep repeating it until we can't anymore. Jake, every able-bodied person in this goddamned hole in the ground is going to have to get ready to fight, ready to fight a war, be fully ready, and be ready now. We can't wait until next week or even tomorrow—this isn't going to be our fucking underground Alamo!"

Jessie stormed out of the room, the door slamming behind her; everyone looked at Sarah who was still.

"I agree with her. If I were you, every single one of us would go down to the fifth level and get geared up. If this is going to happen, it could happen today, next month, or next year. We have no idea, but we can't wait helplessly and hope it won't happen. Like she said, we get ready, we stay ready, and we hope it doesn't happen, but we're ready if it does."

Everyone looked at Jake before the room erupted with everyone talking at once. Sarah looked at the room, shook her head, and left to find Jessie and her daughter. If Jake and the others didn't get ready to fight, they needed to be ready to bug out.

Tatum, NM

James was back, his bicycle left in the yard. Sunlight filtered through the windows of the home, and a dozen people sat in the living room. Lisa was the woman who lived there, Amanda learned, and her husband, Joe, came home about thirty minutes after James came back. Everyone who sat in the living room arrived on a bicycle, some of them new-looking, some of them ancient and held together with some unusual repairs.

"After the gas started going bad a bit ago, we all turned to bicycles. Inner tubes are a bit of a problem. We started with using cans of Fix-A-Flat that we got from the gas stations. Eventually we started using small pieces of rubber from the tire shop as inner tubes. Seems to be working OK," Joe explained.

Amanda nodded, her curiosity quenched. As excited as everyone in the room was, all but Amanda held an open MRE in their hands. All of them appeared thin, and their clothes didn't seem to fit them as well as they had. She quickly learned that of the town's original six hundred or so residents roughly two hundred of them were still living. The roaming herds of the dead hadn't come through town and, within the first day of the attack, the citizens of Tatum banded together to have constant patrols to put down any zombies who came through. Mostly, especially at first, the dead that posed a threat were their own fellow residents. There was an outbreak of suicides about six weeks after the attack, which in the end really brought the rest of the survivors together. They pooled their supplies and made sure that everyone had a firearm and a fair share of the supplies necessary to survive, and they held open discussions about depression and survival. For all that they did well as a community, what the entire town was waiting for was help.

WINCHESTER: STORM

Over the previous weeks, small groups would bicycle together further and further out on patrols looking for other survivors, scavenging for anything of use, and hoping to find answers. The clusters of farms around the county were contacted, a few more survivors found among them. Eventually, they bicycled all the way out to Plains and down to Lovington. There were a few survivors in Plains, but the town hadn't done as well as Tatum. Lovington as a town hadn't banded together, but there were three big survivor groups that held roughly four hundred people of the nearly eleven thousand previous residents of the town. The groups were each led by experienced preppers and, surprisingly, each of the groups had good relationships with each other. Amanda was astonished, expecting a splintered town run by three different factions with different leaders and loyalties to be at a bit of a war with one another. They weren't, and had even facilitated a barter system for trading.

Rumors abounded in Tatum and in Lovington, but no one knew exactly what had happened.

Mr. Finch arrived about the time that Joe finished giving the quick history of Tatum and how they had survived.

"Welcome to our little town, Ms. . . . ." Mr. Finch paused.

"Lampton, Amanda Lampton."

"Ms. Lampton that's quite the truck you have. How is it that it still works, and where are you getting fuel for it?"

"It was stored in a hardened facility in Texas, but it was designed to survive an EMP anyways, as far as I know. Fuel is always a bit of an issue. I tend to syphon what I can find out of semi-trucks' fuel tanks."

"We had a few older vehicles that still worked after the EMP, but fuel began going bad sort of quickly. Some of the guys who used to work the oil field said it was due to the ethanol, and we've run dry of the diesel fuel we did have. Either way, we're pedaling our way around nowadays. Thank you for the food you could share, but we must know, do you know what happened? How did you survive? How did you get here? Where are you going and why?"

Amanda was waiting for that question. She knew it would come, and she had spent the previous half-hour in an internal debate trying to decide how she would approach it.

"First, I do know what happened. The Chinese and North Korean governments launched an attack on the United States. It began with nuclear missiles detonated high in the atmosphere, which caused an EMP, destroying electronics and the country's electrical infrastructure, as you are already aware.

The aircraft you saw fly past after the EMP sprayed what has been named the Yama Strain."

Amanda continued for nearly an hour, explaining that she had been the Secretary of Agriculture, how two agents had come to her house in Little Rock, about the journey to Texas, the facility there and the one in Groom Lake, and the hunt for survivors. Then she extended an open invitation for any to join her on her journey to Nevada, with the intent to return to Texas. Believing that these people, survivors, fellow citizens deserved to know the truth, Amanda left no detail a secret, except that she was now the sworn President of the United States.

Once finished, the room sat in stunned silence, each of the people in the small living room trying to process all the information that was thrown at them, trying to decide how much to believe, if they could believe any of it.

Joe spoke first. "So there is no help coming." It wasn't a question.

Amanda shook her head. "There is nothing in place still functioning that can help, yet."

"And your plan is to drive to Area 51, pick up a group of people, drive back to Texas to get more vehicles, and then shuttle back and forth until all those people are safe underground in Texas? What about people like us?"

"We didn't know about other survivors. Well, some people who had radios that survived were able to contact those in Groom Lake, but no one knows how many people have survived. We don't know how many people died."

Faces around the room, previously elated to have a large meal that equated to more than the typical day's ration of food, now looked defeated. Amanda tried to keep a positive attitude, but the loss of any hope for the future sucked the air out of the room.

Mr. Finch finally spoke. "Thank you, Ms. Lampton. We've survived as a town together so far, and we will survive as a town together into the future, hoping that someday things will get back to some sort of normal that we once knew. Tomorrow we will hold a town hall discussion to let everyone know what we learned from you. If you are going to be staying the night, you are welcome to join us in our meeting tomorrow."

Amanda didn't answer at first. "Mr. Finch, thank you, but it would be best if I continued my journey. Don't give up hope. Don't give up on one another. We will survive, but only if we work together. We now know you are here. I'm sorry we didn't know that before. The task we face is hard but not insurmountable.

Once in back in Texas, I will send a truck to you with all we can spare. I'm sorry that there isn't more we can do more quickly."

When she stood to leave, Mr. Finch stood as well. "Ms. Lampton, let me at least walk you to your truck. Joe, I'll be back in a moment."

Mr. Finch went to the front door and held it open for Amanda, and they walked in silence until they came to the back of the MRAP. "Ms. Lampton, how many other cabinet-level secretaries survived?"

Amanda paused before answering. "None of them."

"That's what I thought. Madam President, God's speed."

Amanda shook his hand, opened the back hatch, climbed into her truck, and passed down another case of MREs to Mr. Finch, "We won't fail you."

Mr. Finch nodded and walked back to the house. Amanda climbed into the driver's seat, started the truck, and drove down the block to return to the highway; turning left, she drove west, the sun low enough on the horizon to shine directly into the windshield.

In the Aviat Husky

Oreo's insistence that they land grew, and the day was getting late, so instead of pushing on and being left to an airplane that smelled like dog crap, Andrew saw the single long airstrip near I-40 and decided to take the opportunity to land for the evening. The town, which sat on the opposite side of I-40 from the airfield, wasn't too large, so he didn't think that there would be too big of a problem, or at least he hoped there wouldn't be. If worse came to worst, he could let Oreo relieve himself and they could fly on, landing on a deserted small highway or somewhere else if need be. Although fueling up was also high on Andrew's priority list, second at the moment only to Oreo's situation.

Banking over the airport to make a final turn for landing, Andrew saw a large concrete arrow by the beacon and smiled. This airport was a part of the original air transport system from the late 1920s. Happy to see that some history had survived even the end of the world, Andrew landed and made the turn-off for the FBO and a small group of hangars. Two white tanks sat aboveground, which was a good sign for easier fueling, but first, after the prop stopped spinning, Andrew climbed out and pulled Oreo out of the back seat. Oreo immediately ran to the taxiway sign and peed on it. Andrew scanned the area. There was no sign of movement, no signs of the dead, although this section of I-40 appeared to have been pushed clear by a massive horde, as had the entire stretch of Interstate since Albuquerque. They appeared to be outbound toward the West Coast. Andrew was following in their path, but he had no way of knowing how far ahead of him they were and if he might catch up. Using the available tie downs, Andrew secured his aircraft and began clearing the closest hangar to find a spot for the night.

Nellis Air Force Base, NV

One recon team was out, and the other team split into two shifts for security; so far the reports weren't good. The entire base was overrun, although they did find the Thunderbirds' F-16s sitting on the flightline. The daylight waning, the recon team was heading back in for the night. Aymond debated staying another day or leaving after the sleep rotation in the morning. The shortwave broadcast was back on, someone repeating the same script and advising a channel switch for other information. The other frequency had another person repeating instructions on how to construct some sort of radio and how to use Morse code. It didn't matter. Aymond was glad to know someone else out there survived.

One more day, if there is anyone here, we're going to need them. Then we'll go to Area 51, which I hope is staffed with military personnel. We have a war to fight.

CHAPTER 9

Outside of Magdalena, NM
April 7, Year 1

Amanda woke unrested, her mind having refused to let her sleep peacefully through the night. The survivors in Tatum, all the others she didn't know about, that no one knew about . . . she had been right. There were survivors, many survivors trying to just live another day all across the country. The longer she took, the more time it took to mount an effort to help, to somehow conquer the reanimated dead, the more of them that would die. After refueling from another abandoned semi-truck's fuel tanks on this side of San Antonio, New Mexico, she drove into the night until she knew she was really making a bad choice due to her emotions by pushing on. She simply stopped in the middle of US-60, turned off the lights, turned off the truck, cracked the roof hatch for some air, and felt utterly and completely alone.

Giving up on sleep, Amanda climbed out onto the roof of the truck. Standing out of the turret, she saw the eastern horizon beginning to glow with the morning twilight, the moon only a sliver of light in the sky. As her eyes adjusted to the darkness, Amanda could see well enough to drive. Scanning the area and confirming that she was actually alone, Amanda climbed down to the pavement, squatting against one of the large wheels before starting her day. She missed the perfect facilities of the SSC, the hot showers and mostly comfortable bunks, but meeting the survivors in Tatum the previous day had galvanized her will, her resolve to win re-energized. Back in the MRAP, Amanda tore open an MRE as she drove. Today was the day, unsafe or not; she wasn't going to stop for the night again, and there simply wasn't any more time to waste.

Saint George, UT

Bexar woke up early, before sunrise, dressed and walked into the garage. The only other person awake was Frances, who was sitting security watch for the last half of the night. He thought it was smart that the group split the nightshift, only five hours per person; the dayshift was seven each. That made the rotation harder with fewer people, but the problem of being too tired during a long shift of sitting in the dark listening to crickets was slightly easier to withstand and still be useful with the shorter shifts. As a rookie, Bexar had worked the nightshift, just as every rookie cop did wherever they might work. The dayshift was for the veteran officers and people trying to buck for a promotion. The nightshift was the fun shift, as long as something was going on. For Bexar, it seemed like every nightshift had something going on; it seemed that without fail he would fall into some sort of fucked-up call. It got bad enough that his sergeant forbade him from making traffic stops after four a.m. because every time he did it would end in a chase, a fight, or having to Taser someone, and other units running code across the city to come help.

Standing alone in the garage over the work bench with his AR disassembled, he slowly cleaned the rifle, inspecting each piece, and removed the bolt carrier and took it apart. Bexar finally realized what his old supervisor had been trying to do. It wasn't about keeping the calm; the reality was that when an officer was a complete shit magnet, the numbers game could catch up, and an officer-involved shooting would follow. Officers never really recover from having to shoot someone. It had been only in the last couple of years that officers were beginning to be encouraged to see a therapist, especially after a critical incident, but before that they were told to man up and truck on. The things that followed were a common script: heavy drinking, failed marriages, and lives ruined for a once proud officer, and that was for the "good" shoots.

Bexar shook his head, absentmindedly dragging the teeth of the small extractor across the back of his hand to see if it left light scratches. Scratches were good; when the extractor became worn, it wouldn't scratch the skin, and failure to extract malfunctions would be soon to follow. The ejector spring felt good, and the gas rings still spun, but they were showing wear.

I should probably switch out parts when we get to Groom Lake and start carrying some spare parts.

He'd always hated cleaning his weapons, a chore, a task after a range day or qualifying, something to be done quickly, efficiently, and be done with. But this morning, Bexar felt a certain amount of Zen in meticulously cleaning and inspecting each part of his rifle before reassembling the bolt carrier and putting it all back in the upper. A light coat of Break-Free covered the bolt carrier and charging handle. After checking the trigger, he set a drop of lube on the edge of the hammer's release, carefully working the hammer back and forth. Someone taught him a long time ago that it helped with a smoother trigger squeeze, and he wasn't sure if it was real or not, but it *felt* like it made a difference, and that was what mattered.

The irony of the concerns about being in an officer-involved shooting wasn't lost on Bexar after reassembling his rifle, making a functionality check, reloading, and making it ready. Not counting the risen dead, he had no idea how many actual living people he'd had to kill in the past few months. Unloading and disassembling his pistol on the bench, Bexar thought about what the number might be and became angry. Angry at each of the bastards that forced him to kill, angry that his little girl was dead, angry that his wife was still miles away, angry that they were going to have to raise a baby in this new and horrible world they lived in. Most of all, he was angry at the bastards that started this whole mess, the faceless attackers, angry that no amount of justice could be taken to reconcile what they had done.

Working faster, Bexar's previous Zen of weapon maintenance left him, and he quickly cleaned, reassembled, and reloaded his pistol, holstering it and walking back into the house. Following the smell of coffee, he found Guillermo sitting at the kitchen table, chatting with Frances, who had apparently finished her shift on security watch.

"Welcome, my friend Bexar, join us." Guillermo gestured to an open chair next to Frances, standing to pour a mug of coffee for the new arrival; two mason jars sat on the table, one with powdered creamer and the other with some artificial sweetener. As preppers go, this group was living the luxurious life. Bexar, Malachi, and Jack's original group plan of canvas tents and country living paled in comparison.

"What are you going to do after you get there?"

Bexar stared into his coffee, his mind wandering in the steam. "I'm, sorry, what?"

Frances smiled wearily, tired but needing to wind down before going to bed. "After you get to Groom Lake, after you are reunited with your wife, what are your plans?"

"Hopefully live a peaceful and uneventful life; raising a child . . . I'm not sure if that can happen."

"If you bring your wife back here, I bet it could."

Bexar smiled. "You guys are really trying for the hard sell before we leave, huh?"

Guillermo grinned. "Wouldn't you? Why leave to live in a hole in the ground in Nevada? What about Chivo? What is your friend going to do, settle down underground with your family?"

"I'll probably do what I've done for the last twenty years, mano: Serve my country with unique and secret distinction."

Guillermo stood and brought another mug of coffee to the table. Frances stood. "Merylin is probably waking up, and it's her day to cook. If I want any time with her before she gets to work and I get to sleep, I've got to get it now. Bexar, Chivo, if I'm asleep when you leave, thank you, thank you for everything."

Chivo smiled and thanked her.

"What about you guys? The compound has eight members once we leave. Are you going to keep on with the same plan or try to branch out for something new?"

"We're not sure, Chivo. Our plan is to keep on the same track, but we're always open to new opportunities, like the chance Angel took with you two. That worked out for the better, even if it was a hard road to travel."

The small talk continued back and forth, drifting from scavenging for more working vehicles or somehow finding horses to replace the ones Chivo and Stan had lost to the dead. They talked about the new weapons and possibly changing the security setup and protocols to include them; Chivo thought it lunacy not to. When you have the ability to deploy automatic weapons and RPGs to deter an invading force, why keep those tools in the back locked away.

"The SEALs do this thing when they encounter a superior force; they fire everything they have, I mean everything, and it is staggering. The enemy force can't respond quickly enough; it's like a sudden wall of death. By the time a counter attack can be mounted, the frogmen have slipped away and disappeared into thin air. While I was in the unit, we tended to use other kinds of support, but we had the Little Birds and the amazing pilots of the 160th. Holy shit, the Night Stalkers would take those fucking helicopters places I wouldn't want to drive a car through, and they would do it in total darkness and in shitty weather. God, I hope they made it through this mess. If we're going to function well enough to destroy the fucking Chinese, we're going to need guys like that."

"Is that where this is going?" Guillermo asked.

"It has to. I don't know what they wanted to accomplish. The only thing that makes any sense whatsoever is the attack being a prelude to invasion, but I don't know how they would conquer the dead to do it. Maybe there's something we don't know. Maybe in a year's time or two years, the bodies of the reanimated dead fall apart. It could be a war of patience and attrition, who knows with those fuckers. Afghanistan I got, I understood those tribes and the centuries of fighting, the same with the drug cartels, and I understood the purpose and the money driving them. This shit we're in now, I can't wrap my brain around it; it's just loco, all of it."

Guillermo shook his head. "Only time will tell?"

"Sure, mano, in a year, maybe two, we'll know. Either things will happen or they won't, and there's shit all we can do except react to it. If there's an invasion, then we need all the survivors and all the equipment we have left to repel it. If it is a war of attrition, we just have to survive, and we'll take the country back. If this was some sort of suicide pact, destroy the world, destroy themselves, or just destroy the world so they have their own slice to themselves, that just doesn't make any sense, but it seems to now. So we're left with the only three things we can do: wait, train, and survive."

Merylin walked into the kitchen, smiled, and began preparing the group breakfast. Each of them had a specific role in the group, but tasks like cooking rotated daily to keep things fair for all. Bexar and Chivo hadn't cooked a single meal since they'd arrived, but Chivo, being experienced with such things, assured Bexar privately that eliminating a threatening rival "tribe" and returning with war booty was all they would have to do even if they stayed for a year.

Chivo excused himself and left to walk outside. The VW sat in the courtyard, next to the massive forklift. The new weapons, ammo, and gear were stored in the garage now that the shop had been destroyed, but the crates remained in the courtyard for the moment. The group had discussed using the crates as crates, or disassembling them to have wood for the fire or wood to construct unknown future projects. A vote hadn't happened yet, so for now, the crates sat empty, stacked against the far fence line. Walking the fence line, Chivo inspected the fence and perimeter.

What they need is a bunch of Hesco barriers, make the compound a true fire base, something that could be defended more easily. Start with the fence line and then gradually extend out the compound's security wall in concentric rings until they "owned" the whole hillside.

A hardened target is a target passed by. Chivo checked the homemade roof rack, the extra gas cans, and their share of the booty, mostly ammo and a few grenades, all unpacked from the bulky crates and jammed into the tiny car. It sat squat on the worn suspension. The best estimate that he had was that it would take them roughly five hours of driving to get to Groom Lake, if everything went right. Roughly two hundred miles, so ten gallons of treated gasoline from the group's stores were in the Beetle's gas tank, and another ten gallons sat in two gas cans on the roof. If twenty gallons wouldn't get them two hundred miles in an old Beetle, then they had issues.

Milan, NM

Oreo nudged Andrew awake, a dusty, dirty couch in the hangar his bed for the night. Andrew pushed his dog away, but Oreo nudged him again, and then Andrew heard voices.

"That's the Husky we saw, so he's got to be in one of the hangars. He isn't anywhere else."

Now wide awake, Andrew leapt off the couch, pistol in his hands; he crept to the hangar's side door, edged against the metal wall and waited, nearly holding his breath. His heartbeat banged in his ears so loud that he was sure that the two men outside could hear it. The doorknob turned, and the door rattled, the deadbolt locked from the inside by Andrew the night before. There was the sound of a key sliding into the lock and then the deadbolt turned with a hard click. The door edged open, daylight burning brightly into the hangar. Andrew shielded his eyes the best he could to keep some of the night vision he had and waited for the men to step inside.

One then the other, both older men in jeans and worn-out tennis shoes, stepped into the dark hangar. Andrew waited, hidden in the shadows behind the opened door. Once inside, Andrew pushed his pistol into the second man's back. "Don't move or I'll kill you." Oreo barked.

"Hey, guy, we're not here to harm you. You're a pilot, and we're pilots, and we live across the Interstate. After we saw your Husky land yesterday, we wanted to come chat. Nothing we have sitting outside will fly again without some work and parts we simply don't have, but really we wanted news, wanted to know if you know anything about what's going on."

Andrew waited for Oreo. If Oreo approved, he would trust his dog. He hadn't been wrong yet. A moment later, Andrew felt a nudge on his leg, and Oreo sat down against him, "My dog says you passed the test. I learned to trust my dog more than I trust people nowadays. Why don't we go outside and chat."

"Sure, or I can push open the hangar doors to get some light in here, your choice."

Moments later the metal doors rattled as the two men pushed them open along the tracks in the concrete, light flooding the hangar and the lone aircraft that sat in it, an older King Air. That plane easily flew higher, faster, and further than his little bush plane, but it took much more fuel and couldn't land on rough fields.

After introductions, Roy and Jay told Andrew the story of their survival in Milan. Twenty-two of them were left after a horrible week last month when a massive group of the dead pushed through on the Interstate. They didn't all stay on I-40; many of them flooded the town, killing thirteen while the rest of the survivors sheltered in place, praying to survive. Canned food kept the remaining twenty-two people alive, days spent scavenging abandoned homes and stores for anything they could find gave them a stockpile to last through the end of the year, but the one thing they didn't have was any information.

Andrew told them about all the other survivors and groups he had met over his travels, about his friends in Arkansas, the home-built radio, Groom Lake, and his desire to get there.

"So Bob built the radio basically out of used car parts?"

"Pretty much. He was a radio geek before the attack and knew what he was doing, so he changed the design a little bit, but that's basically what he did. He made a much better generator design. The antenna was a long run of wire draped over power poles."

"Do you remember what he did well enough to help us build one?"

"I can do you one better, I wrote it all down; it's in the plane."

Both of the men shot up, waiting impatiently for Andrew to take them to the new treasure of information, the ability to have a working radio, a way to talk to the outside world!

Half an hour later, the men were in the hangar, the cowls off the King Air's engines, wrenches turning to remove some of the parts they needed to build a radio. Quickly they decided that the airfield's historic airway beacon would be the perfect perch for the large antenna loop they needed. Promising to return in a few hours while they gathered the rest of the necessary parts and to bring a lunch back, they left Andrew with the key to the padlock on the Avgas tank to refill his plane while he waited.

This was a better experience than he'd had in the weeks before. News was a barterable good, but the directions to build a radio, a chance to communicate, that was more than just a barterable good, it was like having solid gold bars. Andrew wasn't Oprah rich, he was post-apocalyptic rich, which was even better.

After taxiing to the fuel tank and filling the Husky's fuel bladders, he relocked the fuel tank and taxied back to the tie downs to secure the plane. He figured at the least he was going to be remaining in Milan until the afternoon; worst case he might have to spend another night in the hangar. He was close, closer than before and wanted to get closer still to his destination. Not a dusty metal hangar in nowhere New Mexico, but in a real honest-to-God secret underground base that had food, showers, bed, people, and safety. Not that Andrew wanted to stay there forever, but the chance to relax for a couple weeks in what qualified as a five-star resort in the new world was a titillating thought.

Sitting on the tarmac under the shade of the Husky's wing, Andrew flipped through the atlas, ruler in hand. A straight line was roughly five hundred miles and would go right over the Grand Canyon, which was something that Andrew had wanted to see since he was a child. If the winds aloft were in his favor, there was no reason he couldn't make the flight to Groom Lake without refueling, but again, with no way to know, he wasn't about to take that gamble. The Grand Canyon was about the halfway point and could be an interesting stop. He knew that operators in the area offered aerial tours of the Grand Canyon, so there had to be landing strips somewhere nearby, but only the larger airports were shown on the atlas.

Jay and Roy returned, three others in tow, each carrying bags. One of the bags was given to Andrew; it contained a loaf of bread and three sealed mason jars with soup in them. Two cans of dog food were also in the canvas bag.

They didn't offer a can opener, but Andrew had an old P51 opener in his bag for just such an occasion. Oreo waited patiently, drool dripping to the tarmac as Andrew slowly made his way around the opening of the can. Once the top was open, without a proper dish, he simply upended the can onto the tarmac. Oreo didn't mind and quickly ate the gravy-covered processed meat that he had missed for much of the time after the attack. After feeding Oreo, Andrew held the loaf of bread in his hands, a real loaf of bread. Some other survivor groups, the ones that were well-stocked preppers, had the means to make bread, but it had been weeks since he'd had any. Tempted to bite right into the middle of the loaf, Andrew contained himself and tore off a chunk, the chewy meat of the loaf tasting like a piece of heaven, the thick crust tough and crunchy.

Yup, better than Oprah rich . . . much better.

Andrew sat, enjoying one of the jars of soup and the bread while watching the group build the radio and hang the antenna's wire from the beacon's tower. Finishing the bread, Andrew took Oreo and went to nap under the plane, both with full stomachs, until some yelling woke him up.

After a moment, he realized that it wasn't really yelling, but happily excited people. Andrew correctly guessed that the radio worked, and the group had made contact or were listening to another conversation, writing out the letters of each tapped-out word buzzing on and off in the spark-gap radio. Standing slowly, Andrew walked to the group sitting around a folding table in the hangar, wondering if they were excited enough that they might give him another loaf of bread.

"So it works?"

"Damn straight it works, son! This is amazing, just simply amazing!"

"Bob said it was ancient technology, what the original wireless telegraph operators used, long before voice communications."

"Andrew, we don't care. It works, and we made contact. Now we're listening to another group out of . . . where are they out of, Susanne?"

"Michigan."

"Wow, out of Michigan, and they're talking to your friends in Nevada. Area 51, I never thought we had aliens there, but I knew we had something. Thank God for that something."

Andrew looked at the sky; the sun was well-past overhead and endlessly marching toward the western horizon. They would be delayed another day, but if they could fly out at first light in the morning, they could stop off at the Grand Canyon, refuel, and land on the dry lakebed of Groom Lake before sunset.

"Jay, you guys wouldn't happen to have any charts or sections you would like to donate? I'm flying off of a road atlas, IFR all the way; I follow roads."

"Son, we've got a whole stack of charts. You can take the lot or pull the ones you want, and you can always come back for the rest if you need them!"

Jay handed him his keys again, pulling up the key to the FBO with a short explanation of where they were stored. Sporty's Pilot Supply it was not, but it was better than he had, so it was the best that could be found.

Smiling, Andrew left the group to find the sectional charts, while their attention stayed unwaveringly on the radio. If they had all thirty-eight, he would take all of them. It was worth the room and worth the weight to be able to know altitudes, where towers were, actually *plan* a flight instead of bumming around the slow routes of the Interstate system hoping to find somewhere to land for the night. With obstacles, elevations, and altitudes marked, he could even fly at night.

That's it, I'm going to take a quick nap, plot the course, and fly out. If I do it right, I should arrive just after sunrise. Groom Lake is marked on the sectional. All I need is sunlight to land.

Outside of Hurricane, UT

Amanda felt exhausted, the long drive taking its toll on her, but as tired as she felt, she was strangely energized. She still had half a tank of fuel left after siphoning more fuel a few hours prior and, according to the signs, she would be coming out of the highway in the middle of nowhere soon. Following Highway 59, in Hurricane she would take Highway 9 for a bit and, unfortunately, end up on I-15, but not for long before she turned off. The Interstates were not her friends, but not since the night of the huge storm and dodging zombies by lightning flashes had she had much issue on the small highways. Surprisingly, this trip was a longer journey than her trek from Little Rock to the SSC, but it was going much smoother and much quicker than before.

Highway 59 descended into the town, and two turns later Amanda was on Highway 9 driving west through the middle of town. Scanning for signs of survivors or any signs, and excited to see more, she continued on, tired, the

MRAP swerving back and forth on the roadway some as she stared out of the side windows. The hard thunk of something hitting the front bumper brought her attention forward again.

Outside her windshield stood nearly a virtual wall of meandering death, hundreds if not thousands of the reanimated dead milling about in the roadway. Amanda slammed on the brakes and jerked the wheel right, taking the first side street she saw. At first glance, the streets appeared to be in a grid pattern, and Amanda hoped she was right. In the side-view mirror she saw dead shambling in a slow, methodical pursuit, so she turned left, paralleling the highway, slowing and swerving back and forth. There were less of the dead on this street, but more and more followed the movement and the sound of the heavy diesel engine. More dead streamed out from around buildings and homes, blocking her path once again. Turning left, she drove the truck through a chain-link fence, bouncing across a rock-filled field between her and Highway 9.

Back on the highway, Amanda pointed west, slowing down to nearly a crawl, the truck practically driving with the engine at idle as the heavy steel bumper pushed bodies out of the way or under the truck. Frowning, Amanda scanned the gauges; everything from the oil pressure to the air pressure was where it was supposed to be. Feathering the accelerator pedal until the truck slowly sped up, she glanced at the speedometer which showed a brisk five miles per hour; she continued pushing through the middle of the rioting pack of dead with persistence. If something happened and she got stuck, if the truck failed, if any number of things happened, she would live out the rest of her life surrounded by death in a large armored truck.

Saint George, UT

They were getting a later start than they wanted. Originally planning on leaving first thing in the morning, Chivo went outside again after breakfast to find Stan in the middle of an oil change on the Beetle. Trying to be gracious, Chivo agreed that it was probably a good idea, but Bexar was visibly annoyed. The morning slipped by as more things happened. They agreed to stay for lunch, but would leave immediately thereafter, Bexar nearly shaking from the anticipation and anxiety of wanting to get on the road to get to Jessie.

A far cry from Bexar's beloved Wagoneer with its full-length roof rack, the homemade wooden rack did well to hold their provisions, most of which didn't fit in the interior of the car or under the hood of the trunk. Expecting to arrive in a single day's drive, most of what they carried in the way of gear were weapons of war, including Chivo's favorite rifle to reach out and touch someone from a distance. The rifle and case being much too long to even attempt fitting in the car, it sat tied down on the roof rack like a canoe of death. Four MREs and a gallon of water each was all they decided to bring in the way of provisions, choosing to fill the spaces with the weaponry purloined from Frank's group.

Shortly after lunch, they were finally on their way, the loud exhaust announcing their departure to anyone dead or alive that happened to be in the area. Remembering how bad things were just before they turned onto the I-15 frontage road, the windows were only rolled down a little way, even without air conditioning, both of them ready to roll them up quickly at the first undead they encountered.

The tires were old, but they would have to work; the car was loud and slow but was keeping a steady pace as they made a right turn onto Saint George Boulevard, the wide four-lane road that cut through town to Highway 18. The palm trees, an apparent favorite of landscapers in the area, looked withered and sickly, and the median was full of weeds. The close-standing businesses and office spaces did not look much better.

"Amazing, isn't it, how fast everything went to shit?" Bexar nearly yelled over the loud muffler.

Chivo nodded, deftly swerving around a small cluster of dead walking in the middle of the roadway. Flat-topped mountains loomed in the distance, and Bexar silently wondered how their little car would do trying to climb up the hillsides. For all the dead that had been seen on the Interstate and surrounding area recently, the heart of town seemed nearly abandoned by the dead, eerily devoid of lingering hordes veiled in thick black curtains of flies.

Twenty minutes after turning north on Highway 18, the vagabond pair of travelers were free of civilization's ruins and once again on the open highway, winding slowly through the desolate desert country side. Small clusters of homes and ranches dotted the distance along the roadside, which left Bexar questioning what someone could do to be a successful rancher in the uninhabited barrens of this region of Utah.

Passing a subdivision, the reanimated dead that they had missed leaving Saint George were found slowly streaming out from around the sides of the houses and toward the highway. Unlike their drive into Saint George, this time they cleared the growing herd of death before the roadway was blocked and a serious problem occurred.

DAVE LUND

Groom Lake, NV

They had resorted to yelling, the overweight quartermaster trying to protect the cache of supplies that they weren't even finished inventorying yet. Jessie wanted free rein to outfit, arm, and supply every single survivor that lived in the vast underground facility with as much ammo, weaponry, and equipment that they would possibly need to stand their ground against whatever may come. She was done playing the game in piecemeal. It was time to jump feet first into the water and face all that could be with all they had.

"No, even if Jake was standing here ordering me to give you free rein, I would not do it. It isn't fair for the group, it isn't right, and a woman like you doesn't have the first clue how to defend your own home much less a community like we have here!"

Frustrated, Jessie gave the quartermaster a one-fingered salute. Erin, who was with her, stepped close to the overweight man. Her right hand holding a knife, she pressed it against the crotch of the man's jeans, left hand gently brushing the side of his face and simply whispered, "You fuck with us and I'll cut off your dick and shove it down your throat. You don't even have a clue how to defend your pathetic little cock much less all this gear you're hoarding. Walk away and never come back. If I so much as see you in the hallway, you'll have to sit down to piss the rest of your life."

Blood drained from the man's face. He gasped for air, unable to speak, raising his hands in the air as a sign of surrender. Erin felt her right hand get warm and wet. Looking down, she saw that the man had wet himself. "That's just sad, a grown-ass man scared of little ol' me. Run along now, little boy, go on."

The man took two timid steps backwards, away from Erin and the knife she had against his now wet jeans. before he left in a stumbling sprint toward the door.

"Jesus, Erin, remind me not to piss you off."

"I don't think you ever could, Jessie," Erin said with a faint smile.

Ignoring the metal desk piled haphazardly with stacks of papers against the computer, covered in crumbs, and generally disgusting, the pair set out into the dark reaches of the storage area with small notebooks in their hands, donning headlamps to read the box and crate contents, making short notes as they walked, discussing what they thought they would need. Erin wanted more ammo for her 50-caliber rifle and a good spotting scope. Jessie just wanted something, a lot of something, she just wasn't sure what. All the survivors in the underground facility had pistols; they were required to carry them at all times, but the pistols were of all different makes and calibers, a mix of mostly what they'd all brought with them. Rifles were another story. Some had AR-variant-style rifles, some had hunting rifles, a few had some sort of variant of the AK-47, and fewer still, like Jason, had some type of shotgun; although not a rifle, it was at the least a long gun of some sort.

Erin pointed at a large section of wooden crates. "Jessie, I think we should outfit the group with as many of these M-16s as we can, all that don't have some sort of AR. Then at least the magazines and ammo are interchangeable."

"That's a good idea; we had group-standard weapons for the same reasons with our prepper group."

The pair kept walking, reading what they could on the highest shelves of the racking. It felt like they were in a tactical Costco, but instead of five-gallon jugs of ketchup, they had boxes with five thousand rounds of 5.56.

"How did your prepper group start?"

Jessie had waited for these questions to come from Erin for some time, but even expecting and rehearsing the answers to herself time and time again, she got choked up when trying to begin. "My Bexar, we met while I was finishing college. He was working all sorts of odd jobs, and we knew we were in love from the beginning. He grew up with Malachi and Jack, true lifelong friends. They could go months without seeing each other because of life and kids, but when they got together, conversations would seemingly pick up where they had left off, like no time had passed. The jokes, everything. Jake married first, but he and Sandra had dated for years and years. I think even before they went to college. Malachi married last, but he loved that little east Texas girl. For a time she worked in the prison system before she'd had enough of the bullshit that came with it and left. They moved to north Texas, we were in central Texas, and Jack's family was between Dallas and Fort Worth. We all camped together when we had the chance, meeting at random state parks and even out to Big Bend on one occasion, but it was Jack who started us on the idea of prepping. Things got a little out of hand after that, but as crazy as they got with it all, I supported it, Sandra supported it, and I think Amber, Malachi's wife, supported it, although I had the impression she was just mostly playing along. Each of them was good at many varied tasks, but each had their strong points. My Bexar, especially from the training associated with being in law enforcement, was the group's tactics and weapons guy. Malachi was communications and planning; he was a bit OCD about all of that. Jack was good with food storage. Really the three families had the perfect plan."

"If it was perfect, what happened?"

"The fucking dead happened. Bexar heard about the attack from the police dispatcher before it happened and was able to get a group text out to Malachi and Jack before the EMPs hit. He didn't include me on the text because he's forgetful like that, and he abandoned his post and duties to escape home. His motorcycle – he was a motorcycle cop – died near the neighborhood because the EMPs hit. He ran home, we loaded up, and bugged out."

"How did your vehicles still work?"

"We had an old Jeep Wagoneer. God, I hated that thing, but Bexar had it since high school and would probably have divorced me before selling that fucking thing. Anyways, we all had older rigs with no electronics in them for an EMP to kill off. We all left our homes to bugout to a central Texas location where we had all of our supplies. It took us a few days each, but we all got there . . . sort of. Amber had been shot, died, and turned, biting Malachi. He died that night and was found reanimated the next day. Losing Malachi and Amber was the first big blow to the group."

"Why didn't you stay with your supplies?"

"The goddamn dead! We were still too close to Dallas; the night horizon glowed orange with the huge fires ripping through the city, and out of those fires came the first wave of dead. We threw all we had on the roof racks and bugged out again. We decided to head to Big Bend National Park, and eventually we made it there."

"Where?"

"You know on Texas where the Rio Grande goes down then back up before going down again to the Gulf of Mexico?"

"Yeah."

"Well most of that is a national park. Now that place was the good life! It was surprisingly mostly deserted, not too many dead to clear out . . . between some solar panels and some ingenuity, we had power to our cabins in the Basin, the mountain area, and we even had running water as it was spring fed. There were javelina and mule tail deer to shoot and eat. Jack even got an ice cream freezer from the store in the park to work on solar power so we could preserve the meat."

"So why here, and why now?"

"We used Malachi's radio, a ham radio, and contacted Cliff, who told us about this place. A fucking biker gang heard us on the radio and attacked us to raid our supplies."

"What happened? Everyone fled, and here you are. Why did you get separated from Bexar?"

"No . . . we, well, a lot of things went wrong. Our daughter Keeley was killed, and the biker gang kidnapped me. I didn't know if Bexar was alive because he was missing, just vanished, and after realizing I was pregnant and alone, I set off to come here. A lot of fucking good that it did me!"

Jake walked into the cavernous room, looking down each long dark aisle as he passed until he spotted Jessie's and Erin's headlamps and walked up to them with a serious look on his face. "Were you two really going to cut off our quartermaster's penis?"

Erin laughed. "No, but now that he's gone all tattle-tale, I might just have to do it now!"

"Heh, well, I'd ask you not to. He's scared and pissed off and telling everyone about it. After the last outbreak, you all bought some good will, but that won't last if you keep up stuff like that. Anyways, the reason I'm here is that we voted on it, and the towns agree, we fight. But what do we do now?"

"First, we equip. Second, we train. But in the meantime, we figure out what all we have down here in storage. Send us all the people you can spare; we need to figure out everything we've got here, and we have to do it *fast*."

Jake nodded. "OK, let me see who I can scare up and that I trust to help you. I can't have anyone's crotch outty being turned into an inney."

Jake left, and Erin and Jessie continued to chat back and forth. Jessie told her about seeing Bexar in the Basin acting like a madman before she heard what she thought was an explosion; that she was knocked off her feet and into unconsciousness. After that, it was simple planning and building the motivation to actually go.

Erin shook her head. "Damn, and I thought my life was tough."

"Well, to be fair, I don't have Sarah for a mother!"

They both had a much-needed laugh from that; all the while they climbed through crate after crate of weapons and clothing.

Ellis Air Force Base, NV

The team chief, Gunnery Master Sergeant Jerry Aymond, had finally reached his limit. The base was dead, everything was dead, they were done with Nellis, and they needed to leave and point toward Area 51. That might be dead too, but it appeared to be somewhat alive due to the shortwave radio broadcasts. Those transmissions were the first real sign of some sort of surviving civilization that they had found, and the remaining Marines in his MSOT needed good news for a change. Walking out of his makeshift office and into the lounge area that the men had started sleeping in, Aymond cleared his voice loudly, then again, waking the nightwatch patrol.

"Raiders! Load it up to convoy north. We're done here, and it's time we go."

"Think we'll find alien bodies?"

"Who the fuck knows, Happy, but if the recording is true, we'll find people, which I would rather find any day of the week than an alien."

The team quietly worked hard, loading the truck as quickly as they could, stacking the supplies and equipment that they were able to scavenge from the PJs' cache. An hour later, Aymond sat in the passenger seat of the lead M-ATV. With the radar truck taking the middle position, the small convoy drove off the flight line and toward the north. The padlocked chain-link gate to the parking area was quickly disposed of, but the next gate's concrete crash barriers were something they would rather avoid than hassle with. After threading through the parking lot, the heavy block wall gave way to another chain-link fence, which they found had already been cut; it was open wide enough for the vehicles to pass through.

All of them were privy to many secrets; except for Jones, they all held top-secret clearances, but Area 51 was not something they had any knowledge of. Overall, they only had a vague idea as to where it was, trusting that the directions given on the shortwave radio transmissions were correct. The directions were very general, for groups coming from larger areas. Some highway names were given, but without a way to directly communicate with the facility. With GPS being down, they would once again have to wing it.

The directions were for groups coming from the West Coast areas, using I-15 as a general marker that led them to US-95, which was on the northwest side of Las Vegas. Driving out of the fenced perimeter of Nellis Air Force Base, they found themselves on the northeast side of Las Vegas. A simple road atlas was all they had available; the route appeared easy, Aymond following the little lines he marked on the paper, but he had his concerns. After the recon patrols through the large base, it was obvious that Las Vegas was completely overrun by Zeds. Once they were fully fueled, Aymond scaled off the approximate distance that they would have to travel to reach Groom Lake, and he was pleased to see that they shouldn't need fuel while en route. He was tired of the hop-scotching and waiting; they would drive all night if they had to, but they weren't stopping until the convoy pulled into Area 51.

Enterprise, UT

The easy trip had been anything but easy. The handful of tiny towns that they'd passed along the way appeared deserted. If there were any reanimated dead in the towns, they didn't see any; if there were any survivors, they didn't see any of them either. Eerily alone as they traveled together, like a scene from "On the Beach," the countryside remained intact but devoid of life.

On the dashboard of the old Beetle was one large single gauge. It contained the speedometer, an odometer, a fuel gauge that seemed questionable at best, and two warning lights. The one that was marked "OIL" was off; the one that was marked "TEMP" was on.

Highway 18 crashed into a T-junction at Enterprise, a service station at the far side of the roadway junction, which Bexar guessed probably also served as the community meeting place, grocery store, and supply house. Chivo shifted into neutral and let the VW coast into the parking lot, bouncing across the potholes.

"These old air-cooled VWs have a single fan belt that goes from the crank pulley to the generator, which is bolted to the fan. If we've temped out the motor, this punta is either done or the fan belt broke."

"Where the fuck are we going to find a fan belt for a forty-year-old car?"

"We improvise, mano," Chivo said, stopping the VW in the middle of the parking lot. "It's a simple v-belt. We scavenge one off a tractor, a lawn mower, use some rope, hell, you can whittle one out of a piece of wheat for all I care, but we'll figure it out . . . FUCK!"

Chivo launched out of the car. Bexar, not sure what the problem was yet, simply followed his lead, getting out, grabbing his rifle and getting ready to fight. It was quickly apparent what the problem was. Again following Chivo's lead,

Bexar's knife was in his hand and he was cutting the gear lashed to the roof rack free while Chivo threw green cans of ammunition out onto the pavement from the back of the car as fast as he could, the green cans clattering loudly across the parking lot.

Thick black smoke poured from the back of the car. The Baja modification left the car without a deck lid over the motor, so flames quickly lapped the roof of the car.

"Bexar, get this shit on the other side of the building. Do it quick!"

Leaving the car, which was becoming fully engulfed, Bexar scooped up a handful of gear and Chivo's big rifle case and sprinted to the far side of the convenience store, where he dropped the load. He sprinted back to the car, Chivo passing him in the opposite direction, as the whole back of the car burned, flames reaching high above them. Thick, caustic black smoke filled the air.

Chivo and Bexar passed each other again, Chivo yelling at Bexar, "Stay back there!"

The hand grenades, some of the ammo cans, and a handful of rounds for the RPG they'd brought were still in the car. Chivo ran back behind the convenience store and slid to a stop. Bexar was doubled over, coughing and trying to catch his breath.

"Keep your mouth open!"

A small pop sound preceded the explosion. As the windows shattered, pieces of shrapnel and German steel that was once their car rocketed past their mostly safe position behind the brick wall.

The pressure wave toppled the metal awning over the gas pumps. Ears ringing, Bexar couldn't hear Chivo, who grabbed his head, turning it from side to side, looking at his ears before giving a thumbs up. It dawned on Bexar what Chivo meant to keep his mouth open; it prevented his eardrums from bursting from the explosive concussion. Chivo tapped Bexar on the chest, pointed to his eyes and then pointed out. Pointing to Bexar, he pointed left; pointing to himself, Chivo pointed right and then raised his rifle. Bexar nodded, remembering again what one of the elaborate hand signals he and his motor buddies had made up mocking the SWAT team, which usually involved which taqueria they were going to eat at after working the morning school zones.

Rifle up in the low ready, Bexar followed Chivo around the corner of the building. Staying close, Bexar took responsibility for the left side of view, scanning the fields and the highway; the destruction was incredible. The convenience store was on fire, the fuel pumps were on fire, and it seemed that everything was on fire. Chivo stopped, tapped him, and gestured back to where they had come. The ringing in his ears starting to fade, Bexar could faintly hear the popping sounds of the growing fire. Chivo picked up his rifle case and grabbed a few ammo cans, Bexar picked up what he could carry as well, following Chivo into the desert beyond the burning convenience store, once again moving what they had left away from a growing fire.

Chivo yelled, "At least this time I don't think this damn thing will explode!"

Bexar nodded. "I'm getting really fucking tired of shit blowing up near me!"

"Seriously, you're like an explosion shit magnet. What the fuck is wrong with you?"

"It's my wonderfully pleasant personality."

"Personality like a rabid raccoon!"

They both laughed. The demanding world that now existed was something to be laughed at only because all that anyone could do was laugh. Anything else would result in madness.

In the MRAP, UT

Thick black smoke stood as a lone pillar on the horizon. Ending her quick tour of Central, Utah, where she'd been looking for survivors, Amanda feared that the black smoke was the result of survivors running afoul in their cooking or some other means. She now believed, more than ever before, that the country was full of survivors, enough to repel the dead, to conquer Yama.

On the edge of the town lay a rancher's field. Under an awning, she found a few tractors, and next to the tractors was a metal tank sitting about six feet off the ground, fuel nozzle dangling. The gate was unlocked so, after pushing it open, Amanda drove the big truck along the dirt path to the tractors and the fuel tank. Rust combating the painted surface, barely visible was the stenciled "DIESEL FUEL ONLY" on the front of the tank. Hopeful, Amanda rapped the tank with her knuckles; the tank sounded like it had fuel in it. How much, she had no idea, but with the sun quickly approaching the western horizon, she would take any fuel she could find. Especially if she was going to drive through the night; she was no longer willing to spend another day resting or waiting.

The fuel tank didn't quite top off the MRAP, although it nearly did, but it was quick and easy, taking only about ten minutes. It was much quicker than her usual fueling sequence of siphoning from a semi-truck's saddle tank, with the added blessing of not having to wash the taste of fuel out of her mouth.

Back on the highway and pointed north, she drove toward the growing pillar of thick black smoke, wondering if any others were doing the same.

SSC, Ennis, TX

Clint lifted the last box of MREs he was bringing into the MRAP. Loaded with ammo, food, water, and enough fuel to make the trip without having to scavenge for any of it, he was ready to leave. His first thought was to set some IEDs for any surviving visitors who might arrive, that is if any would be left, but in the last message his handlers were quite specific that they wanted the facility deserted and intact. This was to be one of the primary operating bases for running their new providence once the invasion was complete.

Clint was indifferent; his newly revised mission was peculiar but not totally unexpected. His first thought was to drive to the southern edge of the fields in northern Colorado, but his orders were very explicit in that he was to travel to Montana. That would mean he would have to play a new role instead of just breaking into a dead facility.

Apparently there were other plans for the flights of ICBMs in Colorado and Wyoming. They didn't explain, and he didn't really care. Orders were orders. All it meant was that his travel time would take longer and would involve more snow. Early April was springtime in Texas and could still be very much winter in Montana. Well-provisioned, the stores from the SSC facility gave him the cold-weather gear and even the proper Air Force uniform to wear in case by some miracle some missile crew had survived and was still manning the control panels. If he had been someone in that position, the temptation to rogue launch against Korea and China would have been too great. Since that hadn't happened, Clint didn't expect to find anyone, but the best prepared were always the luckiest.

The soft orange glow of the late afternoon sun edged into the dark tunnel as the hatch opened, grass and dirt falling onto the ramp. The hidden exit was the same that Amanda had used, except that Clint knew exactly where he was and which way he had to travel. His route was meticulously planned, as was each of the rest of the steps. He didn't want to travel far at night, but he had to get started immediately if he was to make his rendezvous on time.

Las Vegas, NV

The journey on Highway 215 around the northern side of the city began easily enough. It was not very developed, not like the thick swarming city to their south, but the highway dove into the heart of the northwest corner of the city. Needing to reach Highway 95 to get pointed north and to their destination, they found the Zeds on the highway a virtual roadblock, forcing the convoy to slow to a virtual crawl as the Zeds bounced off the bumper of Aymond's M-ATV.

Aymond keyed the radio. "We're going to stop. Jones, bring the radar truck alongside my truck. Kirk, think you can get into the back of that thing and get it running?"

"Roger that, Chief, can do."

Jones stopped with the back of the radar truck next to the driver's side front wheel of the lead M-ATV, the remote turret firing controlled bursts, clearing the swarming Zeds, but unable to get the angle needed. The dozen or so in close range, next to the trucks, would have to be killed by hand.

Gonzo opened the driver's door, raising his pistol and firing. Kirk opened the back door and stepped out, doing the same, moving quickly but smoothly. He heard Gonzo's pistol rounds snap past him, dropping Zeds in his path. Kirk turned and fired, clearing his immediate path, careful of his backdrop, not wanting to put a round into the radar truck. As quickly as they had started, it was over. All the doors were closed, the big flat transmitter raising and rotating forward, and the rioting swarm of Zeds fell to the ground. The thick cloud of black flies also fell from the air around them, the radar truck killing them as readily as the Zeds.

"Jones, drive forward slowly and stay in the center of the road. Kirk, rotate the dome as we roll, but keep it facing forward; it even killed the flies, so I don't want to see what it would do to us if it gets pointed back toward us."

"Roger, Master-Guns."

"Gotcha, Chief."

As they drove onward slowly, the sea of dead before them fell. Trying to avoid them the best they could, they drove over the bodies, hoping the bones wouldn't puncture a tire. Heavy rubber-run flat inserts were in the tires, and the onboard air system could keep the tires inflated if there was a minor puncture, but a serious failure would be a show stopper.

The deeper they traveled into the city, closer to their turnoff, the more they found that the city was completely in ruins. It was amazing that Nellis was as intact as it had been. Aymond observed the destruction, the ruins, the swarming Zeds, and the bodies that they drove through, and found himself hoping that they would actually find real people at Area 51.

Groom Lake, NV

Two dozen people now worked in six teams, organizing the massive stores. The numbers of variety of weapons was staggering to Jessie, most of which none of them had any idea how to use, except for the rifles. The M2 machine guns seemed simple enough to use. Even if Major Wright had survived, she doubted he knew how to use most of this gear. What they needed were some survivors who were combat vets, infantry, anybody with the experience to teach them how to use most of this gear. The M-16s were easy enough; the three of them had plenty of experience with AR-15s or M4s. Somehow the group of survivors that had amassed underground in Groom Lake were regular everyday people, the kind of people one would hope would survive the end of the world, but still people with no training or tactics, not that Jessie held her level of training in any sort of high esteem. All she had was a bit more than most of them, which was all they had for now, so that was what they would use.

The remaining airmen worked primarily in the radio hut, electronics and communications being their trained jobs in the Air Force. Since Wright's death, they had mostly stopped wearing their full uniforms. With civilian clothing not being readily available, and no shopping malls to be had, they switched to wearing untucked T-shirts with their utility trousers, practically a hippie rebellion in their world, which Jessie was both happy and sad to see. Happy for her belief that this, of all times, was when people should be comfortable and have some level of happiness where they could find it; but she was sad to see the loss of the only remaining functional piece of the mighty United States military.

Glancing at the clock on the wall, Jessie realized that they had been at it for more than six hours. They had missed lunch, and if they didn't act soon, they would miss dinner as well.

"Hey, Sarah?"

Sarah finished taking notes from the group reporting to her before walking to Jessie.

"Yeah?"

"We've been working for quite some time. I don't want to stop. Think we should see if the mess hall could send down some sort of boxed dinner or something?"

"Sure . . . Erin!"

"What, Mom?" Erin yelled from somewhere in the darkness.

"I'll be back in a few. Take my place!"

Sarah walked toward the door and handed her clipboard to Jessie, who sat down, absentmindedly rubbing her growing baby belly. She was tired and hungry, her feet swollen and aching, her back ached. and she wished she could go out for a pedicure.

"You going to make it?"

Jessie handed Sarah's clipboard to Erin. "Well I don't really have a choice in the matter, do I?"

Enterprise, UT

Sunset was over, twilight and the starry sky battling for domination overhead. Chivo and Bexar were trying to settle into their overnight accommodations, not far from the still smoldering gas station. The afternoon had been spent locating and clearing a good spot to sleep, after first looking for a usable vehicle. Giving up on finding a vehicle before the end of the day, shelter became the primary goal. Found and cleared, they began moving the surviving gear from the desert field to the metal building they had chosen for the night. Working together, they moved slower than they had the first two times that they moved the gear because the urgency and danger were gone from the situation, outside of the handful of gathering reanimated dead, attracted to the area by the blast and fire, coming from who knows where.

Chivo held his arm out, stopping Bexar. "You see that, mano?"

To the south, bright lights grew out of the desert, slowly coming closer, appearing brighter as they came.

"What the fuck is that?"

"That's a truck."

"No shit, Chivo, but what sort of Mad Max bullshit is it?"

"No, mano, that's a fucking MRAP."

"Like a Cougar?"

"Yeah, well, that's one kind of MRAP."

"The sheriff north of us got one of those surplus for the tactical team; fucking huge."

"And heavy, armored, and armed."

"How do we play this?"

"That's our new ride, mano . . . I've got a plan."

Groom Lake, NV

Jessie sat at the desk and ate her dinner. The mess hall had sent down enough vegetable soup and "orange drink" for all who toiled deep in the dark corners of the storage area. The soup was good, and the beverage again tasted more like the color than an actual orange. It dawned on Jessie that she would probably never eat an actual orange again unless she happened across one somewhere out in the wilds. Her baby wouldn't have an orange, or limes, or lemonade.

My God, what about scurvy?

Taking a deep breath, Jessie felt distant enough from the situation momentarily to recognize the edge of a soon-to-be-mother freak-out. She was happy that she wasn't far enough along to start nesting yet; she couldn't see if the storage area had baseboards, but if it did she was sure they were filthy. She remembered their little house in Brazos County, their first house; after painting Keeley's room bright blue early on in the pregnancy and then finding out that they were having a girl, Bexar repainted the room for Jessie more than anyone. The baby wouldn't know the difference, but Jessie *had* to have the right paint and crib and covers and decorations . . . a couple's first baby was a big deal. She laughed to herself. This time her entire pregnancy was a different story.

She was on the fifth level, or five floors underground, but Jessie didn't really know how deep they really were or how stout the underground facility would be against an attack. Tipping up the plastic bowl, finishing the rest of the broth, she watched Sarah run the show. Erin went back and forth between groups, taking notes and also making a pile of gear for the three of them. Watching all the activity, activity she and Sarah were responsible for, Jessie wondered if they were making the right choice. If the SSC went offline, if there was an invasion, would it be better to be holed up in an underground fort on the frontier, or was there a better option?

Originally, their bug-out plan with Malachi and Jack was supposed to work. They had made all the right choices, stored all the right stuff, and built the right vehicles, and everything still went to hell. The plan failed because it was a single plan; it didn't have any contingencies. This plan didn't have a contingency, and she needed one for herself, Sarah, and Erin, and they needed one fast.

"Hey, Erin, could you come here for a moment?"

For all the activity in the vast storage area, the noise level was manageable; Erin heard Jessie from a few hundred feet away and began walking toward her.

"What's up?"

"Tell your mom that you're coming with me for something, and we're going topside. There's something I need to do with the FJ."

"OK, like what?"

"Plan B."

"Isn't that the morning-after pill? A little late for that now."

Jessie glared at Erin, who laughed and jogged away toward Sarah. A few minutes later, they stood in the hangar next to the FJ, wearing what had become their small-group-standard aboveground expedition kit, which contained significantly more gear and ammo than what consisted of their EDC, everyday carry, while underground.

Inside the MRAP, UT

Amanda slowed as she approached a T-intersection. Checking her atlas, she saw she needed to turn left. A lone reanimate stood in the roadway, right in the middle of the intersection. Veering to drive around it, she was startled when it started waving its hands over its head. Amanda slammed on the brakes, the heavy air brakes hissing in protest.

It was a man, not a zombie, and he was yelling at her, waving his arms, trying to get her to come to him. She couldn't hear him in the truck, but it looked like he was yelling "Help." Amanda drove forward, stopping very close to him, his chest barely visible over the high hood. He was yelling help and waving frantically. He wore a pistol, a dirty T-shirt, and pants, but appeared to have nothing else. Amanda left the truck running and cracked open her door to stand on the step to hear what the man was saying.

As she opened the door, her feet were ripped out from under her. Hitting her head on the step as she fell, the world around her went dark.

PLA Reconnaissance Position, NV

After driving north from S4, the APC turned and followed the dirt road, meandering up the western side of the mountain. Reaching their planned destination and confident of the lack of persons alive or dead in their surroundings, the four-man team left the APC just below the military ridgeline. They now lay under netting to break up their outlines and set a rotation behind the powerful tripod-mounted spotting scope. As they slowly scanned each of the buildings, the only movement the team could find was from the dead trapped in what the intelligence reports listed as onsite apartment housing for some of the facility staff. The location they were most interested in was the northeast white hangar next to the edge of the dry lake bed and the numerous other escape routes and hatches around the complex.

Encrypted satellite communications kept the recon team in contact with the small assault force. The elite of the expeditionary special reconnaissance teams of the PLA, the Siberian Tiger unit specialized in survival skills in harsh environments. They were the initial recon and assault team to clear out pockets of resistance and special facilities to be followed by the sweeper and cleanup teams comprised of mixed units from the PLA and the Korean People's Army. This mission was easy: simple sabotage, infect, load up, and fly out. The sweeper teams would come through in the next few months, neutralizing the Yama-infected imperialists.

The assault set to launch just before dawn, the team continued to update their commander with status reports every hour. So far, each of the six reports was a simple one-word transmission indicating that the situation was unchanged and that no enemy imperialist movement was detected on the surface.

Groom Lake, NV

Jason joined Jessie and Erin, at Erin's insistence. Her quick idea turned into another four hours of Erin gathering essential items to take with them. After her plan was outlined, Erin didn't want Jessie to do any heavy lifting, which it was that, heavy, so the three of them drove out of the hangar, looping around to the west and heading south toward the shooting range. Dawn was only a few hours away. Although the canvas wall tent, the only remaining original group-standard tent, was dyed a flat-green color from the natural bright-white color of the canvas, Jessie wanted to find a spot where the tent would be close enough to get to, far enough away to possibly be missed, and amongst enough clutter to possibly be overlooked. Up the hillside from the shooting range stood a tank farm, and those five tall tanks would give Jessie all that she wanted in a discreet intermediary bug-out location.

None of them had any idea what was in the tanks -- it could have been flying-saucer fuel for all they knew – but bouncing up the dirt road in the darkness, they couldn't even see the tanks yet, even with the bright off-road lighting that Jack had installed on the FJ; the darkness was a thick veil around them. Jessie drove, with Erin sitting in the passenger seat and Jason behind her. Erin, hyper-vigilant, found her mind wasn't on Jason but on the surrounding darkness. Her "big rifle" rode on the roof rack, which was where she planned to go if the shit hit the fan. With the short-barreled M4 in her hands, she absentmindedly kept tapping her right thumb against the safety, checking that it was flipped up and on safe. Jason's weapon of choice remained his shotgun.

After what felt like an eternity in the darkness, the tanks grew out of the desert hillside ahead of them. Driving to the westernmost side of the tanks, Jessie stopped the FJ and turned off the lights and the engine, and each of them sat quietly in the interior, waiting for any reaction, any shambling dead to approach. Still not having the opportunity to practice with any of the night optic devices that they had located in the storage area, each of them clicked on their headlamps; the dim LED lights left the interior of the bug-out vehicle awash in red light.

Mostly confident that they were alone in the expanse of Groom Lake, they climbed out of the truck.

"Jason, the tent is in the case on the left, and the poles are in that PVC tube," Jessie said, pointing to the roof rack. She began to reach for the PVC tube to start pulling out poles when Erin stopped her, reminding her that she was to hold security; she and Jason would do the work.

Grunting, Jason and Erin flopped the tent out of the case and down from the roof rack, and it fell with a dull thud onto the desert floor. Jessie and Bexar could set the tent up in about an hour, as they found out in Maypearl. They could pull the tent down in ten minutes when pressed, although not as neatly as they would typically. The EMT metal tubing clanked, sounding as loud as gunshots to the three of them in the darkness; they were trying to be quiet, but the tubing simply wouldn't cooperate.

When the metal angle pieces were arranged and the strong tent frame assembled, Jason and Erin pulled the heavy canvas tent over the frame.

"Just like the pioneers, huh, Erin?"

"No wonder they had fucking wagons and donkeys and shit. If this is their state-of-the-art lightweight camping tent, what did they cook with, lead?"

"Cast iron, and, yes, it's heavy too. There's a skillet and a Dutch oven in the case in the back of the truck."

"Isn't a Dutch oven when a guy . . . ."

Jason snorted. "Yes, but it's also a cast-iron pot with a lid."

Erin and Jason kept bantering back and forth, at a whisper. Jessie walked around the bug-out site for another security sweep, but also to get a feel for the layout if she had to come up here in complete darkness.

In the MRAP

Chivo drove. To say he was familiar with the different models of vehicles all classified as the mine-resistant ambush-protected vehicle would be an understatement. Ironically enough, they ambushed and took this one, but the lone driver, a woman they knew and were surprised to find in BFE Utah and alone, lay flat on her back in the rear of the truck. Bexar tended to her. Although she had been knocked out from hitting her head against the thick metal side step, she came around quickly and with a severe headache.

After listening to both of them apologize profusely, Amanda had the pleasure of listening to a lecture on patrol tactics and safely using an MRAP from Chivo. Sipping water, he offered to give her a shot from the medical bag in the truck that he promised would take away all the pain, but Amanda opted to take a handful of 800mg Motrin instead. Chivo smiled slightly. If she was going to eat the 800mg "grunt candy," then maybe she could become a warrior president yet.

Two hours after the ambush, President Lampton was awake, the MRAP was loaded with the remaining provisions that Chivo and Bexar had saved from the doomed VW, and they were once again pointed north, driving through the night at Amanda's insistence. Beginning with the short version of events, Chivo wanted to know all the details about Clint and the two facilities.

"What about Cliff? Clint sent him a message, some sort of random numbers radio broadcast; he was supposed to go to Granite Mountain. We haven't heard from him since you guys radioed your message from Cortez to Bill and them at Groom Lake."

"Fuck Cliff."

"Now, Bexar, sure he fucked us, but he also saved us, so I'd say that leaves him close to neutral," Chivo continued, telling Amanda the whole backstory about Cliff sabotaging their exit and the group in Saint George, which surprised Amanda because she'd driven through the same towns they had, including Saint George, and hadn't seen that survivor group. They also told her about Cliff's partial redemption by saving both of them so Angel and his group could get to them.

"So why didn't the other group . . . ."

"Frank's."

"So why didn't Frank's group just ask for help? If they had helped you, why wouldn't they help them?"

Bexar quietly listened to the conversation, wishing Chivo would speed up; they were closer to Jessie than they had been since Big Bend, and his heart ached to see the love of his life again. Especially now that even President Lampton felt it necessary to overland to Groom Lake, jeopardizing her life for the idea that an attack might be imminent.

"The two groups knew each other, or knew of each other at least, before the attack. Frank's group didn't think Guillermo and Angel would help them, so the story went."

"How did you figure all of that out?"

"We captured one of their members during an attack, and I asked him."

"And he told you?"

"Yes, ma'am."

Bexar chortled. "He fucking waterboarded him . . . uh, Madam President."

Amanda raised her eyebrows. "Did it work?"

"The enhanced interrogation techniques worked well, ma'am."

Faintly smiling, Amanda thought to tell him to simply call her Amanda, but her pounding head made her want to let him sweat it out a bit longer.

Chivo slowed and stopped after turning south onto Highway 93.

"Dude, why are we stopping?"

"Are you a medic?"

"No, I always called for medics."

"Then chill out for a bit. I know you're excited, but it is time to medically evaluate the President again. You can put your happy ass in that seat for a bit if you can't wait five minutes."

Chivo laughed and slapped Bexar on the ass as he climbed over him to get to the driver's seat. The dash looked about like any semi-truck that Bexar had ever seen. He pushed the yellow diamond valve in, and the parking brakes released; he looked for the gear selector.

"It's a push button, mano," Chivo called from the back.

After pushing the button for drive, they were off at what felt like a breakneck pace from his seat behind the driver's wheel, but topping out at fifty-five miles per hour according to the needle. The powerful lighting turned the dark highway in the middle of nowhere into near daylight. As heavy as the truck was, it felt more nimble behind the wheel than Bexar would have guessed, as he gently swerved around an abandoned semi-truck in the roadway. Smiling, he felt invincible in the big armored truck sitting so high above the passing pavement.

Mercury Highway, NV

"Master Guns, I'm telling you I saw fucking headlights! They turned away from us and then disappeared."

Aymond turned to Kirk, who sat behind the driver's wheel. The entire team having heard Jones' radio transmission, the convoy sat motionless, all their lights extinguished as a precaution. The lighting selector even disabled the brake lights. "We're in the Nevada Test Site. Think it might be a patrol from Area 51?"

"No dice, Chief, why would they flip their lights off if they're a friendly patrol, especially after inviting everyone to come visit on the shortwave?"

"The PLA didn't have night optics."

"The PLA and KPA that we fought *so far* didn't, but who's to say that these guys don't have them?"

Aymond knew Kirk was right and knew the answer before he had even asked it. The trip out of Las Vegas had taken much longer than anticipated, darkness falling on them hours ago; the convoy had remained at a slow speed with the radar truck leading, the dome on and blasting away at nothing but empty desert for a good while. They hadn't seen a single Zed since turning off of Highway 95, so the need for the dome being up and in use seemed moot, especially with possible tangos in the area.

WINCHESTER: STORM

"Gonzo, drop the dome and get back into this truck. Jones, fall into the second position. NODs on, keep the lights off. If they're PLA tangos and headed north, we need to catch them before they get to the base."

Buildings appeared out of the desert, awash in the green-and-black glow of the night optic devices as the team quickly drove by. Jones was the only one who hadn't had a lot of experience with the NODs until the MSOT found him and Simmons holed up in an aircraft hangar, a mechanic not having a high need for using them even if every Marine was a rifleman.

The lead M-ATV's remote turret, controlled again by Gonzo, swept back and forth as they passed buildings and facilities in the secret weapons test area, but the turret always faced toward the front. In the rear M-ATV's remote turret, Snow kept rear watch at the controls. The Marines were in combat patrol mode, although Gonzo secretly wished for a Rip-It to make it feel like old times.

CHAPTER 10

PLA Scout Position, Groom Lake, NV
April 8, Year 1

The reconnaissance team had noted the vehicle in their report a few hours prior, but after the lights were turned off, they didn't see any movement from it again. The four PLA special forces soldiers quietly debated the purpose of being next to the fuel tanks. They would not be safe for any sort of fighting position, although they could be used for a security watch point. The grainy green-and-black world magnified large through the spotting scope didn't have the resolution they needed to see what anyone was doing or how many people were there. Although there had only been a single vehicle, it appeared to be military in nature.

Guard Shack, Groom Lake, NV

"Look, mano, the sign says to stop and dial the number, so we'll stop and dial the number."

"Why should we waste our time with that?"

Amanda answered before Chivo could, "They could have a security patrol or guards."

"She's right."

Bexar conceded defeat on the issue. They all climbed out of the truck and stretched their legs while Chivo dialed the number and made contact with the facility.

"OK, the instructions are to follow this road down the mountain and around the dry lake bed. After reaching the south end of the lake bed, we turn left and drive onto the flightline and into the northeasternmost hangar."

"Couldn't we just drive across the lake bed?"

"I don't know, buddy, but when a secure facility tells you to enter a certain way, you enter a certain way. You don't know what they've got in place."

Bexar took his spot behind the steering wheel again with Chivo riding in the front passenger's seat coaching him on how to navigate the poorly maintained gravel road up the mountain; they were surprised to find that near the guard shack and beyond the fence line the road was nicely paved.

"Who in the world did they get to build a secret paved road into what is arguably the most famous top-secret base in the world?"

"My people, mano."

"Jesus, that's kind of racist."

"Yeah, probably him too."

Both of them laughed while Amanda staring at them with a bit of bemused curiosity. When they had met at the SSC, Bexar was banged up and fairly reserved. This was a different man than before, they both were, and they had obviously been through some tough times together.

Mercury Highway

Aymond watched the craters pass as the convoy ripped through the desert as quickly as they dared. Gonzo and the forward-looking infrared display of the remote turret were their first line of defense through the darkness. Aymond threw out what they'd learned of the invading force from San Diego and their contact with them in Yuma. If they really were chasing a blacked-out enemy patrol and they did have NODs, then he had to assume they would have FLIR capabilities as well. If that was the case, then all they had on their side was surprise. Aymond hoped that would be enough, but hoped even more that Jones had been mistaken.

Wall Tent

After the long ordeal of erecting the tent, from concept to finish, Jessie was exhausted, and she hadn't even done any of the hard work. After the strong winds and sandstorms they had experienced before on the surface, Jessie made sure Jason and Erin hammered a stake into every available loop and that each of the guy-lines were staked and taut. The last thing she needed now was for her tent to take flight and blow away into the desert.

Erin and Jason were tired but sort of wired; two cases of MREs, a five-gallon plastic jug of water, and two cases of 5.56 joined the single case of 50-caliber rounds for Erin's rifle inside the tent. All the prepper provisions, the cast-iron cookware, and the rest remained in the FJ. This was all a hunch on Jessie's part—one she hoped would prove to be untrue. The eastern sky was beginning to lighten with the approaching dawn; Erin convinced Jessie and Jason to wait for dawn. Jessie sat against one of the FJ's wheels, slowly eating one of the MREs. She found it odd, but the MRE was sort of tasty compared to the food they had been eating from the mess hall. She gave the kitchen crew credit for stretching rations and cooking every day, but the improvising apparently gave way to some blandness. Or Jessie was tired and hungry, which was a winning combination to make a bad meal into the best meal of the day.

Erin sat next to Jason a little further down the hill, in front of the tanks, both of them eating an MRE each for breakfast.

He's a little old for her. She's only fifteen, and he's four years older than she is . . . so is Bexar, Bexar's four years older than me.

Tamping down her suppressed high school teacher instincts, Jessie realized that the law prohibiting a relationship between the two of them no longer existed and, in a few years, as they grew older, the difference in age wouldn't have even batted an eye before the end of the world.

Jessie felt a slight mixture of hope and sadness for Erin; the pickings were sort of slim after the dead started shambling around, but humanity always finds a way. Throughout the known history of civilization, no matter what plague or event befell the weary, they always found a way. Noah had his ark.

Is this our own ark? It's the damned Fort Apache amongst the native undead is what it is, but my John Wayne isn't here yet.

Light flashed to the north, the shockwave of an explosion blasting across Jessie and her motley duo of armed teenagers. Jessie stood, looking at the rising fireball. Erin sprinted toward her, climbed on top of the FJ and ripped open her rifle case. Jason stood still, awestruck by the sight.

In the MRAP

"What the fuck was that?"

"You and things blowing the fuck up, mano. Fuck it, go across the lake bed, go now, go!"

Bexar slowed and turned the wheel left, bouncing over uncut desert toward the edge of the lake bed. Reaching the hard surface, he pushed the accelerator all the way to the floor, the turbocharged diesel roaring in response.

Chivo flipped on the communications radio mounted in the MRAP. The electronic display illuminated dimly and he began punching in commands to the keypad on the front. Bexar only glanced at him, a crashed C-130 passing by their window bringing his attention forward. Racing toward the rising fireball, the quickened adrenaline heartbeat of racing to a robbery in progress or a man with a gun call felt like home, those associations being pushed out over the last few months. Bexar's eyes narrowed; taking a deep breath, he was a man racing to a battle.

MSOT Convoy

"Holy shit, Chief!"

Aymond nodded. Apparently Jones was correct, and they were running behind. The nimble M-ATVs were already racing as fast as they could; the closer they got to the fireball, the closer to the battle, the more careful they would have to be, but until then the trucks kept along at their governed speed, bouncing along the paved road now winding around the mountains. The internal debate about the radar truck in the convoy was one that would have to be decided quickly. If they cached it, they might lose it. There weren't exactly a lot of hiding spots out in the open. If they charged into battle with it, the valuable truck might be a combat loss. It wasn't armored, and Jones could be KIA as well.

Aymond pressed the transmit button on the handheld team radio he wore. "Jones, in the next two klicks, find a spot to stash the radar truck, get on board with the trail unit, advise when back en route."

"Roger, Master Guns."

"Roger, Chief."

Aymond turned to Kirk. "What do you think, high ground or flank?"

"Flank, Chief."

"North or south?"

"That fireball is north of the road, so I say south."

Aymond nodded. "Do it."

In the MRAP

"Who the fuck was that on the radio?"

Chivo smiled. "I don't know, but they weren't fucking speaking Mandarin!"

Amanda unlatched the roof hatch and began to climb up to the turret.

Chivo yelled over the noise, "Lampton, get your ass back in here!"

Amanda looked down at Chivo, who now spoke with a calm, firm voice, "Madam President, why don't you climb down and take my spot. We have friendlies on the net. Bexar drives, you talk on the radio, and I man the turret."

It wasn't a request. Amanda climbed down, Chivo already climbing into the back of the truck yelled forward before climbing into the turret, "Bexar, tell her what you want to say. We're playing this one fast and loose. I don't know . . . fuck, treat it like a bad cop situation or some shit. Good luck, mano!"

If they had been wearing proper combat gear, they could have plugged in their headsets, but they lacked proper in-vehicle communication.

Bexar glanced at Amanda. "Say what I say: 'Who are you, and what's your twenty . . . location?'"

Amanda held the handset and keyed the radio: "Friendly forces, what is your position?"

After some back and forth on the radio, Amanda turned to Bexar. "They're Marines!"

"Yeah, I can hear the radio, too, but now what?"

Amanda returned to the radio. After another series of transmissions, she lowered the handset. The Marines knew they were on the lakebed, and they wanted the MRAP to charge straight for the fire.

MSOT Convoy

Aymond frowned. *Fucking civilians charging into battle, going to have to save their asses . . . .*

The entire team wore the MBITR radios and had heard the radio transmissions; there was a mix of emotions amongst the team in response to the radio traffic. Kirk keyed on the net. "Chief, we're about a klick behind you, over."

"Get out on the lakebed, intercept, and assist the civilians to the north; we're taking the south, over."

"Roger."

Still frowning, Aymond press-checked his rifle, slapped the assist a couple of times to make sure the bolt was all the way forward, and spoke over his shoulder, "Talk to me, Gonzo."

"Shit, Chief, can't see shit with the FLIR, except the fire. Can't see anymore because of the buildings."

Kirk slammed on the brakes, the tires chirping on the tarmac as he turned sharply to race in between what looked like barracks, across the flightline, and into the desert. Gonzo swung the turret as they bounced past the buildings. He yelled, "Got two APCs, about a dozen tangos piling in. Holy shit! Someone just dropped one of the tangos."

"The civilians?"

"No, I see them, looks like an MRAP; they're about a klick and a half out and coming fast."

Aymond keyed the radio. "Two mounted patrols, a dozen combatants visible and bugging out."

The Tanks

Jessie stood on the roof rack. The last time she had done that was the first day she'd met Sarah and Erin. This time she wasn't on the wrong end of Erin's steady aim. Erin had climbed on top of the easternmost tank and lay prone with her rifle. Jason climbed the ladder with the green can of 50-caliber ammunition for her rifle; apparently she thought she would need it.

"Jessie, some truck just hauled ass out into the runways!"

"Shit."

Jessie nearly leapt off the roof. Climbing into the driver's seat, she started the FJ, left the lights off, and drove toward the rising sun, straight across the desert, to the taxiway. Turning north, she floored the old FJ and drove toward the hangar until she saw movement to her right.

That's the truck.

It was large and tracer fire streamed out of the weapon mounted on the roof. Big trucks sat near the hangar and looked like something out of a Chuck Norris movie from the eighties. Trusting her instincts, she turned hard right and raced toward the truck driving across the runways.

The Hangar

The PLA special forces saboteur team's mission was done. The teams came out of the blast door and into what remained of the hangar after their initial attack. Suddenly taking heavy fire, they piled into the armored personnel carriers, turned and drove north as fast as the heavy trucks would accelerate.

In the MRAP

Amanda excitedly repeated what was broadcast on the radio.

Bexar nodded, concentrating on his task. He saw odd-looking armored trucks driving away from the fire. He was going to tell Amanda to ask Chivo what to do, but the big M2 in the turret opened fire, rattling with controlled bursts. Spent shells dinged against the armored roof, some of them falling into the interior of the MRAP.

It took a moment to realize that the sound he heard was enemy fire hitting the windshield. Lights started coming on in the dashboard; glancing down for a moment, Bexar saw one that looked like a tire pressure warning. The others he didn't have time to think about as the truck pulled hard right.

Amanda held the radio handset and repeated the Marine's transmission, yelling, "Friendly coming from our right. He said slow down, the run flats will keep us rolling, and turn off all of your lights."

Shadows of men piling out of the armored trucks still close to the burning hangar danced across the desert floor as muzzle flashes burst from the running men like strobe lights.

Bexar let off the gas and found the button for the lights, turning all of them off. Looking up, he saw a familiar orange streak coming toward the windshield. Out of instinct, he ripped the wheel to the left as something rocketed past him, barely noticing an explosion behind them in the remaining mirror.

The controlled bursts Chivo was using before gave way to long streams of fire. Chivo yelled at Amanda to bring him ammo. To their right, another dark vehicle appeared, which looked vaguely American, but Bexar wasn't exactly an expert on military vehicles. The tracer fire was beginning to be hard to see, dawn giving new perspective to the world around them, but the truck that pulled alongside his position streamed high-cyclic death from its turret-mounted weapon.

Chivo stopped firing; Bexar stopped the truck and could hear a voice calling to cease fire over the radio. An SUV shot across the runways toward the ruined armored trucks, the bodies, and the shell of a hangar. The doors were gone, the roof was mostly gone, and most of the hangar was simply gone, burnt, ravaged by the fast and heavy battle; a thick concrete hump in the back was all that was left. Bodies lay in ruin around the armored trucks that they had been attacking, which smoked, each of them badly damaged.

Is that . . . is that Jack's FJ? I haven't seen that since The Basin. The bikers had it; we left it there when Chivo's crew pulled my unconscious ass out of that firefight.

"Jesus, my God! Jessie, what the fuck are you doing?"

Bexar slammed his foot to the floor. The truck, both front tires flat, was slow to respond, but began to pick up speed. The hangar appeared to be about a half mile away, and Jack's old Toyota FJ was going to beat him there.

The FJ

Jessie slammed on the brakes, sliding to a stop on the tarmac outside the ruined hangar. The two armored trucks of the attacking force sat destroyed; men and pieces of men lay on the tarmac near them. As the SUV stopped, Jessie climbed out of the truck, held her rifle and walked briskly into the remaining shell of the hangar. The blast door was damaged and open.

"Shit. Sarah!"

Behind her one of the dead PLA stood, shakily stepping toward the interior of the destroyed hangar.

The Tanks

Erin cursed under her breath and squeezed the trigger. Jason couldn't hear anything but the loud ringing in his ears; he was worried that he might not be able to hear again after the massive muzzle blasts of the Barrett rifle being shot in rapid succession. Erin rose up, slapped an empty magazine on the tank, and picked up the fresh one. Jason pulled the rounds out of the green ammo can, each over five inches long. Ten rounds were loaded in the magazine and set next to Erin.

After swapping out magazines again, Erin stopped firing and made very small adjustments back and forth, scanning the scene for more threats. She watched as the truck came to a stop next to the FJ, and four men in uniform, battle gear, and thick beards stepped out of the truck. Concerned, Erin watched as they quickly formed up and cleared the ruined trucks they had all been firing at. Each of the Chinese attackers lay dead for good, their heads ruined by Erin's sharp skills.

Her ears rang loudly too; looking at Jason, she could see him talking but couldn't hear him. She pointed to her ear and shook her head. Jason pointed to himself, to his ears, and also shook his head. She switched out the magazine on her 50-caliber rifle with the fully loaded mag that Jason handed her, then gave him a kiss before stepping toward the ladder. As she climbed down, a rifle as long as she was tall smoking in her arms, he loaded the second magazine and quickly followed. They quickly walked toward the hangar. She was worried about her mom but trusted Jessie.

MSOT

"Clear!"
"Clear!"
"Clear!"

Aymond keyed the radio. "Kirk, get Jones back to the radar truck, and get that damn thing over here. Then go back to where Jones saw the headlights and try to find where these PLA assholes came from."

He saw the damaged MRAP accelerating across the lake bed toward the hangar. The truck ground to a stop against the parking brake and the engine died. The windshield was pockmarked from rifle fire, and both the front tires were flat. The MRAP had seen better days. The driver leapt out of the truck while it was still moving. Ragged and thin, the man yelled, "Jessie, stop!" while sprinting toward the woman, ignoring Aymond and the MSOT, his rifle swinging by the sling as he ran.

The woman turned and fell to her knees. The man slid to a stop, helped her up, and held her tightly. In return, she wrapped her arms around him. In the midst of the damage and ruin, the two held each other, crying.

The Hangar

"Bexar, my sweet Bexar, it's really you. I never gave up; I knew you would come to me!"

"I'm sorry, baby. I'm so sorry. I'm sorry about Keeley, I'm sorry about Big Bend, I'm sorry about Maypearl, I'm sorry about it all."

Tears streaked down Jessie's cheeks. Bexar placed his hand on her stomach, wiping tears off his face as he did so. Chivo walked past the Marines, who stood still both watching the scene unfold and scanning for any new threats. Amanda followed Chivo in joining Bexar and Jessie.

Chivo looked at Jessie gravely. "Ma'am, I want to apologize. I was in Big Bend as a part of the rescue force and saw you, but I thought you were dead. Our orders were to get the survivors, and Bexar was the only one we saw . . . but I made a promise, and I brought him back to you."

Jessie wrapped her arms around the man. She didn't know him and couldn't even say thank you she was crying so hard, so she just hugged him.

Aymond walked to the group and stood silently for a moment. Once Jessie finally released Chivo to stand next to her husband and hold his hand, Chivo glanced at the uniform, read the name tape, and smiled.

"Master Gunnery Sergeant Aymond, may I present to you the President of the United States, Amanda Lampton." Chivo gestured toward Amanda, who stood there, a large lump on the side of her head, her hair blood-matted, and bruising on her face.

"Bullshit."

A lively discussion began in the ruined shell of the hangar, none of which concerned Bexar; nothing else could, he had his wife back.

Jessie looked over Bexar's shoulder.

"What's wrong, baby?" Bexar turned to see a teenage girl walk toward the hangar, a rifle like Chivo's held across her shoulders, a short- barrel M4 hanging from a sling, A teenage boy with a shotgun was with her. Chivo looked at Erin and chuckled; she responded by flipping him off. Erin walked past Jessie and to the ruined blast door, peering through the entry way, observing dark scorch marks on the interior walls.

"What's her deal, Jess?"

Erin nearly held her breath, trying to listen. Nothing. She could hear nothing at all.

"Bexar, there are over a thousand people down there; the attack might have finally done this place in. The computers were under attack for weeks."

"Jessie, let's just get to Level Five. We get Mom, and we get the fuck out."

"Get out to where, back to Texas? If they know about this place, they have to know about the SSC. They'll be there next if they aren't there right now!"

Jessie turned, walking back toward the FJ to retrieve her chest carrier and spare magazines. Bexar followed along. "You're not going down there."

"Like hell I'm not!"

"I just got you back; I'm not going to lose you again. I can't lose you again!"

"Look, chica, you should stay. You have your Bexar. You have your baby, and I'm going for Mom and coming right back, in and out."

"There is no in and out. The last outbreak was a shitstorm all from one person. There's no telling what's happened now ... you have no idea if she's still on Level Five, it's been hours since we left her there. She could be anywhere in that damn place!"

Jones drove up in the Chinese-made radar truck, which resulted in a lot of rifles being raised and Aymond standing in between the rifles and the truck. "Whoa, easy now, this one is ours."

Chivo spoke first. "What the fuck is that, Aymond, radar?"

"Something like that. We commandeered it from the PLA in San Diego. It kills the Zeds."

Amanda looked surprised. "Sergeant . . . ."

Chivo interrupted her. "Master Gunnery Sergeant. Marines get really testy when you shorten it like that, ma'am."

Amanda gave Chivo a hard sideways look. "Thank you, Chivo. Mr. Aymond, what PLA in San Diego?"

"The short brief is that there is roughly a battalion-sized force of PLA, a container-ship flotilla, and they used airborne to secure the San Diego airport. We destroyed the container ships, blocked the harbor, demo'ed the runways at Halsey Field, and stole the radar truck. Although we had a successful guerilla campaign, we couldn't sustain it, so we began working our way toward the interior looking for other military units."

An explosion rumbled across the mountains. Aymond keyed his radio and spoke quickly. After the reply, Aymond excused himself to climb into the M-ATV as a small yellow aircraft taxied to a stop by the trucks.

Chivo shook his head. "Area 51, a fucking el circo. Aliens are next."

No one else spoke. The aircraft's engine shut off, the propeller jerked to a stop, and a man climbed out of the small plane, joined by a black-and-white dog, tail wagging, "Holy shit, did you guys hear that aircraft crash?"

Aymond looked at the new visitor, the morning being one of constant surprises for the Marine. "We did. Where was it, and what happened?"

"South. There's another dry lake bed down near Mercury; looked big, whatever it was. It wasn't one of yours? I was circling overhead for the last hour waiting for dawn. Dammit! You guys shot the shit out of those guys! That was one hell of a firefight."

Aymond wasn't listening. After the news about the other aircraft, he keyed his radio and spoke rapidly and climbed into the M-ATV with the other MSOT team members. Ordering Jones to stay put with the radar switched on, they drove off rapidly.

Muffled sounds of gunfire could be heard from beyond the ruined blast door.

"It's been a fun morning, but it's time to go." Erin set down her large Barrett, grasping her short-barrel M4. Jason followed her to the door.

Jessie clicked on the headlamp she still wore from the previous night. "Honey, Bexar, are you coming with me or not?"

"Those are my only two choices?"

"That's it."

"If that's it, then there is only one choice. I'm going with. Chivo?"

"Yeah, mano, why the fuck not."

Amanda began walking toward the blast door. Chivo held up his hand. "Corporal . . . ."

"Jones, sir."

"Corporal Jones, welcome to the party. If you wouldn't mind escorting President Lampton to my broke-ass MRAP for her safety until the Master Guns returns? If we don't come back, she will direct you and your team back to another secret facility in Texas with her. I suggest you listen to her. Right, ma'am?"

"Thank you, Chivo," Amanda replied, without masking the sarcasm and annoyance in her voice.

"Now, Mrs. Bexar, if you don't mind, I'd like to go first."

"Chivo, the goat, is it? First of all, I don't know you, and, secondly, you don't know where the hell you're going! I do."

"Baby, he should go first. Chivo and I . . . we've been through a lot together, trust me."

"Mrs. Bexar, you can whisper directions in my ear as we go." Chivo smiled at Bexar as the reunited and newly expanded team stacked on the door to enter.

Chivo looked over his shoulder. "Slow is smooth, smooth is fast, got it?"

Jessie, Bexar, Erin, and Jason responded in order. Chivo stepped inside, and the rest followed in a tight formation.

S4

The reconnaissance patrol watched in horror as the massacre unfolded in front of them, unable to help and not close enough to respond in time to render any aid. All they could do was radio support, directing their teammates' weapons fire to the approaching enemy. This mission was a failure, their team in shambles. A brief report was returned to their command chain via their SATCOM. Returning to their APC, they drove down the mountainside to the awaiting commander. They could hear the jet engines of the transport aircraft already starting in the distance. They all knew what the response was going to be if the team's mission failed; they had to leave immediately. The four men watched in disbelief as their transport lifted off without them, and then smoke began trailing from one of the engines and then another. Just fifty feet off the ground, the tail began to drop, the right wing falling lower, before the aircraft cartwheeled across the lakebed in a growing ball of fire.

Rapidly, the four men formulated a plan and drove toward the south as fast as their APC could maintain.

CHAPTER 11

Near Ulm, Montana
April 8, Year 1

Cliff sat in the MRAP at a rural crossroad, the heater running, thick snow
still covering some parts of the countryside. Away from the computers of the
SSC, he had a shortwave radio on the console, and a notebook and pen in his
hand; he wrote down the seemingly random letters and numbers, a female
voice coming across the scratchy transmission.

Transcribing the cypher, Cliff wrote down the coordinates on a smaller
piece of paper, retrieved a cigarette lighter from the breast pocket of his flight
suit, and lit the first piece of paper on fire, holding it out of the open door until
it burnt to his fingers and he let it drop.

Driving another ten minutes south, he turned the MRAP into an unmarked
but obvious driveway, drove past a helipad, and stopped at the heavy gate. The
missile-alert facility plaque still hung on the fence, the Officer In Charge and
the Non-Commissioned Officer In Charge placard slots missing the names that
changed with each watch-duty rotation. Glancing at the poles on the corners
and the video cameras, he assumed that if the Launch Control Center was still

online, and since the Launch Control Support Building was still standing and the fence was still intact, that the cameras were still operational as well.

A loop of wire hung from the red-and-white radio tower, which was odd. Assured by his handlers that the hardwire launch control workaround would actually work, all he had to do was actually get in the facility. For him to accomplish that, it all started with a single button push on the intercom.

ACKNOWLEDGMENTS

Writing a novel is often a solitary pursuit; continuing into the fifth book of a series takes a legion of friends, family and readers who not only read, but give the author support. Winchester: Over wouldn't have been a success without all of you and we wouldn't be on Book Five in two years without all of you. However, most of all my wife has been and continues to be my biggest fan, though that wasn't in the vows. Without her support, Book One would have never have been written, much less the whole Winchester Undead series and "Take Control of Your Camera" (not to mention Winchester Undead Book Six and the planned upcoming releases). Thank you, all of you, and thank you, Morgan.

Keep your go-bags packed and be ready, I ride with Bexar!

-Dave

Website: http://www.winchesterundead.com
Facebook: https://www.facebook.com/winchesterundead
Twitter: @WUzombies
Instagram: https://instagram.com/f8industries/
Tumblr: http://winchesterundead.tumblr.com/
Pinterest: https://www.pinterest.com/f8industries/

The *Author Dave Lund Tales of Adventures, Winchester Undead Newsletter* is the place for unique content. To gain access to the custom-made full Winchester Undead plot location map, special contests and tales of adventures, you have to sign up here: http://talesofadventures.net/newsletter/

ABOUT THE AUTHOR

My name is Dave Lund. I hail from Texas and am a former Texas "motor-cop." My family and photography round out my usual day-to-day passions, but post-apocalyptic zombie stories really fire me up. Before my previous stint as a motor-cop, I was a full-time skydiving instructor and competitor (in Canopy Piloting, aka swooping) with over 3,000 skydives. I am no longer an active skydiver so I can focus on my family, photography, and writing.

The characters in the Winchester series comprise some personality composites of people I have known or met in my life, but no character is based on a single real person or even two people combined. They are a complete work of fiction and do not represent any actual people, living or dead. Yes, that includes Bexar! Many of the themes, objects, weapons, tactics, and locations in the Winchester Undead series are pulled from my past and experiences, as many writers are apt to do, including my love of Big Bend National Park in Texas; although I have to admit there is no secret cache site in the small Texas town of Maypearl. At least none that I had any hand in creating. Although the secret base from the SSC is probably true . . . .

ABOUT THE AUTHOR